SECOND CHANCES

GEORGE LEE MILLER

FRIO PRESS LLC

This is a work of fiction. Names, characters, places, and incidents either are the product of the author's imagination or are used fictitiously. Any resemblance to actual persons, living or dead, events, or locales is entirely coincidental.

Paperback ISBN: 978-1-7341564-3-0
Hardback ISBN: 978-1-7341564-5-4
' ISBN: 978-1-7341564-4-7

Cover design by Lance Buckley
Interior design by Lisa Gilliam

Published by Frio Press LLC FRIO 2020

For Kyle and Ruby and all that is just and true and good.

"Even as I have seen, they that plow iniquity, and sow wickedness, reap the same."

—Job 4:8

PROLOGUE

Maya Chavez and her new friend Lori Kostoch held hands to keep from falling as they raced down a narrow dirt path that led to a secluded beach on the Pedernales River. The girls wore cutoff jean shorts, flip-flops, and T-shirts over the skimpy bikinis they hoped would turn heads at the party. It was August and still warm despite being close to midnight. There was a new moon, and the Central Texas sky was clear and far enough from any big city for the Milky Way to blanket the heavens with pinpoints of light.

Maya carried a red-and-white canvas tote bag she'd been given at senior registration. It was stenciled with the stylized head of a billy goat, their high school mascot. Inside was a bottle of cheap vodka she'd stolen from her mother's closet and two plastic quarts of lemonade that Maya insisted was the best thing to use for mixer.

The girls were in a hurry because they were late for the party. It was Maya's fault. She had to wait until her grandparents were asleep before she could sneak out. They hustled toward the glow of a bonfire on the horizon and the sound of a strong bass beat. The well-worn trail wound through cactus and mesquite brush like a white snake in the dark.

Maya's foot slipped on a loose rock, and Lori caught her before she could fall.

"Don't break the bottle," Lori said, pulling Maya upright.

"I've got it," Maya said, holding the bag proudly above her shoulder. "Besides, it's plastic." She reached into the bag and brought out the vodka bottle.

Lori noticed the seal was cracked and there was an inch of clear liquid missing. "You started without me."

"It was like that. I didn't drink any," Maya protested. She stole the booze to impress Lori and the other students at her new school. She was a transfer student from San Bernardino, California, and hadn't told anyone she was actually born and raised in Fredericksburg. She liked being known as the *chick from Cali*.

Lori took a drink. "Gross."

"You have to mix it with lemonade," Maya explained.

Maya had been reluctant to go to the party because it was so far outside of town, but Lori said the river was where everybody went. Kids had been partying there for as long as anybody could remember because it was isolated—if the local cops tried to bust them, it was easy to escape. Besides, Lori explained, the senior guys would be there. Maya didn't think much of the local boys but decided to go along. Lori was the only friend she'd made since her mother had dragged her back to Fredericksburg to be near her grandparents.

Maya had to sneak out, but she didn't care. Her grandparents were too strict. It was like they lived in a different century. No one had to be home by ten anymore. She'd never had a curfew in California because her mom was always passed out by ten and left her to do whatever she wanted.

The girls paused to catch their breath on the sandy bluff overlooking the wide bend in the river. The opposite side was a stone's throw away and chock-full of willows and cottonwood trees. In the late summer, the water level was low, but the bend formed a pool that was nearly always at least four feet deep and perfect for swimming. The beach side of the river was covered with twenty yards of sand scattered with white limestone rocks that glowed yellow in the firelight.

"I thought this was a senior party," Maya said, studying the figures around the bonfire. She didn't recognize anyone from registration.

"It is," Lori said. "Don't worry, the guys we want to impress will be here."

"You mean Owen?" Maya teased as she followed Lori down the bluff to the sandy beach.

"What?" Lori pretended innocence. She *was* trying to impress Owen Bauer, not only with the tiny bikini but by promising to bring Maya, the new girl from Cali. Owen was a senior on the football team, and Lori'd been trying to get his attention since she was a sophomore.

"Don't *what* me. I saw you talking to him at registration," Maya said and poured some of the clear vodka into the lemonade bottle and shook it up. "That's how it's done," she said. She had a lot of practice mixing drinks for her mother. "Here, take a drink."

Lori hesitated.

Maya pushed the bottle to her lips. "Come on, it's a party, right?"

Lori took a drink. "Tastes like lemonade."

"It's supposed to, stupid," Maya scolded her. "What do you guys drink out here, beer?"

"Yeah," Lori said.

"That's disgusting."

Maya focused her attention on the guys circled around the bonfire.

"Watch this," Maya said. She set the bag in the sand and slipped out of her T-shirt. Her bikini was bright red, with spaghetti straps and triangles of thin cloth that barely contained her small breasts.

The girls had giggled while they were trying the suits on at the mall in San Antonio. They knew the impression they would make and the looks they would get. The style was Maya's idea. She said it was what all the girls in California were wearing.

"Come on. Your turn," Maya teased.

"Give me some of that," Lori said, reaching for the vodka mix. She took a drink for courage, then pulled her T-shirt off, revealing a strapless kelly-green bikini that was similar to Maya's.

One of the boys from the firepit walked toward them. He was six feet tall with an angular body and muscular arms. He had a shock of disheveled blond hair that covered his ears and reached to his suntanned shoulders. Around his neck he wore a braided shell necklace.

"Hey, Lori," the boy said when he got closer. "Didn't think y'all 'd show."

"Told ya we'd be here," Lori shouted over the loud music. "I brought Maya."

Maya arched her back so that the teen boy could get a good look at her swimwear.

"Wow!" His eyes settled on her bikini top.

Lori slapped him on the shoulder. "Hey," she shouted. "What about me?"

He put his arms around Lori and kissed her. "Easy, you did good," he shouted. "Did you bring the booze?"

Lori nodded. "Maya got it."

He put his arms around each girl's waist and led them toward the bonfire. "Come on over to the fire. Y'all can't have any fun standing out here in the dark."

The music was deafening. The throbbing bass vibrated deep in Maya's bones. She expected to see familiar faces. Instead, she saw a group of men in their twenties. They wore long shorts that sagged well below their waists. A few wore wife-beater T-shirts. Most were bare-chested, showing off a collection of tattoos. They were circled around two older-looking women in sequined bikinis who gyrated their hips as if they were on stage at a strip club. This wasn't what she expected.

One of the men broke away from the pack. His blond hair was long and tied in a thick ponytail. He was bigger than the others, and his hairless skin was bulky with muscles and covered with tattoos. The most dominant one was a red-and-green dragon that wrapped around his chest. The head of the beast was above his right breast, and red tongues of fire shot down his chiseled six-pack abs.

"This is the Dragon," Owen shouted above the music. "Maya brought vodka." Owen held up Maya's bottle.

The Dragon grabbed it and took a gulp. "Nasty," he said, and smiled, looking directly at her red bikini top. His voice was a raspy baritone. He made no attempt to hide his stare.

Maya felt the skin on her neck and cheeks turn red and hoped the others didn't notice in the dark. She wondered if she'd taken her *Cali Chick* image too far.

"You look like you're ready to party, girl," the Dragon said. He took Maya by the wrist and turned her in a circle like he was handling a child. His powerful hands grabbed one wrist and then the other like she was a marionette being spun on a string.

She was repulsed and excited at the same time. He had an alpha-male cockiness that gave him total control of everything around him, nothing like the high school boys here or in California.

"Take off your shorts," the Dragon said. It wasn't a request.

Maya glanced again at Lori, who had taken a step back and stood beside Owen.

"Come on, girl. Show me what you got," he demanded.

There was no way to turn back now. She wanted to fit in more than anything and hated the feeling of being an outsider in a new school again. She thought it was some kind of test for the new kids, and she was determined to show them she could pass.

Three or four of the other men gathered around Maya and waited for her to strip out of her shorts. She smiled, hiding her nervousness, and unbuttoned the top button of her jean shorts. Two of the men tilted their heads back and howled like wolves.

The Dragon grabbed Lori and tossed her beside Maya. "You too, girl," he shouted.

Lori looked to Owen for support, but he just smiled. Lori undid a button on her shorts. Maya suddenly wished she had gone with the more modest version of a swimsuit. The one she first tried on had come up over her hips and covered a lot more skin. She'd only suggested the tiny version because she though Lori would say no.

With one quick movement, she pulled the cutoffs down over her butt and let them fall to the sand. Lori did the same.

All the men howled, then closed in around her. A hand grabbed the string that held the tiny red top around her neck. She crossed her arms as the flimsy material suddenly slipped down. The men laughed. She smelled them now. All around her. Body sweat and cheap cologne. One of them slapped her butt. A hand tugged the string holding her bikini bottom. Her throat was tight. She felt panic. This wasn't supposed to be happening. Maya clung to the bikini bottom with one hand and held her other arm across her breasts. She tried to scream, but she couldn't make a sound.

Someone grabbed her hair.

Then, as quickly as it began, it was over. The Dragon was beside her. The man who had grabbed her hair was on the ground, bleeding from his nose.

The Dragon put his hands on her shoulders. "Sorry. These dudes're animals." He picked up her shorts and handed them to her.

"Thank you," Maya whispered and pulled her shorts back on.

The Dragon lit a joint and inhaled a huge breath, holding the smoke in his lungs for what seemed like a full minute. When he let it out, he smiled and handed the joint to Maya.

Maya hesitated. She'd tried it before, in California. Everybody did it at her old high school. She put the joint to her lips and inhaled deeply, imitating the man's actions. She tried to hold in the smoke, coughed violently. This stuff was stronger than any she had ever tried.

The Dragon laughed. "You gotta relax your throat, girl," he said, and brushed her long dark hair over her shoulder. His smile was warm and friendly.

She tried the joint again. This time she followed his advice. Maya looked around the bonfire for Lori. She glanced toward the river and in the shadows of the bluff, but Lori was gone. It was strange, but now she didn't care. She felt herself relax. A warm sensation slowly crept from her head to her fingers and toes.

"You're the Cali girl?" the Dragon asked, as if she was the only one on the beach.

"That's right," she said, smiling for the first time since she'd been back to Texas.

The Dragon put his thick, powerful arm around her.

CHAPTER ONE

I OPENED MY EYES TO GENERATIONS of Fischer ancestors staring down at me from dark photographs lining the ancient limestone walls of my small childhood bedroom. Some were tintypes, some sepia tone, some black and white, and others were color prints yellowed with age. All the faces were stern and unsmiling. I had read once that the firm expressions in old photographs were the result of the extended period of time it took to expose the film. The subjects had to pick a pose they could hold, or risk blurring the image. As a kid, I always thought the old folks were frowning at me because they could somehow read my mind and disapproved of whatever scheme I was cooking up to escape my ranch duties. For a time, I thought Grandpa had hung the pictures in my bedroom to make me feel guilty, then I realized that he had slept in the same room as a boy. I wondered if the photos made him feel guilty or if guilt was just a trait that ran in the Fischer family. It was one of the many things I never got a chance to ask him before he was murdered.

The photos stretched back over the 150-year history of my family in Texas and covered every wall in the house. I wondered if my picture would one day be on the wall, and if my grandson would one day see it from this angle. I was the last of the Fischer line, and I was sleeping in my childhood bed after a fifteen-year absence because I'd been wounded on my last case and needed downtime. The anchor of the family, my grandpa, had also taken a bullet. He didn't make it. Continuing the family tradition fell on my shoulders. So far, I hadn't been able to hold onto a girlfriend long enough to add any more branches to the family tree. My Fischer Private Investigations business took all my time and energy.

The sound of silverware being placed on a wooden table downstairs reminded me there was someone else in the house—an uninvited guest who was disrupting my planned rehabilitation. It was two weeks after my grandfather's funeral. Family and friends had drifted back to their own houses, leaving me to recuperate and deal with the family land. I was the only direct descendent, and Grandpa, God rest his soul, had left a will granting me rights to the house and property.

"Breakfast!" Helen, my uninvited guest, yelled from the downstairs kitchen.

The smell of pancakes and sausage mixed with coffee permeated every room in the house. She must have gotten up before sunrise to have everything done before I woke up. I was normally an early riser, but the gunshot wound courtesy of a corrupt state politician had altered my normal routine. I ended his life, but not before he wreaked havoc on my partner and my family.

Helen hadn't bothered to show up for my father's funeral when I was sixteen. But she felt compelled to show up for Grandpa's, and I got the feeling she wanted to stay. Not just the night but indefinitely. Something about wanting to take care of me, at least until I got on my feet. The wounds were sore as hell, but I was able to move around and didn't feel like I needed any help, especially from a woman who hadn't been around to take care of me since the seventh grade.

"Nicky, are you gonna sleep all day?" she yelled again. She sounded like she used to when I was in elementary school.

What irritated me the most was that when she called me Nicky, I felt like I was back in third grade trying to think of an excuse to skip school. It added to the odd feeling of seeing my ancestors staring down at me from the limestone walls. They all seemed to want the answer to one burning question: *What's next?* Would I keep the family ranch and stay in my old hometown, or would I sell out and return to San Antonio? Would I continue my private eye business after nearly being killed on my last case, or return to law enforcement, or maybe finish my last year of law school and pursue a less dangerous profession?

If I sold out, I wouldn't have to worry about maintaining the ranch or paying the taxes. On the other hand, the property had been in the family for five generations. If I did keep it, I wouldn't be able to make a living raising goats and cattle. Small farms and ranches were a thing of the past unless the land had oil and gas. The Fischer ranch had plenty of deer, hogs, and cedar brush, but no *bubblin' crude*. I would have to get back to San Antonio and start lining up paying clients or pursue another day job.

Helen's sudden interest in me was motivated by money. She didn't have to spell it out. Grandpa's ranch was over four hundred acres along Grape Creek, less than fifteen miles from Fredericksburg, Texas, a town that had become a German-themed tourist destination. Before he was murdered, Grandpa had turned down several very generous offers to buy the place. The prospective buyers wanted to turn the 150-year-old limestone house into a bed and breakfast.

"Nicky?" Helen called again.

I could hear her designer boots on the ancient stone steps and quickly slipped on a pair of jeans. She was my mother, but I had stopped thinking of her in that capacity twenty years ago, and I wasn't about to let her walk in on me in my underwear.

"I'm coming," I said and hustled into the bathroom. I closed the door before she could reach the upstairs landing.

"Do you need some help with your bandage?" she called through the door.

"No thanks, Helen. I can manage." I stripped the bandage off my chest and winced in pain when it caught the new growth of chest hair. The edges of the wound were still red and raw, remnants of an infection that I couldn't seem to shake. The .38 slug was going to leave a nice scar about three inches above my left nipple. I checked the other wound on my upper arm where I'd been hit by a .308 rifle bullet while jogging down the San Antonio River Walk.

I wasn't feeling sorry for myself. I was counting my blessings I had survived. I held my arm up so that the wound was visible in the mirror over the sink. If I kept adding new scars to the constellation of marks across my forehead that I'd picked up on my final overseas deployment, I'd look like Deadpool before I turned forty. Maybe I'd start wearing red tights and a mask.

Helen knocked on the bathroom door. "You all right in there?"

I had been asked that more times in the weeks following Grandpa's funeral than I'd ever been asked in my entire life. The two bullet holes had taken their toll. The doc at the hospital had reluctantly let me go home with a truckload of antibiotics and some extra strength pain meds. I had been lying in bed for a month and was getting antsy. Grandpa's ranch house didn't have television reception or internet, and I'd already read the collection of history books I'd brought from my house in San Antonio. I wanted to be outside. Starting on the ranch chores would be a great way to step up my rehabilitation program.

Helen knocked again. I could hear her pacing the wooden floor.

"I'm fine, Helen," I said, irritated. I finished applying fresh bandages to both wounds, then waited till her footsteps retreated back down the stairs. I'm not sure which riled me more, her pretending to care or me pretending to be nice.

When I walked into the kitchen, Helen served me a plate of sourdough pancakes topped with three sunny-side-up eggs, fresh hash brown potatoes, and a side of venison pan sausage. It was my favorite breakfast as a kid, and other than migas or taquitos, it had always been my go-to morning meal.

"Thank you for breakfast," I said. It was a meal that needed to be followed by a day of manual labor. I had intended to saddle my horse and ride out to the property boundary to fix the broken wire on the fence, but something told me I wouldn't get that far.

Helen sat and watched me use my fork and knife to reposition the eggs on top of the pancakes. I reached for the ketchup, not looking up, waiting for the inevitable questions I knew would eventually emerge like the tomato sauce from the upturned bottle.

"Would you like some juice?" She held up an orange juice bottle.

"No, thank you."

She poured herself a glass of juice and sat down to watch me eat. She wore jeans tucked into stylishly sequined cowboy boots and a white, long-sleeved shirt. She had a silver bracelet embedded with turquoise and a matching pendant that hung from her tanned neck. At fifty-five she wore her dyed blond hair pulled into a girlishly ponytail, and the only weight she'd added in twenty years came from silicone gel implants. I'd heard rumors of other boyfriends over the years, rich rancher types, but she claimed to be single now.

"I thought I'd go to town today and pick up something for dinner. What would you like?" she asked, sitting in Grandma's place at the other end of the table near the stove. She had served me in Grandpa's place at the other end. I wasn't ready to take over his place and definitely didn't want Helen taking over for Grandma.

"Let me get through breakfast first." I knew she was filling in dates on the calendar as far ahead as she could. It was another one of her calculated moves to ensure her place on the ranch.

"Since I'm going to town anyway…" She let the sentence trail off while she grabbed Grandpa's stovetop percolator and poured us both fresh coffee. It smelled rich and delicious, and strong enough to float a horseshoe. Grandpa would have approved. "I don't know why Grandpa never used a regular coffee maker," she said, and filled her cup with French vanilla creamer. "I think I'll pick one up in town today."

"When are you going back to Colorado?" I asked. I decided to plunge into the deep end and sink or swim. I was raised by a no-nonsense Texas lawman and a taciturn rancher grandpa who were both blunt and to the point. When I left home, I'd served four years in the Marine Corps, not the best place to learn social graces. My last girlfriend tried to teach me the art of idle chitchat to improve my people skills, but I wasn't that interested. It was one of the reasons she was my ex-girlfriend.

Helen stirred the creamer into her coffee, not looking at me.

"Don't you want me to stay?" she finally asked.

I took another mouthful of egg and pancake while trying to decide how best to put into words what I wanted to tell her.

"No," I said, as tactfully as I could.

Helen went to the sink. Grandpa didn't have a dishwasher. There wasn't room to install one in the ancient kitchen, and he scoffed at the idea of wasting water.

"You need someone here. You're not fully recovered yet, Nicky." She made a half-hearted attempt to scrub the pan, pretending to be helpful. She was never handy in the kitchen.

"I've been taking care of myself for a long time," I said.

"That's not fair. You know your father had a lot to do with my leaving." Her voice had that familiar edge to it.

I took a bite of venison sausage. I didn't want to get into an argument about why she left Dad, or why she didn't make any effort to contact me until after I got out of high school. I was over it.

"I'm sorry," she said. "I just thought…" She stopped working and leaned her back against the sink. "I just thought that with Grandpa gone things would be different."

I looked up from my last bite of pancake and egg. Tears were forming in her hazel eyes. She was going to pull out all the stops. I stood and handed her my empty plate.

"Why don't you cook that roast that's in the refer?" I said. I was only putting off the inevitable, but I didn't want to start my day bathed in alligator tears.

Before she could respond, tires crunched on the gravel driveway. I wasn't expecting company. From the front window I could see Helmut Geisler's Dodge Ram coming up the driveway. Helen saw him too.

"I forgot to mention, Mr. Geisler called the landline this morning before you got up."

"Why didn't you tell me?" I found my boots by the front door and slipped them on.

"It was so early, I wanted to let you sleep."

I found my hat and waved to Helmut through the window.

"Nicky, I know what he wants. You shouldn't get involved. You're not ready to go back to work."

I didn't bother to reply.

CHAPTER TWO

HELMUT GEISLER SLOWLY UNFOLDED HIMSELF from the cab of his dusty Dodge Ram four-wheel drive pickup. He reminded me of a twisted piece of rawhide wrapped in Wrangler jeans and a faded blue western shirt. His weather-beaten face was shaded by a sweat-stained Stetson Rancher hat. Helmut and my grandpa had been friends since long before I was born, tied together by proximity and a shared livelihood. The Geisler family had been in the area almost as long as the Fischer family. He was one of the few left, now that Grandpa was gone, who still spoke Texas German and loved to tell stories about early settlers to anyone who would listen.

"*Guten Morgen. Wie geht's?*" he asked, delivering his German with a Texas accent.

I understood him because I'd grown up around my grandpa, but if things got more complicated than "good morning," I was going to have to remind him that I wasn't fluent. By the time I went to high school, the language was out of fashion.

He extended a callused palm and shook my hand with the grip of a much younger man.

"Sorry I missed your call. I didn't get the message till just now," I said. "Want some coffee?"

He looked past me to the front window, where Helen stood staring at us.

"Is it safe then, to go inside?" he asked with a twinkle in his eye. He knew my family history as well as I did. There weren't many secrets around the old-timer network of which, until recently, my grandpa had been an intricate part.

"She was just going to town for groceries," I said and winked.

"In that case, I could use a cup," he drawled, as if his indicator light had come on showing he was a quart low.

"Good that Otto got his hay in the barn." He was going to add, *before he died*, but he stopped himself.

"Think it'll last the winter?" I asked, shifting the direction of the conversation away from the raw subject of Grandpa's murder.

Helmut rubbed his bony chin. "Almanac says it will be a cold one."

We made our way to the porch, where Helen stood.

"Good morning, Mr. Geisler," she said.

"*Morgen*, Helen," he said and tipped his hat.

"How's your wife?" she asked.

"She's up and around now. Busy with the fall garden. Says death will come when it comes." Helmut's wife had lived through her fourth heart attack.

"Let us know what we can do to help," she said, then put a hand on my arm. "I'm going to town. If you think of anything you need, call my cell phone."

Helmut and I watched while she climbed into her white Chevy Tahoe with Colorado plates and drove toward the front gate in a cloud of white dust.

"So, she's here now?" he said, following me into the house.

"Well, she's here *for* now. I'll put it that way." I tested the coffee pot to see if it was still hot, then poured us both a cup.

Helmut seemed to be waiting for me to add to the family gossip. When I didn't, he moved on to the reason he was here.

"My granddaughter is missing," he said matter-of-factly. He took a sip of coffee. The twinkle in his eye was gone, replaced by something cold and serious.

I waited for him to fill in the details.

"Her name's Maya Chavez," he said.

He held up a picture that looked like it was clipped from a yearbook. Her dark hair was long and flipped over her right shoulder. She had intelligent eyes, and her smile revealed a youthful touch of defiance that stood in stark contrast to her stern Hill Country grandfather.

CHAPTER THREE

HELMUT GAVE ME THE DETAILS of Maya's disappearance. It wasn't the first time she'd run away from home. Anna, her mother, was a drunk, and raising her daughter had taken a back seat to maintaining her daily alcohol level. I sympathized to some extent. I'd used Jack Daniels to mask the pain of reentry from my final deployment. I got through it, but not without a kick in the butt from Grandpa.

I knew Anna's story. She never got the kick she needed and, as those things usually go, ended up ruining more than just her own life. When Maya was ten, Anna took her daughter and moved to San Bernardino, California, to live with Maya's father. She blamed her drinking on the lack of opportunity in Fredericksburg. She always thought she was destined for bigger and better things but the small town was holding her back. She discovered life was just as hard in the big city. When Maya's father left the family high and dry, Helmut tried to convince his daughter to move back to Fredericksburg so at least Maya could have a stable home. Anna refused until Helmut threatened to cut off his support. She must have sobered up long enough to realize that her daughter would be better off in a small town close to her grandfather.

Helmut said Maya wasn't overjoyed to leave her friends in California for her senior year. She'd spent eight years in very busy Southern California, and now she was confined to a town of eleven thousand where the biggest event of the year was an October festival celebrating the town's German heritage. Maya was only half German. Her father's name was Chavez, and she inherited her dark hair and olive complexion from his side of the family.

Helmut had filed a missing person report with Officer Zeller from the local police department. Zeller had made a few phone calls and talked to the students who knew Maya at the high school and to her mother, but he couldn't find evidence of a crime. Since Maya had just turned eighteen, he said there was nothing else he could do. Zeller told Helmut that Maya had probably returned to San Bernardino, where she felt more comfortable. Helmut didn't buy it.

"Did Zeller check her cell phone records?" I asked.

He looked puzzled for a moment. Like my grandpa, Helmut had a landline connected to his kitchen and still wrote the occasional letter by hand to his cousin in New Mexico.

"Oh, yes," he said, remembering. "I gave him the number I had. He said it wouldn't help. Something about the kind of phone it was."

"A *burner* phone?" I asked.

"Something like that." He dug out a wad of paper from his shirt pocket. "I have the number here." He sorted through the scraps at arm's length, not bothering with reading glasses, then handed me a number written on the back of a gas receipt. Like Grandpa, Helmut used his shirt pocket as a filing cabinet.

I told him I would look into it. Helmut offered to pay up front, but I told him I wanted to be sure there was something I could do before we signed an agreement and made it an official case. He understood that private investigations were my business. He was an old family friend, but also a rancher, which meant he was in debt up to his eyeballs. If it turned out I could be of some help, we would have to negotiate payment. Grandpa's cattle would need hay for the cold winter if I decided to keep the herd. Helmut also raised goats and domestic hogs. I might not get a mortgage payment from him, but if I took the case, I would have plenty to eat.

"Ten years ago, I would have gone after her myself," he said, his voice displaying emotion that he wasn't accustomed to using.

I could remember when he and my grandfather seemed to stand ten feet tall. There was nothing they couldn't hunt, ride, fix, or drive. If someone needed help, they were there. If there was trouble, they took care of it. Now, it was up to me.

"*Halt dich munter*," he said when he climbed back in his dusty Dodge Ram. It was a salutation I'd heard all my life. Grandpa said it meant *keep your chin up*.

"*Halt dich munter*," I said.

CHAPTER FOUR

It was the first weekend in October, which meant it was festival weekend, the biggest event of the year. Every weekend brought tourists from Austin and San Antonio, but on Oktoberfest weekend, tourists tripled the population. The Fredericksburg Chamber of Commerce advertised the town as *the polka capital of Texas*, implying there would be plenty of beer on hand. You couldn't have one without the other. Main Street was bumper to bumper and parking was scarce, so it seemed the slogan or the implication was working to attract visitors.

Maya's mother, Anna, worked at a motel near downtown. Helmut wasn't sure what her schedule was and didn't have her cell phone number, because both changed every few months. Maya was in the processes of moving in with her grandparents. She was going to live with them during the school year.

It was midmorning on a Friday, and I parked my pickup near the Super 8 motel entrance. The parking lot was already full. People had gotten to town early to see the parade that kicked off the Oktoberfest celebration. I recognized a woman in her forties with stringy blond hair pushing a service cart between rooms. She stopped to light a cigarette and stare at a family of four piling out of a minivan as if she resented the extra work they represented. She wore jean shorts and a Metallica T-shirt and looked like she could use a beer.

"Hey, Anna," I said, getting out of my pickup and taking a few steps toward her. I didn't want to come on too aggressively for fear she'd bolt into one of the rooms. She had a reputation for being flighty and probably owed money to half the people in town.

"Hey yourself, Nicky," she said.

"Busy weekend, huh?" I was working on my friendly chitchat.

"You come by to tell me that?" So much for idle prattle.

"Actually, I came by to ask you about your daughter, Maya. Your dad came by the ranch and said she was missing. He hasn't seen her since the middle of August. The tenth, to be exact. Have you heard from her?"

"Guess that kinda proves the old man couldn't handle her either." She blew smoke through her nose and cocked her left eyebrow. The menthol smoke smelled like it was laced with cheap vodka. If she was fishing for sympathy, she wouldn't catch any from me.

"So, you haven't seen her?" I asked.

"I told Zeller what I knew. What's it to you?"

"You know I'm a private investigator. Helmut thought I might be able to help. He's worried about her. I told him I'd look around. He said y'all weren't speakin' to each other."

"You got that right. The old bastard took my daughter away from me. What do you want me to say to him?"

"You're not concerned that Maya's been gone for six weeks?"

"Maya's not my responsibility anymore. Helmut took me to court."

"I didn't know," I said. That was something Helmut hadn't told me. "Do you think Maya ran away?"

"I did when I was her age. I know what that old fossil is like. He never goes anywhere or does anything except work that worthless patch of limestone rock he calls a ranch." She was bitter at the world for not treating her right.

"Did you ever think he was working all those long hours to support you and your mother?"

Anna looked at me like I'd just slapped her in the face, not expecting to be called on her bullshit.

"Didn't you move back here because he threatened to cut you off?"

"He owes me. I'm his only daughter."

"He doesn't owe you a damn thing." I let my anger get the best of me.

Her bottom lip trembled. She covered her face to hide her tears. She didn't want to listen to what I had to say. There was obviously more to the story than Helmut had told me.

I tried to soften my approach. "Do you have any idea where she might have gone? Was she close to anybody back in California? Maybe your husband's family?"

"She didn't get along with them. They didn't want us there." Tears streamed from her bloodshot eyes. "I don't know… I don't know… Can you find her?" Somewhere beneath her bitterness, she was concerned.

"I'll do what I can. If she does contact you, give me a call." I tossed my business card on her maid service cart and got back in my pickup. Before I started the engine, I saw her sneaking a sip from a pint bottle of vodka hidden under the clean towels.

CHAPTER FIVE

THE SECOND PERSON ON MY list to talk to was Lori Kostoch. Helmut said Maya had mentioned her name after she had gone to the school to register for classes. I knew the Kostoch family and called their house first. I explained to Lori's mother who I was and that I was looking for Helmut's granddaughter. I told her Lori might have run into her at registration. Her mother said Lori had a job at the German café on Main Street and was there now helping out for the busy festival weekend. Since it was almost lunchtime, I figured it was a good time to have a chat with Lori and see if the *jaeger schnitzel* was still as good as I remembered.

On the way, I called my partner, Skeeter. He was house-sitting for me in San Antonio and recovering from a gunshot wound of his own. The last case had almost taken out the entire Fischer Private Investigations firm—all two of us. His specialty was online research and, my worst nightmare, social media. I was the last generation not to be born with a cell phone in my hand. I didn't get one until after I got out of the Marine Corps and was still baffled by all the ways the younger generation kept in touch. Skeeter was my age but suffered no such confusion. If Maya left a digital footprint, he could track it, and he would post on Facebook and the missing persons sites. I gave him Maya's burner phone number in case there was anything he could do with it.

There was no place to eat within a ten-mile radius of downtown that didn't have four or five tourists waiting to be fed. The German Café was no exception. While I stood in line, I searched for Lori. Her mother said she was tall and slim and had blond hair. Several of the waitstaff matched that description, so I asked the hostess if Lori was working. She pointed out a teenager hustling out of the kitchen carrying two plates of German sausage with generous sides of potato salad and red cabbage.

When it was my turn to be seated, I steered the hostess to a table near the kitchen that looked like it was part of Lori's territory.

Lori stopped at my table a little out of breath and flashed a cheerleader smile. She was appropriately dressed in a blue cotton dirndl. Everybody was German on Oktoberfest weekend. I wore a baseball cap pulled low over my forehead scars to appear more approachable but slipped off my sunglasses and set them on the table.

"Hi, I'm Lori. What can I get you to drink?" she asked.

"Hey, Lori," I said, flashing what I hoped was a friendly smile. "I'm Nick Fischer. I was a *battlin' billy* back in the day.

"Oh, yeah…" She recognized the name. Fredericksburg was still a small town. "Come home for the festival?" She was distracted and in a hurry to move to the next customer.

"Actually, I'm a professional polka dancer, now. Giving a demo at seven in the American Legion tent. You should stop by."

Her face lit up. I had her attention.

"Really?"

"Do you like to polka?" I asked.

"Of course." She was a true daughter of Fredericksburg.

"I'm just kidding. Actually, I'm looking for Maya Chavez. Her grandfather asked me to help him find her. She hasn't been around since August. I'm a private investigator." I dug out my license and held it up. I saw a little twitch at the corner of her mouth. The cheerleader smile disappeared. "Her grandfather said you two were friends."

"Her grandfather?" Her eyes darted to the front door.

"You're both seniors. She was a transfer student from California."

"Yeah. I think I do remember her." She glanced around the jam-packed café again as if checking to see if anyone was watching our exchange. "No, I haven't seen her." She tugged at the calico apron on her costume.

"When did you see her last?"

"I only met her at registration. I didn't know she… she had any relatives in town. She said she was from California."

"The police didn't talk to you?" I asked.

"No," she said quickly. "Why would they?"

"Because she's missing, and her family is concerned. Her grandfather is Helmut Geisler." The color drained from Lori's cheeks. "You know Mr. Geisler?"

"Yes, of course. He… he bought my steer at the junior livestock show last year." She stood wringing her hands on the apron. She seemed not to know what to do or say next. I handed her one of my business cards with the words *Semper Fi* written under my name. She studied the card.

"My dad was a Marine," she said.

"I knew your dad," I said.

Her smile returned. She knew what Semper Fi meant. Her dad had been killed in action in Afghanistan. She had more information but for some reason was too scared to share it with me.

"If you think of anything that might help me find her, give me a call."

"Sure thing, Mr. Fischer," she said.

I had to stop myself from looking around the table to see if she was talking to me. Nothing brings home the inevitability of aging more than returning to your hometown after fifteen years and being called "mister" by the local teens.

"How's the *jaeger schnitzel*?"

"Still the best in town," she said, getting her confidence back.

"Sold. And bring me a Spaten Doppelbock." There weren't many places that had dark German beer on draft. I figured I would take advantage of it.

"Anything else?"

"*Nein danke*," I said.

She rolled her eyes. Everybody tried to speak German on Oktoberfest weekend. It was like going to a Mexican restaurant on Cinco de Mayo and ordering with a Spanish accent.

When she brought the food, I thought she might add more details about Maya. Instead, she pasted on the cheerleader smile and made a point of not making eye contact.

I drank the beer and polished off the schnitzel. It was as good as I remembered. If I kept eating like a ranch hand, I would eventually have to do some work. When I was in San Antonio, I kept up a regular routine of running with my Labrador along the San Antonio River Walk and working out at Lucky's boxing gym. Since I'd been shot, all I had been doing was eating, sleeping, and reading history books.

I finished my meal and waited for Lori to reappear with my bill, but she never came back. Another waitress brought my check. The café was too busy to look for her, so I took the check and walked to the register. Lori had written her name on the bottom in girlish script with a heart in place of a dot above the *i* in her name. Below that, she'd written, *ask Owen Bauer*.

CHAPTER SIX

I WAS LOOKING FORWARD TO THE Fredericksburg Oktoberfest not only because of the high concentration of beer and sausage but because Kelly was driving down from Lubbock for the weekend. She was an old friend I'd first met in the Marine Corps and who had helped me on my last case. She was there when I took a bullet in the chest and stuck around until I was released from the hospital. I had promised her a polka dance at the festival and hoped it might lead to something more intimate after the oompah band went home. Since Helen extended her stay at the ranch house, I had to scramble to find a room at the Best Western, which is normally booked months in advance. It wasn't exactly a romantic love nest, but Kelly was a farm girl and didn't seem to be impressed by excessive shows of money—a welcome change from my last girlfriend.

My reunion with Kelly would be a little complicated now that I was working on a case, or at least looking into it. Nothing had convinced me that Maya would be easy to find. No one, so far, had told me everything they knew. Like any other case, I proceeded with the idea that the more people I talked to, the closer I would get to the truth. There was no such thing as disappearing without a trace.

Lori had given me a name. Owen Bauer. If he was from the same Bauer family I knew growing up, he wouldn't be hard to find. The Bauers were a fixture in Gillespie County. Like the Geislers and the Fischers, the Bauers traced their family roots to the original settlers. They farmed, raised cattle, and at one time owned a dry goods store on Main Street.

I had also read Owen Bauer's name in the local sports section. He was the senior quarterback for the football team and had an outstanding game against rival Kerrville last week. As an alumnus, I always tried to keep track of the team, and the current head coach had been my teammate.

I drove to the high school and parked behind the *Battlin' Billies* stadium. When I wasn't getting into trouble or hunting, this was where I spent my time in high school either waiting for football practice, on the gridiron, or drinking beer.

It was early afternoon in October and still hot outside. Not the sticky, humid-hot of San Antonio because the town was sixty miles further away from the Gulf of Mexico and a thousand feet higher in elevation, but hot enough that watching the football team do wind sprints made me break out in a sweat.

Rocky Velosic was the head coach. I could see him on the field wearing one of those straw field-hand hats with the extra-wide brim, torturing the team with blasts of his whistle—every time he blew it, the players hit the turf, then jumped up and ran in place. It was the same drill we both hated when we were on the team together. It was a cakewalk compared to boot camp, but at the time, all my teammates thought we would die.

I didn't want to stroll down memory lane with Rocky before I got a chance to talk to Owen, so I waited in the parking lot until the team was finished and the coaches and players ran into the locker room.

Twenty minutes later, I spotted Owen walking out of the gate under the stadium. I recognized him from his picture in the paper. He had thick blond hair that was damp from a shower and tucked under a red team hat. The brim was flat, like he'd just picked it off the shelf, and he wore it covering the tops of his ears as if the team had somehow ordered all the caps in extra-large.

"Hey, Bauer," I called through my window before he could reach his brand-new Ford F-250 4x4 pickup. His family had one of the larger peach orchards north of town, and his grandpa was one of the first to put in domestic grapes and cash in on the Texas wine craze. He turned toward me as if he expected the paparazzi and dropped his team duffle bag to the parking lot.

"Do I know you?" he asked. The kid had a chip on his shoulder that could have held up the north end of the stadium.

I got out and walked over to him. "Nick Fischer. I used to play football here back in the day." We shook hands. "I was on your coach's team." That got his attention. "How's the team look this year?"

"I think we're going all the way," he said, putting on a goofy grin and launching into what sounded like a rehearsed speech. "If our frontline can give me the protection I need, I'm going for Coach Velosic's passing record." Rocky was a local legend. It wasn't enough to win us the state championship, but it did launch his college career at North Texas, and it eventually landed him the head coaching job at his alma mater.

"Enjoy it while you can," I said. It wasn't what he was expecting to hear. His goofy grin faded, and I caught him focusing on my forehead scars and the bandage on my upper arm.

"Who are you again?" he asked.

"Nick Fischer. I did play with your coach, but I'm a private investigator, now." I showed him my creds. "I was wondering if you'd seen Maya Chavez."

His tan face turned crimson. A little switch went off in his brain. He blinked a few times in rapid succession before the goofy grin returned.

"Maya who?" he said. The kid needed to work on his lying if he was ever going to be a superstar athlete.

"Chavez. New student. Her grandfather's Helmut Geisler. You know him?"

"Sure. Everybody knows Mr. Geisler." He picked up his bag and tossed it in the back of his pickup. "I'm drawing a blank on the girl."

"Maya. Maya Chavez."

"Yeah. Why're you lookin' for her?"

"Mr. Geisler's worried about her. Hasn't seen her since August."

"Maybe she went back to California," he said and got into his pickup. He was in a hurry to go.

"Why would she do that?"

"I thought that's where she was from."

"I never said that."

He opened a can of wintergreen-flavored snuff and packed his bottom lip while the wheels in his brain tried to come up with a good comeback. He stayed silent. Evidently, nothing came to mind.

I handed him my business card through his open window. "If you hear from her, give me a call."

He glanced at the Marine Corps motto. Clueless. He spit brown tobacco juice into an empty plastic water bottle.

"Sure thing. You're a private investigator?" he asked. It was finally sinking in. "Must be serious."

"I just wanna be sure she's safe." I held his gaze. Most of his cocky bluster had faded.

"Were you any good? In high school, I mean. When you played football with Coach V."

I smiled at him. "Who do you think caught all those passes he threw?"

"Where'd you play college ball?"

"I didn't. I joined the Marine Corps."

CHAPTER SEVEN

Owen Bauer was anxious to get out of the parking lot. He definitely knew Maya, and he definitely lied about it. He could have been in a hurry because he had a hot date—it was Friday night on Oktoberfest weekend, and the Battlin' Billies had a bye week, but it seemed more likely that something I said touched a nerve. He didn't like hearing Maya's name or that she was Helmut Geisler's granddaughter. He and Lori were both surprised by that connection.

I followed him down a residential street that ran parallel to Main Street. All the locals knew to avoid downtown because the road would be bumper to bumper and stay that way until after midnight when the festival shut down. I slowed to let him get a block ahead of me, but I didn't think he would be expecting a tail. He was a high school football jock, not a CIA agent or a hardened criminal.

With any luck, Maya wasn't far from home, and she had kept in touch with her high school buddies while she was taking a break from her alcoholic mother and stern grandpa.

Owen parked his new F-250 on the side of the road near the rear of the restaurant where Lori Kostoch worked. I checked my watch. It was after four thirty. Maybe he was hungry after practice, or maybe Lori was his girlfriend.

He hurried to the back door and let himself in. I found a shade tree across the street and waited. I was supposed to meet Kelly at the motel by six o'clock. I wanted to go back to the ranch and shower and change before she got there, but I also didn't want to miss finding out what Owen Bauer was up to.

Letting work interfere with our relationship probably wasn't the best way to start things off, but I couldn't help it. Either Kelly would understand, or she wouldn't. Besides, with any luck, I would find Maya before Kelly arrived.

Five minutes later, Owen came out the back door pulling Lori by the hand. I watched them argue back and forth, not knowing what they were saying. Owen was doing most of the talking. Lori stared down at her shoes and played with her blond hair. If I confronted them while they were together, they both would lie to me again. The question was, which one would lead me to Maya the fastest? It seemed likely that one of them would finish the argument and pick up a cell phone, or even better, go talk to Maya in person.

My phone rang. It was Kelly. "Hey, gorgeous," I answered. Ever the charmer.

"You don't sound like you're home in bed," she said, sounding a little disappointed.

"I'm flat on my back, saving all my energy for you."

"Liar. I hear traffic. You're going to have to do better than that. You're supposed to be recuperating."

"Okay, you caught me. I came to town so I could get the keys to our love nest for the weekend."

"You promised me a night of polka dancing."

"I was thinking we could limit ourselves to beer and brats. I'm still really sore."

"Oh, no. Put on those lederhosen, Mr. Fischer. Don't play the wounded warrior with me."

Kelly was explaining her choice of outfits for Oktoberfest, when Owen slapped Lori hard across the mouth. It was all I could do to stay in my pickup and not rush across the street and put the teen quarterback on his ass. Lori covered her face with the costume apron. The arguing stopped. Owen took a step back. Lori sat down on a metal bench.

"Nick, what's happening?" Kelly asked.

"I'll tell you about it when you get here."

"You're working on something, aren't you?" she said. "You're supposed to be resting. The only work you were going to do was on the ranch."

Owen sat down beside Lori and put his arm around her. She stood abruptly, said one last thing, and stomped back inside the restaurant. Owen watched her go, then walked back to his pickup.

"Nick, are you still there?" Kelly asked.

"I gotta go," I said and disconnected. I had to make a choice—confront Lori while she was reeling from a slap in the face, or squeeze the truth out of her boyfriend?

I chose Owen. Dealing with tearful females wasn't my specialty. I followed him east out of town. The road paralleled the Pedernales River through prime farmland and dozens of new businesses. Everything from wineries, produce stands, antique shops, to an upscale brewery popped up here because it was the main road to Austin, where most of the weekend tourists came from. Owen's family had property here and in a half dozen places around the county.

When he turned north on a gravel road, I fell back a few miles. His dust cloud was easy to follow, like chasing a tornado across Kansas.

I passed stock ponds and rocky pastures full of sheep, goats, and cattle before the column of dust began to settle. I looked at my watch. Five fifteen. If I turned around now, I could make it to the motel by six, in time to meet Kelly. I wouldn't be showered or checked into the room, but I would be on time.

Life was full of choices. Meeting Kelly was going to have to wait. I pulled to the side of the road. Owen's pickup turned off, went over a cattle guard, and disappeared into the brush. The terrain was steep, rocky, and covered with cedar and post oak trees. The temperature was October hot, which is to say you wouldn't get sunstroke, but it felt better standing under a shade tree. I turned off the engine, unrolled the windows, and listened to the hot engine tick.

The stretch of road seemed familiar. The contour of the surrounding limestone hills lined with dense brush sparked a memory that danced on the edge of my consciousness. I watched two turkey vultures float in a leisurely circle, searching the road for their evening meal. Their black wings tipped just enough to keep them moving forward. Then I realized where I was.

This was the same remote area where my dad was murdered. He was serving a warrant on a drug operation that was set up in an old trailer house. The site was maybe a mile west of where I was sitting. The deputy who brought us the news had said not to visit the area because there was nothing to see but the burned remains of a trailer—some melted aluminum siding and a dozen or so blackened cedar trees. Naturally, I had to see it for myself.

Since the incident involved the county sheriff, the Texas Rangers had conducted an investigation. They said the fire was probably sparked by gunfire from one of the suspects and accelerated by volatile chemicals they were using to cook meth. It was before anybody really knew what the drug was and the cooks could still buy all the necessary ingredients at the local drug store.

The Rangers found the remains of five bodies. One was a fourteen-year-old girl, and one was my dad. The girl was the reason he had gotten a warrant to search the trailer.

The fire burned so hot that it melted his 1911 .45 pistol down to the ivory handles. The other weapon he carried was a Mossberg shotgun. There was nothing left of it but a twisted piece of the barrel. I kept the ivory handles on my fireplace mantel in my house in San Antonio as a reminder of his sacrifice.

My cell phone rang. I snapped out of my musing and glanced at the caller ID. Kelly. It was five forty-five.

"Are you ready to polka?" she asked.

"Who isn't?" I said. She was bound and determined to get me on the dance floor.

"Where are you?"

"On a dirt road about ten miles out of town." A flash of sunlight reflected off a piece of glass or metal about five hundred yards from the road. "Hold on one sec." I dug my binoculars from the console, put the phone on speaker, and tossed it on the dash.

"What are you looking at?"

"I'm not sure yet." I put the glasses on the brush-covered hillside. I saw the outline of a double-wide trailer. The flash of sunlight must have come from the front door swinging open. Most of the yard was invisible to the road unless you knew where to look. With the Bushnell ten-power binoculars, I could make out two figures standing by the door. They were only partially obscured by the surrounding brush. One was Owen, and the other was a big guy with a blond ponytail that hung down to the middle of his bare back. His muscles were well defined, like a body builder's, and covered with tattoos. When he turned, I saw the head of a red-and-green dragon decorating his right breast. He was laughing at something Owen said. The butt of a pistol protruded from his tight jeans.

"You still there?" Kelly asked. "I'm on Main Street now. Wow, it's like downtown Lubbock on game day. You weren't kidding about Oktoberfest being popular."

Ponytail stepped back into the trailer and shut the door. Owen had already stepped behind a tree. I could hear a pickup engine start.

"Keep going through town. The motel's on the east side. I'll be there in twenty minutes," I said and disconnected.

If I waited by the side of the road, Owen would pass right by me. I didn't want to lose the element of surprise, so I started my pickup and made a U-turn in the gravel and headed back to town. If Maya was hiding out in the trailer house, I wanted to stop by unannounced and get her side of the story.

CHAPTER EIGHT

There was a bevy of German-themed motels in Fredericksburg complete with Bavarian murals on the outside walls and cuckoo clocks in the rooms, as well as dozens of bed and breakfast rentals catering to Oktoberfest visitors, but they were all booked several months in advance. I'd put my name on a waiting list and been lucky that the Best Western had a cancelation. The franchise owner had tastefully added an edelweiss flower painting to the lobby along with the usual western kitsch to give the place a local flavor.

The alternative would have been for Kelly to stay at the ranch, but I didn't want her and Helen under the same roof. I'd learned at an early age that sound travels well in a stone house with wood floors. I could never sneak out, talk on the phone, or do anything private that escaped my dad's or later my grandparents' attention.

I spotted Kelly's Dodge Ram pickup parked in the shade near the motel entrance and pulled up next to her. She wore her short blond hair loose and had on a red Texas Tech T-shirt and khaki shorts. As always, she looked like she could ace the Marine obstacle course.

I wasn't sure of the current status of our relationship. We first met in the Marine Corps when we were both stationed in Afghanistan. We were attracted to each other then, but she was an officer and I was enlisted, so there was really nothing we could do about it. Four years later, we met for beer at the VFW along the San Antonio River Walk. At the time I had just started dating my law school classmate. Kelly was just mustering out of the Marine Corps and moving back to her hometown of Lubbock, where she got a job working for the campus police. Fast forward two years, and I called her to help me with a murder case. She ran a test on her sophisticated Rapid DNA equipment that helped me track down the killer. Oktoberfest weekend was going to be our first reunion since she had left to return to work the day after my release from the hospital.

I looked at my dirty T-shirt and sweat-stained baseball cap in the rearview mirror. I hadn't showered or put on clean clothes. So much for getting off on the right foot.

"You look amazing," I said, trying to sound suave and debonair. She wrapped her arms around me and kissed me hard on the lips. My dirty shirt and sweaty cap didn't faze her at all. "Sorry about the T-shirt. I—" Thankfully, she didn't let me finish.

"I've missed you," she murmured.

We were barely able to get the key from the slightly embarrassed desk clerk and make it to our second-story room before we had our clothes off and our arms and legs wrapped around each other like two high school kids on prom night.

By eight p.m. she informed me it was time to polka. She modeled the dress she'd found for the occasion. It was a modern version of the traditional dirndl that fit her like a glove.

"I can't believe you don't have any lederhosen. You're all into your German heritage."

She seemed a little disappointed.

I confessed that I did have a pair but that I'd grown out of them in high school. I'd never bothered to update my wardrobe.

"We'll have to fix that." She went into the bathroom to put the finishing touches on her outfit. "I'm going to buy you a pair for next year," she called from the open door. "Will you wear them?"

I didn't commit one way or another. Kelly put on some country music while she worked on her hair and makeup. I figured I had a year to form an acceptable negative response.

Next year. I liked the way she said that, like us being together until next year was a given.

CHAPTER NINE

I PARKED ON A SIDE STREET near the town square, and Kelly and I followed a line of people to the ticket booth. Every year on the first weekend in October, the Marktplatz across the street from the county courthouse was fenced off for the weekend festivities. The night was usually warm. Fall weather comes late to Central Texas, something I'm sure it took the first German immigrants a while to get used to. Most of the attendees wore shorts and T-shirts. There were dozens of men wearing lederhosen, and double that many women wearing dirndls. Some of the costumes fit well. Others were new and stiff and obviously purchased for the weekend occasion. Everybody was in a festive mood.

As we stood in line, I admired Kelly's blue-and-white dirndl that extended to her mid-thighs and showed off her tan athletic legs. She caught me looking.

"You'd look good in leather shorts," she said. "I'll bet they sell them here."

"I heard they were sold out. We'll have to wait for next year."

Her laughter made me glad she was here. The stars were visible above the glow from the tents and food booths in the square and added to the friendly small-town feel. The family in front of us included four generations who had probably never missed a festival.

"Are any of the parties involved in your missing persons case going to be here tonight?" Kelly asked.

"Everybody shows up at the Oktoberfest," I said.

She looked a little disappointed. "Does that mean you're working?"

"Maybe I can solve the case during the polka dance."

"You're not getting out of dancing."

I slipped my hand in hers and smiled. "We can always go back to the motel room."

Her smile reappeared. "Don't expect special treatment every night."

"If it's because of the bullet wound, I'll get shot more often."

"Don't even say things like that," she said, and spit between her fingers.

"What was that?"

"What?"

"You just spit through your fingers."

"To ward off bad luck." She smiled mischievously.

I paid for a couple of tickets, and we shuffled through the crowd to the beat of tuba and accordion music. We passed the octagon-shaped Vereins *Kirche* Museum—a replica of the original community church—and a giant-sized beer stein that served as a welcome sign and photo opp. I led the way to the food court, where I bought a German sausage sampler plate for us to share, then we moved on to the *biergarten* for a couple of souvenir cups filled with German beer. I pulled my baseball cap down low over my eyes, hoping not to have to talk to too many hometown people I knew. So far it was working. I'd passed a dozen people I grew up with who didn't seem to recognize me. It helped that Kelly was with me. Most of the looks we got were focused on her. When we reached the main tent, my hope of anonymity ended. Every table was full, and every table held someone who knew me and wanted to shake my hand. They weren't fooled by the baseball cap.

The old-timers reiterated their condolences for Grandpa's passing. His funeral was less than a month ago, so it was fresh on everybody's mind. What I dreaded most was having to retell the stories of Grandpa's murder and my shootout with Marcus Lopez, the corrupt San Antonio attorney who was running for governor without regard to ethics or legality.

Telling that last story was easier because Kelly had been there. She wasn't shy about filling in the details. She was a police officer and had been a Marine MP, so she was very good at giving the facts. At the end of the story, most of the listeners would shake their heads and say something like, "*It's a wonder y'all 're still alive.*" I wondered that too but tried not to think about it for too long.

Thankfully, the band was loud enough under the tent to restrict conversations to short periods when they were on a break. Kelly was serious about dancing, and we did our best imitation of a polka dance along with the throngs of college kids, locals, and tourists from all over.

When they started the "chicken dance," I was happy to take a breather and step outside the tent. The warm October night had us both sweating. I was about to suggest that we call it a night and sneak back to the Best Western when I heard a familiar voice.

"Fischer, you ol' scallywag!"

I knew that high-pitched, nasal voice anywhere and immediately felt like I was back in high school stepping out of the locker room.

"Rocky V," I said and raised my beer. "*Prost*. You remember Kelly." Everyone had met Kelly during Grandpa's funeral.

He wore the red cap with the Battlin' Billies logo, red polyester shorts that stretched over his beer belly, and a white polo shirt with Coach V stitched above the breast pocket. He also had two prominent front teeth that gave him a permanent smile.

"Sure do." His eyes were glassy even in the dim light. "You look prettier than a Munich barmaid."

Kelly held out her hand, but he went in for the hug. It was awkward. He planted a wet one on her cheek. When he untangled from Kelly, he grabbed my free hand and shook it like a workout rope in the gym.

"Easy," I said. "I'm still in recovery." I knew I would be sore in more places than one when the sun came up.

"Sorry. Keep forgettin' you're Wyatt Earp."

His wife followed a few steps behind him. She hadn't been to the funeral because she was the head volleyball coach and was with the team at the time on an out-of-town game. This was wife number four for Rocky. I was best man at this first wedding because it had come the week after high school graduation. The bride, his high school flame, was three months pregnant.

Wife number four was younger than Rocky by ten years, which would put her in her early twenties. Rocky had met her when she transferred from Round Rock as a senior in high school. She had a matching polo shirt that was a size too small.

"This is my wife, Gwen," Rocky said. "She just got her boobs done."

Gwen stuck out her chest for us to admire. "Nice, huh?"

"Nice to finally meet you." I held out my hand, trying to avoid eye contact with her implants.

Gwen skipped the hand and went in for the hug. I gritted my teeth. She pushed her enhanced boobs into my chest.

Kelly rolled her eyes.

Gwen turned to her. "I just love your outfit, honey," Gwen said. She tugged at a handful of Kelly's dress like she was examining a mannequin at Walmart. "Aren't you a tiny little thing?"

"What'd ya think of our little celebration?" Rocky asked her.

Gwen didn't wait for her to answer. "I saw you two cuttin' a rug out there. Are y'all takin' lessons?"

They fired questions from both sides, but neither was sober enough to care about the answers.

Kelly smiled and took my hand. "This is our first dance."

"Aren't you two just the cutest couple?"

Kelly's smile got a little bigger.

"Have you seen Jimmy or Castro? They're around somewhere. Allison's here too. Three sheets to the wind. She's lettin' it all hang out, if you know what I mean." Rocky winked at me.

Gwen slapped him on the shoulder. "You stop that, now."

"It's true," he said.

A group of high school kids passed us, giggling a little too loudly. "Hey, Coach V," they said in unison.

Rocky and Gwen both turned to them and waved. Owen Bauer was in the group. He had his head down, trying to go unnoticed. Lori wasn't with him, neither was Maya.

"Saw you in the parking lot after practice," Rocky said. "Why didn't you stop by the locker room?"

Gwen grabbed Kelly's arm and pulled her away. "Let the men catch up for a minute. Follow me to the little girl's room," she said to Kelly.

Kelly's eyes pleaded with me to intervene, but I wanted to quiz Rocky about Owen, so I just smiled.

"Here's some tickets. Bring us a round of beer when you come back," Rocky yelled over the crowd noise. He thrust a roll of concession tickets at his young wife.

"I heard about your little interrogation," Rocky said. He sounded a little irritated. "Why 're you pickin' on my star quarterback?"

"I just asked him a few questions about—"

He cut me off. "Maya Chavez. I know. Word gets around fast, or did you forget? Owen didn't know she was old man Geisler's granddaughter."

"What difference does that make?"

"Just sayin'. Did you talk to Zeller? He was around asking the same questions a few weeks ago."

Les Zeller was a Battlin' Billy a couple of years ahead of us in school.

"I followed the Bauer kid after I talked to him. He went to see Lori Kostoch. They argued, and he belted her in the face."

"Doesn't mean anything. You know how these kids are. It's high school. Tomorrow they'll be partying at Lori's mom's house."

"I had just talked to her about Maya. She's the one who told me to talk to Owen."

"Still doesn't mean he knows anything," Rocky said.

"Then he hauled ass out the creek road past his old man's place. He talked to a tatted-up dude in a double-wide trailer stuck out in the brush."

"So what? The guy probably works for Mike. Most of that part of the county is Bauer land. There's three or four older brothers and a bunch of cousins scattered around out there."

"I think Owen knows where Maya went."

"Things have changed since we went to school."

"What d'you mean?"

"All the new folks moving into the county. Twenty years ago, we knew everybody that came through that gate." He pointed to the ticket booth. "Now, I don't recognize half of them."

"I still saw a lot of folks I know," I said.

"Yeah, that's 'cause you're famous. Everybody wants to shake your hand."

"What's this have to do with Maya?" I asked.

"Things have changed is all I'm saying. In the old days, our families ran the place. It's not like that anymore. If you're thinking of staying on at your grandpa's place, you need to know that."

"I haven't decided whether I'm gonna stay or not. Right now, I wanna find Maya."

Rocky drank the last of his beer. I could see him searching for the right words to tell me something. His lips closed over his buckteeth. I knew him too well. That was a sign he was serious.

"Owen Bauer is my star player. The kid's a natural. Reminds me of you before you threw it all away to go shoot terrorists." He put his hand on my shoulder and leaned in close to me. I got a strong whiff of hops and German sausage. "I don't want anything to happen to him. We got a good chance of gettin' to regionals this year, if not further."

"Congratulations," I said. "Tell him to come clean about Maya, and I'll leave him alone."

"Damn it, Nick. I'm askin' as a favor. The kid's sensitive. If he's worried about you followin' him around, he'll fuck up in the game next week. I can't have that. We're playin' Boerne. They're tough this year."

"All I want is the truth," I said.

"Still the same hardheaded German. I swear to god, I never met anyone as stubborn as you."

"I'm talking about a missing girl. Helmut's granddaughter. You're talking about your football season."

"All right. Let me talk to him. Will you do that? You come on like Rambo. Hell, the kid's shittin' bricks."

"He's got nothin' to worry about if he tells the truth."

The girls elbowed their way through the crowd. Both held a cup of beer in each hand.

"I didn't think we'd ever get through the line," Gwen said, handing a beer to Rocky.

He quickly exposed his buckteeth and slipped back into happy-go-lucky coach mode. "Thanks for the beer, baby," he said and planted a sloppy kiss on her lips.

Kelly handed me a beer.

"To old friends," I said.

"*Prost*!" we said together and tipped our plastic cups to the full moon.

"The band's playing again," Kelly said. She pulled my hand toward the tent.

"Don't take too long," I said to Rocky. "I need some answers." I waved at Gwen. "Nice to meet you, Gwen."

Rocky closed his lips over his buckteeth. "I'll talk to him."

CHAPTER TEN

Kelly and I walked back to my pickup under a full harvest moon. Tired couples, some carrying sleeping kids, some following grandparents, dispersed toward side streets looking for their own parked vehicles. We'd spent the last thirty minutes dancing and watching a grandmother teach her four grandchildren how to polka. They were all under ten years old, wearing traditional costumes, and didn't seem the least self-conscious. I'd learned to dance the same way.

Kelly squeezed my hand when we reached the passenger door.

"You're thinking about your grandfather," she said. I don't know how she knew.

"This was his one social event of the year."

"I'm sorry I didn't get to meet him," she said.

We drove in silence back to the motel. My chest and arm were sore from dancing and shaking hands with everybody I knew.

I parked in the back of the full motel parking lot and went around to open Kelly's door. We leaned against the fender, looking at the moon that had just cleared the oak trees. I felt her breath and her heartbeat all at once.

"You gonna be all right?" she asked.

"Yeah. It'll take a while. He was my father, mother, and grandpa for a long time."

"Wouldn't hurt you to let it all out. I promise I won't tell anyone."

She tilted her face up and kissed me on the lips.

"Remember the first time that happened?" she asked.

"Of course," I said. The first time we kissed was in Lubbock while we were waiting for her lab to run a DNA test. The process took three hours on the state-of-the-art, Rapid DNA testing equipment. While we waited for the results, she had invited me out to dinner. Afterward, we made out in the parking lot until the call came about the positive DNA match.

"Did you really leave me that night because of the case?" she asked.

I wasn't sure which answer would get me in more trouble. If I said I left her in the parking lot so I could pursue the case, she might think I would always choose work over her. On the other hand, if I told her I left her because at the time I still thought I could work things out with my girlfriend, she might think I wasn't completely committed to her. I had never been very good at negotiating the dating world.

"It took all my willpower to walk away from you that night," I said.

She smiled. "Good answer."

Maybe I was learning.

"There's nothing holding you back tonight," she said, and kissed me again. We made out for another minute. A family of four with teenage kids pulled into the empty parking space beside us. I opened my eyes and could see the two young boys in the backseat of the minivan pointing and giggling. Their mother said something to calm them down, but it didn't help. The product of too much cotton candy. It would be a while before they went to sleep.

This time, we managed to get to our room with most of our clothes intact. Kelly wanted to show off the new undergarment she bought for the occasion. It looked like something I'd seen in a Frankfurt strip club, but I didn't tell her that. The material was shear, except for very small German flags in strategic places. I was impressed. It was enough to distract me from thinking about Grandpa and Maya Chavez for another hour.

When we had showered and lain back down on the king-sized bed, we could hear the hyperactive kids bouncing off the walls in the next room.

"Are we always going to have to stay in a motel?" she asked.

"Of course not. I'm gonna give Helen a deadline."

"I didn't mean that you should kick her out. You have more than one room at the ranch house."

"I'd rather not have to put up with her interruptions while I'm with you," I said.

"I wouldn't mind. She seems nice."

"Yeah, well, we have issues. She almost walked in on me in the bathroom this morning. She wanted to check my bandage."

"She's your mother. That's sweet."

"Not exactly the way I would put it." I didn't want to talk about Helen. Owen Bauer's trip to the country had me wondering what or if it had anything to do with Maya.

"What else is bothering you?" she asked, snuggling beside me. I was quickly learning that Kelly wasn't going to ever let me cut her out of my thought process. In the short time we'd been together, she seemed to be able to read me like an open book. "You're thinking about that girl, Maya Chavez, aren't you?"

I admitted I was and told her about my conversation with Rocky. "Rocky seemed more interested in Owen's performance on the field than getting any information on her disappearance."

"A girl's missing and he's worried about his football season? The guy sounds like a real piece of work," she said.

"I promised him he could talk to Owen, but I didn't say I would stop looking for Maya."

"What're you thinking?"

"That trailer I followed Owen Bauer to out in the country. He met a guy with a ponytail and a chest full of tatts."

She slipped off the bed and started getting dressed.

"What are you doing?" I asked.

"You think Maya's out there. If I don't go out there with you, you'll go on your own." She pulled on a pair of jeans and sat on the bed. "We need to know tonight." She slipped on a pair of tactical boots and laced them up. Kelly not only knew what I was thinking, she was willing to go along.

CHAPTER ELEVEN

THE FULL MOON MADE THE narrow gravel road easy to follow at night without headlights. The dangerous part was avoiding the herds of deer and wild hogs grazing along the fencerow. Kelly was holding my hand across the console in the dark pickup cab. It was an odd sensation. Kelly caught me looking at our hands linked together.

"What?" she smiled. "You don't like holding hands?" She tried to pull away, but I held firm.

"No. I like it." I smiled back. "I was just thinking that I'm not used to PDA."

"Well, get over it." She leaned over and kissed me on the cheek. "Besides, we're in the middle of nowhere on a gravel road without headlights. Whatever we do out here wouldn't be considered a public display of affection."

"I see your point."

"I'm starting to think you brought me out here just to take advantage of me."

"If I wanted to do that, I'd have kept you in the motel room."

"If we don't find what we're looking for, can we get naked in the backseat?" she asked.

"Deal," I said.

"Don't make promises you can't keep, Mr. Fischer."

"That's something I never do."

I pulled to the side of the road at the cattle guard where Owen Bauer had crossed that afternoon. There were lights in the brush and muffled music. The night was still and warm. We unrolled the windows and listened to a barn owl hoot his preparation for the night's hunt. The pulsing music didn't seem to bother him. I pulled out my binoculars and swept the brush around the trailer.

"I don't hear any polka music," Kelly said.

"Not much dancing going on either." I spotted two bodies standing by the door of the trailer. They both had shaved heads and wore sleeveless jean jackets. I guessed they were guards, and I wondered what they were guarding. There was a fire burning in a fifty-five-gallon drum about twenty feet away from the trailer. It was cut in half and lying on its side. "I see two thugs by the door watching a barbecue pit. The brush is too thick to make out anything else."

"Let me see," she said, and took the binoculars. "It's a stash house."

"You're sure?"

"It's hidden out in the brush. The windows are closed. Couple of guards outside. Couldn't be a better place to hide a shipment of drugs or whatever's goin' on with those women."

"I forgot you were a policewoman. What was Owen Bauer, star quarterback for the Battlin' Billies, doing here?" Despite the warmth of the October night, a chill ran down my spine. Something in the back of my memory was tapping at the front door of my brain. The sensation gave me an uneasy feeling. That afternoon I remembered the shootout near here that had killed my dad, but there was something else that happened here. Something older. Something that reminded me of Maya.

"What is it?" Kelly asked, staring at me in the moonlight.

"Something happened here that reminded me of Maya. It's been bugging me since we crossed Palo Alto Creek." I stared at the moon for a full two minutes before I realized what it was. "We're hunting a missing girl within a few miles of where Anna Metzger was abducted by Indians and her sister was murdered."

"I didn't think there were any natives left in Central Texas."

"It happened in 1864."

"Oh, some of your ancient history again. I was getting worried."

"The girl survived nine months in captivity. Her fourteen-year-old sister was murdered on the spot. They shot her with arrows, stripped her clothes, and scalped her while her little sister watched."

"Wow, no wonder you were thinking about her." She crossed herself.

"What was that for?"

"Keeps the ghosts away." She smiled. "You said a girl was murdered."

"You're afraid of ghosts?"

"There are some things a pistol won't protect you from."

"Like evil spirits?"

She nodded. "What happened to the girls?"

"They had gone to visit their older sister at the Nimitz Hotel on Main Street. It was February, and there was snow on the ground. They were on their way home at dusk when they spotted riders on the road. They thought it was someone they knew and waved, then realized too late that the riders were a Kiowa raiding party. One of them grabbed Anna and strapped her on the front of his horse. The older sister resisted."

Kelly chewed her bottom lip, waiting for the rest of the story.

"When she fought back, they shot her full of arrows. Anna watched the men strip her sister's clothes and scalp her blond hair. Her family found her body the next morning."

"Oh, my god. What happened to Anna?"

"The Kiowas rode north for twelve days, stopping only briefly for river crossings. Anna wrote about it later. The story also came out in the Austin newspaper. The only food she was given was raw liver. She said her tongue got so swollen from lack of water she couldn't speak."

"And she survived?"

"Yep, survived nine months in captivity. She lived to be eighty-one years old. Married and moved down the road to Mason. The first settlers were a very tough bunch."

She crossed herself again. "You think Maya was kidnapped?"

"The thought did cross my mind. I'm starting to think she didn't leave on her own."

I pulled my Springfield XD .45 pistol from the glove box and checked the magazine. I had a spare that held thirteen rounds.

"What did you have in mind?" she asked.

"Let's go do a little recon," I said.

She pulled a SIG Sauer P226 pistol from her purse and clipped it on her belt. "Dating you is going to be interesting."

"So... We're dating? Is it official?" I asked.

"Are you kidding? We already danced the polka and made love in a Best Western. It doesn't get any more official." She leaned over the console and kissed me. "Let's go see what's going on in that trailer."

We hopped the barbed-wire fence and made our way through the brush toward the lights of the trailer. The moon provided plenty of light to avoid major rocks and the spiny cactus. Pulsating music rattled the aluminum on the trailer. A coyote yipped, followed by a dozen or more. They were on the hunt tonight too.

We crept to within fifty feet of the trailer. The two skinheads were still outside. One was tending to a large piece of meat on the barbecue pit. The other sat in a folding chair drinking a beer. There were two tricked-out Super Duty pickups fitted with chrome roll bars and a new black Jeep Grand Cherokee with oversized mud tires parked in the driveway.

"What do you think?" I asked Kelly.

"I'd like to know what's going on inside."

All the curtains on the trailer were closed. There was the added noise of a diesel generator creating the power for the lights and the air conditioner mounted on the top of the trailer.

While we listened to the noise and watched the skinhead turn the meat, the tattooed guy I saw with Owen stepped out of the trailer. He had his shirt off and his hair in a ponytail, just as he did earlier. Even in the dim firelight, I could see the distinctive dragon tattoo across his chest. "That's the guy I saw with Owen Bauer."

"Looks like a gangbanger," Kelly said.

"Yeah. What the hell's he doin' out here?"

"Drugs, most likely. Whose land is this?" she asked.

"I'm pretty sure it belongs to Mike Bauer, Owen's daddy."

A young girl stepped out of the trailer and onto the wooden pallet used for a porch. Her cutoff jean shorts were tight, and she wore a black tank top. I guessed she was in her early twenties or was small and skinny for her age. Her hair was dark and stringy and clung to her head like she hadn't washed it in a week. The girl lit a cigarette and stood looking down at the meat on the barbecue pit.

"What d'you think you're doin'?" The guy with the tattoo said.

"I just came out for a smoke," the girl answered.

"Do it, then get your ass back in the trailer and finish business," he said.

"He stinks. Besides, I'm done. He's passed out."

The guy with the tattoo laughed at her. He was six two or three and probably tipped the scales at around two forty without an ounce of fat. He was definitely the man in charge.

"You stink." He grabbed the lit cigarette from her lips and tossed it in the barrel. "You're done. I don't want you seen out here."

The girl hesitated. Tattoo raised his hand as if to strike her.

I took a step forward. Kelly grabbed my arm.

"Wait," she whispered.

The girl cringed as if she expected to be hit, but Tattoo didn't swing. The girl retreated into the trailer.

"If you go over there, somebody's gonna get hurt."

"That's the idea," I said.

"You're forgetting about the hole in your shoulder."

"We need to look in that trailer. Maya may be in there." I wanted to slap some sense into Dragon Tatt after watching the girl's reaction, but I understood Kelly's point.

"I'll create a diversion," she said. "Work your way around back."

She stood up and walked directly toward the circle of light surrounding the trailer.

"Hey," I said. "What're you doin'?"

She turned back to me. "Go look for Maya."

I didn't like what she was about to do, but I couldn't stop her. I knew she was armed and could take care of herself. She made it to the edge of the brush before the man with the dragon tatt saw her.

"Well, well, well," he said in a loud voice.

"Easy, big boy," Kelly said. Her voice carried over the music. "I'm looking for Mike Bauer."

While Kelly distracted them, I ducked around behind the trailer and searched the edge of the windows for a crack. I found a small tear in the white plastic covering. Inside, the room was small with warped wood paneling and a mattress without sheets. The young woman I'd seen outside was lying on the bed staring at the screen of her smartphone. There was a naked man sprawled on the bed beside her.

I moved to the next window. It was smaller and higher off the ground. The plastic on this one was raised a couple of inches. I could see a sink full of dirty dishes and a table against the opposite wall. Two women sat smoking. Each had shorts and tank tops exposing a number of tattoos. There was a half-empty bottle of tequila in front of them. I peered around the small space looking for other bodies but saw nothing. The TV was on, tuned to a reality show. There were dirty clothes tossed on the floor, along with black plastic trash bags stacked to the ceiling against one wall.

I didn't see Maya.

I moved to the rear of the trailer. Here, the covering was taped down to the edge of the window. The light inside caused the white plastic to glow. I heard muffled voices but couldn't make out what was being said. They were feminine voices engaged in a serious conversation. I put my ear to the metal frame but could only hear the buzz from the loud music in the front room. I couldn't leave without knowing if Maya was in there.

I took out my folding knife and slowly lifted the edge of the glass window. The frame was old and oxidized, and the window easily opened half an inch. I grabbed a mesquite branch and wedged it under the glass to hold the window open. I paused to listen. They were speaking Spanish, but I didn't know if Maya knew the language. She had grown up in Southern California with her father's family.

I made a tiny incision through the white plastic covering and put my eye to the hole. There were two young women Maya's age sitting on a queen-sized bed. They were dressed like the older women in shorts and tank tops. I smelled the distinct odor of marijuana. The women had long dark hair hanging over their shoulders. Both wore heavy makeup with dark eyeliner. Neither was Maya, but I wondered what they were doing there and what they were talking about.

One turned to the window. Their conversation stopped. They sensed a presence watching them. I ducked away, took the twig from the window, and slipped into the surrounding brush.

Kelly was waiting for me when I got back to the pickup.

"What'd you find out?" she asked.

"No Maya, but there're four other women in the trailer. The

one we saw talking to Mr. Tattoo was entertaining a naked guy or had just finished. He looked passed out."

"Any drugs?"

I told her about the plastic bags stacked against the wall and the smell of marijuana. She seemed to think it was probably drugs. She'd been in on more of those kinds of busts than I had. We got in the pickup, and I made a U-turn in the road and headed back toward town.

"What'd you say to the tattooed guy?" I asked.

"Told him I was looking for Mike Bauer. I showed him my campus police badge. He didn't seem impressed. The big dragon tatt on his chest looks like a prison job. The two skinheads were stoned. They're all ex-cons who definitely shouldn't have drugs or weapons, but the big guy didn't seem shy about showing off."

"What'd he say about Bauer?"

"Said he works for him. And that he would be back in the morning. He offered me some barbecue and a joint if I wanted to wait."

"How generous."

"That guy's evil. I do know that."

"Why do you say that?"

"His eyes. Cold. Dead. No empathy. A prison stare. The kind of guy that makes my skin crawl." She crossed herself. "Don't go up against him alone. Not now. Not with that hole in your chest."

Something told me I wouldn't have that option.

CHAPTER TWELVE

THE NEXT MORNING KELLY AND I stopped by the local police station to see if Officer Zeller had turned up anything new in Maya's missing person case and as a courtesy heads-up that Helmut had asked me to help him find her. We found Zeller eating a blueberry kolache and talking on the phone at his desk. He looked like he could happily put away a dozen of them and had been doing just that since I'd seen him in high school. He had instantly recognized my name when I called to make an appointment and agreed to give me a few minutes of his time on the busy Oktoberfest weekend.

Zeller motioned us into a couple of metal chairs and held up two fingers, which I took to mean give him two minutes to finish his phone call. The other party seemed to be doing all the talking. Les was nodding as if the caller could see him and grunting responses through blueberry-stained teeth. He pointed at a large white pastry box on the desk. I took that as an offer to help myself and selected a pastry filled with cream cheese.

Kelly declined.

I would pay for it when I finally got back in the gym, but for now it was fun to eat like a teenager again and pretend the fuel would help me heal more quickly.

"Well, you two look like newlyweds," Les said, hanging up the phone.

Kelly rewarded me with a bright smile.

"This is my girlfriend, Kelly Hoffman. She was at the funeral. We spoke with your dad."

Kelly shook Les's hand.

"Pleased to meet you," she said. "I'm a police officer in Lubbock."

"A fellow officer." He sized her up from top to bottom before turning back to me. "We were all sorry to hear about your grandpa. Otto was a real fixture around here."

"Yeah, I'm gonna miss him," I said. Most of the town had come to the funeral. At least, everyone that had lived there more than twenty years. Les's father had been a deputy in the sheriff department under my father and recently retired and moved to Rockport.

"Too bad about the SAPD detective," Les said offhandedly.

I wasn't quite sure what he meant. Was he sorry the detective was a dirty scumbag, or was he sorry I'd killed him? The SAPD detective killed my grandpa, put a bullet in my partner, and shot my dog. I wasn't sorry he was gone.

"Yeah, the bastard was dirty." My blood pressure rose, and the hole in my arm from the good detective's .308 sniper rifle throbbed.

His phone rang before he could respond. Les listened to the caller. He held up his hand, signaling for me to wait again while he took the call.

I stared at Les and considered his comment about the SAPD detective while he chatted on the phone. The fact that I had killed an SAPD detective during the course of the investigation, regardless of the officer's obvious criminal conduct, rubbed some law enforcement officers the wrong way. Cops didn't like dirty cops, but there were a few who didn't like anybody outside the fraternity doing anything about it. They wanted to punish their own. Les seemed to think that way.

"Give me five minutes," Les said into the phone and hung up.

I figured that was the time he was giving us, so I let the SAPD remark slide for now and plunged in with my story. "Like I said on the phone, I'm here about Maya Chavez. Helmut Geisler told me about his granddaughter. He's worried. I told him I'd look into it."

Zeller nodded. "You workin' the case?" he asked, sounding surprised.

"We haven't officially signed papers, but there does seem to be cause for concern. She hasn't been home since August."

Les put his hands on the desk and laced his fingers together, gathering his thoughts.

"I appreciate you stopping by and sharing your concern. Helmut's been in here to talk to me a couple of times. I like Helmut. He's a good man. But I think he's way off base with Maya."

"What makes you say that?" Kelly asked. She didn't like the way this was going, and neither did I.

"Here's the deal with Maya," he said. "She's what you might call a wild child. I spoke with my counterparts in San Bernardino and Riverside County. Maya had a history. Picked up for truancy. Runaway. She had gang ties. Her father's side of the family."

"She was born here, Les."

"She spent eight years in Southern California. That had to make an impression on her."

"I spent five years in Iraq and Afghanistan," Kelly said. "I'm still a Texan."

Zeller sighed. "You know what I mean."

"Doesn't matter. She's still missing," I said.

"She's eighteen. It matters. There's no law against her leaving home. You did it."

"Yeah, I joined the Marine Corps. It wasn't a secret. Everybody knew where I was going."

"The thing is, as much as I'd like to help, we don't have the manpower to chase down every runaway case we get. We notify the hotline and wait for a tip. If she committed a crime or she was a victim, and we knew she was still in town, we could go after her. We have to have probable cause." He said this last part like he was explaining it to a third grader. "That means that we could—"

"I know what it means, Les." I could feel my face getting hot.

"The rules have changed, Nick," he said. "We follow the law."

"What the hell's that supposed to mean?"

"I read about your last case. I got the call the day you killed the detective. You played fast and loose with the law."

I suppressed the urge to put a right jab into Les's smug expression. "It was an ambush, Les. I didn't pick a fight, and I didn't fire first."

"We just wanna know who you talked to about Maya," Kelly said, interrupting the escalating tension. "You called the hotline, but did you track her phone or put anything out on social media? That kind of thing?"

Zeller wiped his face with a paper towel. "We opened a file." He held a manila folder up as evidence. "The phone number Helmut gave me was a prepaid phone she bought herself. I talked to a couple of her classmates down at the school and her mother. Nobody'd seen her. We don't have the time or the resources to do social media."

"Was one of them Lori Kostoch?" I asked.

"Yeah, I believe one of them was Lori," he said, reading from the file.

"What about Owen Bauer?" I asked.

"Yeah, him too."

"I talked to him yesterday. He got into a fight with Lori Kostoch, then drove out to a trailer house past Palo Alto Creek."

"The trailer looks like a stash house," Kelly said.

"Now, wait a minute." Les laid his cubby hands flat on the

desk. "That's all Bauer property. You can't be out there without Mike's permission."

"Mike Bauer dealing drugs these days?" I asked.

"You saw drugs in the trailer?"

"I saw plastic bags stacked to the ceiling. The windows are closed. Get a warrant and go check it out. I smelled marijuana, and they had firearms."

"No law against havin' guns," he said.

"Unless you're a felon," Kelly reminded him.

"There were also some females in the trailer. You can take a wild guess why they were there," I said.

Les's face turned red. He stood up. "I need more than that to get a warrant to search Mike Bauer's property. This ain't your daddy's county no more. You can't run around here like you own the place."

"Who owns it now, Les? You? Mike Bauer?"

"I've got work to do, Nick. Nice to meet you, Kelly. Enjoy yourself at the Oktoberfest. I saw you out there on the dance floor last night. Y'all have some fancy moves." He smiled and put on his hat. "Just be sure you keep those moves on the dance floor. I understand you have a legal license to investigate, and Helmut can retain your services. But don't bother Mr. Bauer or his son."

"And what about Maya?" I asked. I faced off with him. We were about the same height. He had thirty pounds of fresh kolaches on me.

"Sometimes kids just run off. Give her a month or two. My guess is, she'll get tired of partying and come home."

"Thanks for the kolache, Les. Say hi to your daddy for me. He was a good man and a good deputy."

CHAPTER THIRTEEN

It was close to noon, and all the German eateries on Main Street had lines out the door. I had promised Kelly schnitzel and red cabbage for lunch but didn't want to wait all afternoon to get it. Every year, the Oktoberfest celebration seemed to get bigger. Grandpa would say that was a bad thing. People like Mike Bauer and everyone with a business on Main Street loved it.

Kelly reached over and took my hand.

"I'll settle for a hamburger. Didn't Germans invent that?"

"Probably. It's got the two things we love, bread and meat."

"Throw on a potato and you'd be in heaven."

"Now you're talking dirty."

I pulled into the Whataburger and got in the drive-through line. It didn't matter where we went, there was a line of hungry tourists.

"Why do you think Les got defensive when you mentioned Bauer?" Kelly asked while we waited to order our burgers.

"He's a city cop. Bauer's on the council. He knows who signs the checks."

"What about Owen?"

"Everybody supports the football team, and Les is good buddies with Rocky. You can bet they will have a conversation about our visit. He's probably on the phone with him right now."

The voice behind the intercom took our order. I cut my engine. My ten-year-old pickup was pushing 200K and had started making a clacking noise at idle that was driving me crazy.

"This is a small town. The people who run it are a close-knit group. They all talk to each other. They may not all like each other, but they all talk."

"I always thought of Lubbock as a small town."

"Compared to San Antonio. Not compared to Fredericksburg."

There was a tap on the glass. When I turned, Lori Kostoch was standing by the door. I unrolled the window.

"Mr. Fischer, can I talk to you?" She seemed apprehensive and kept glancing over her shoulder toward the street. Her blond hair hung loose, and she wore a blue T-shirt from the German Bakery.

"Sure, Lori. Get in."

She glanced at Kelly. "I'd rather it was private."

"It's okay. She's working with me. She knows about Maya."

Lori opened the door and hopped in the back seat.

"Is everything okay?" I asked, studying her in the rearview mirror. I could see the fresh cut on her lip where Owen had slapped her. She had covered it with red lipstick, but it was still swollen.

"This is Kelly Hoffman. You can talk in front of her. She's a police officer from Lubbock."

Lori seemed a little unsure.

"Would you like anything?" I asked.

She shook her head, so I pulled forward to the window. Lori ducked behind the door, hiding her face from the teenage cashier. She would know every teenager in town, and she was obviously concerned about being seen with me.

I drove around the city block to see if we were being followed, then pulled into the parking lot of Fort Martin Scott, the restored army outpost built in a vain attempt to protect settlers from

Indian raids in the nineteenth century. The location was on the edge of town and had just enough tourists to keep us from looking conspicuous.

Lori was still anxious. I took a cheeseburger from the sack and offered it to her.

"Hungry?" I asked her.

"No, sir. Thank you."

I was starving but wanted to give Lori my full attention, so I reluctantly put the burger back in the sack.

"Did you think of something else?" I asked, waiting for her to work up the courage to speak.

"I did see Maya," she said, looking down at her hands. "The night she… The night she left. I was with her."

Kelly raised her eyebrows, shot a glance at me.

"Tell me about it," I said.

"We went to a party on the river before school started."

"Do you remember the date?" I asked.

"The tenth," she answered without hesitation.

"Y'all still go to the river bend on the Pedernales?"

"Yeah, everybody goes there. But this was different."

I waited without speaking. Lori glanced out the widows at the other cars in the parking lot, then scanned the faces of the group of tourists standing beside the historical marker. She seemed to be expecting someone to jump out and approach the pickup at any moment.

"You're safe here," I said.

"We can help you," Kelly added.

Lori focused her attention back inside the pickup. "There were a bunch of guys there I didn't recognize. Older guys. They wanted us to dance for them, like strippers. It was disgusting. One of them grabbed Maya and pulled her top off." The words tumbled out of her mouth and left her gasping for breath.

"Slow down. Who were they?" I asked.

"Owen's friends. He's the one that told me to go and bring Maya. I barely even knew her. I swear to god, I didn't know she was Mr. Geisler's granddaughter. Owen said to bring her and some booze."

"And you were tryin' to impress him?" I asked.

She nodded. "Yeah."

"Did they hurt her?" Kelly asked.

"One of them stepped in. I'd seen him before. He works for Owen's dad. He has this big, like, tattoo of a dragon on his chest. It's, like, green with red flames. He hit the guy who took Maya's top off and made him give it back to her."

"What happened to Maya?"

"I don't know. That's what I wanted to tell you. When that guy stepped in, I took off. I ran back to my car. Maya and I went together. I picked her up in town. I waited by the car for like an hour. When Maya didn't come, I just left. My mom was waiting for me. That was the last time I saw her." She looked down at her hands, then out the pickup window. "I didn't know what to do. Owen said she was all right."

"Right now, we need to focus on finding Maya," I told her. Everything about what she said was wrong, but I didn't want Lori to go off the deep end. "I saw you with Owen yesterday. What did you argue about, behind the restaurant?"

"He didn't want me to say anything."

"Is that why he hit you?" Kelly asked.

She chewed her swollen lip and nodded.

"Does he know what happened to Maya?" I asked.

She shook her head. "He said she left with the Dragon."

"The Dragon?" I asked.

"That's what Owen called the guy with the tattoo," Lori said. "I'm scared." She put her hands on the back of the seat. Looked me in the eyes for the first time. "Will you find her?"

"I'll find her." I wished I was as confident as I sounded. I fished a business card out of my glovebox. Kelly took it and wrote her name and cell phone number on the back before handing it to Lori.

"That has both our numbers on it," I said. "Call us if you think of anything else. We're staying at the Best Western for the weekend. Room two thirty-six."

"Don't let Owen touch you again," Kelly said. "If he does, I will personally kick his ass."

Lori smiled at that. She knew Kelly wasn't kidding.

CHAPTER FOURTEEN

We dropped Lori off on Main Street near the old Nimitz Hotel and the bronze statue of Admiral Nimitz, one of the town's most famous sons. It was two o'clock in the afternoon, and I drove back out of town on Highway 290 to find the Bauer winery. Mike Bauer was Owen's father, and I wanted to ask him about the workers living in the trailer on his property. I was never a wine enthusiast or connoisseur, so I never paid much attention to the local industry, but sometime during the last twenty years the business had tripled in size from a dozen wineries to more than forty. I grew up seeing wild grape vines growing along the creek banks, but now, farmers like Bauer were putting in wine grapes and cashing in on thirsty tourists.

"Ever been to Napa Valley?" Kelly asked as we drove past a brewery that had recently opened for business. It looked like a good place for men to spend a few hours while their wives did the wine tour.

"No, but I imagine it's a little more crowded."

"Not by much. I drove up while I was stationed at Pendleton."

"I'd rather go to the brewery."

"You're a beer snob. Don't Germans make wine?"

"Sure, but just to make money off the French."

"Funny guy."

Fertile farmland stretched out on both sides of the highway in the wide Pedernales River valley. To the north, the rough outline of limestone hills was a constant reminder that we were in the Texas Hill Country. We passed the turn to Luckenbach, the town made famous by a song Waylon Jennings put out in the seventies. They served cold beer under giant oak trees and usually had a live band on weekends that drew a big crowd.

"Did you grow up with Bauer?"

"I've known him and his family all my life. Mike went to school with my dad. His family's been here forever. He donated his great-great-granddad's log cabin to the pioneer museum. Had it dismantled and reassembled on Main Street. If Grandpa were around, he could tell us the full history. I know Mike's involved with the city council and is big in the Catholic Church. Their family were town folks. When the first German settlers came to the area, those who were part of the church settled in town. The intellectuals set up ranches and communities further south."

"So, the Fischers were intellectuals?"

"That's right. We fought for governmental reforms in the old country. When that didn't work out, we came to Texas."

"Isn't that an oxymoron?"

"What?"

"German intellectuals?"

"Now who's being funny? Ever hear of Luther, Nietzsche, or Kant?"

She smiled. "Hitler, Kaiser Wilhelm..."

"Fine, I get it."

"I think there's a connection there."

"You're gonna mock my heritage?"

She laughed again. "Not mocking... just noticed that all those Germans are very serious folks."

"And?"

"And so are you," she said.

"Guilty," I said. She had a point.

I pulled into the Bauer winery parking lot. The tasting room was built like an oversized nineteenth-century wooden barn complete with an exterior of distressed wood and a roof made of rusted metal. The newly paved parking lot and the tasteful landscaping reminded me of the faux western buildings at Knott's Berry Farms.

"Feels like I've been here before," Kelly said.

"I think that's the general idea." All the new tasting rooms built in the last ten years seemed to be either going for the old-world Italian look or the retro farm style. Bauer went with the latter.

Inside, there were shelves full of wine for sale, along with caps and T-shirts and other wine-oriented merchandise featuring the family label. The room had high ceilings complete with exposed wooden rafter beams. In the center of the room was an open bar where three gray-haired couples stood listening to a young hipster guy with a beard and round glasses deliver the vintner's speech. Something about temperature and the acidity, and which part of the tongue tingled when you drank it—all over my head.

A lady in a new Fredericksburg T-shirt and short-cropped salt-and-pepper hair dutifully swirled a half inch of red wine in her glass and then took a big whiff. Her husband looked at her skeptically. A younger couple at one of the tables had skipped the tasting and gone straight for a full glass of wine.

I didn't see Bauer and was about to explore a hallway that led to a back office, when a woman in her early twenties wearing jeans and a western shirt cut us off.

"Here for a tasting?" she asked, flashing a big country-girl smile. "I'm Brenda. Y'all from out of town?"

"Actually, I'm looking for Mike Bauer. I'm an old friend of the family. Is he in today?"

She frowned. Her eyes lingered on the scars across my forehead, trying to judge the likelihood of me buying a case of wine. She probably got paid in tips and commissions.

"But while we're here, we might as well try your wine," I said and winked.

This brought her smile back with a slight blush.

Kelly shot me a curious look.

"I'll go see if he's in," she said, and hurried down the hallway.

"Were you flirting with her?" Kelly asked.

"Working on my people skills."

"Ahh… Well, just a little warning. I'm the jealous type," she said with a straight face.

Mike Bauer followed Brenda out of the back office. He was a big bear of a man in his fifties with a dark beard streaked with gray and a full head of frizzy hair that reached to his shoulders. He wore khaki pants over orange Crocs and a tie-dyed winery shirt.

"Nick Fischer," he said, striding down the hallway. He had a loud, booming voice and held out a large paw for me to shake.

"Mike, it's been a long time."

"Sorry about your grandpa. I wish I could have made the funeral, but I was out of town. Wine business. This place keeps me busy."

"This is Kelly Hoffman, my girlfriend from Lubbock."

Kelly held out her hand, and Mike took it between his thumb and index finger and held her fingers to his lips.

"Pleasure to meet you. Lubbock, eh? We buy a lot of grapes from Lubbock. Not as susceptible to fungus." His eyes lingered on Kelly's formfitting jeans and white Oxford shirt that she left untucked to cover the butt of her SIG Sauer pistol.

I tried to distract him. "I know you're busy, Mike—"

"Not at all." He cut me off and held up both hands, gesturing around the mostly empty room. His eyes were still focused on Kelly's jeans. "In fact, I've been meaning to call you. Do you have a card or something?"

I produced one of my private investigator cards and handed it to him.

He looked it over and smiled. "Semper Fi. Nice. I read about your last case in the paper. Come into my office, will ya?" He turned without waiting for my answer and gestured to Brenda. "Bring us a bottle of reserva, Brenda," he called to her. He put his arm around Kelly's shoulders.

If he slid his hand any lower, Kelly would put him on the floor.

"You're gonna love this wine," he said to Kelly. "Gold medal at the livestock show in Fort Worth."

I followed them down the hall and into his office, which looked just like the showroom, only smaller and with a lower ceiling. It had an oak desk cluttered with papers and a wall dedicated to wine awards and pictures of him receiving them. The opposite wall was dedicated to his son, Owen. He seemed to match his father trophy for trophy, only his were for baseball, basketball, and football. The kid was a hometown hero judging by the framed headlines from the local paper.

Brenda brought the wine and three glasses. I knew I wasn't going to like it, but I decided to go with the flow. Brenda filled the glasses and left the bottle on the table. Mike handed one to Kelly and me, then held up his own.

While his eyes lingered on Kelly, he said, "To Oktoberfest."

We clicked our glasses and drank. "*Prost*!"

"What'd you think?" he asked, anxious for a compliment.

"Wonderful," Kelly said.

"Yeah, best I've had in a long time," I said. I wasn't kidding. It was the only wine I'd had since my last communion in high school.

Mike refilled our glasses. He made a point of touching Kelly's hand while handing her a full glass.

"I knew you'd like it. I can't keep it on the shelf. Wait till this afternoon. All those folks headed to the Marktplatz will stop by when they see the weekend promotion—free tasting. They buy it by the case. You know, we should have Oktoberfest once a month."

"Then it wouldn't be Oktoberfest," I said.

"Hey, we have Christmas in July." He talked like a used car salesman with a new lot full of lemons to unload. "People don't care. Give it a German name, and they'll come. Why do you think they invented Oktoberfest?"

He looked at us, waiting for an answer. I let him fill in his own punch line.

"To sell more beer," he said, and laughed at his own joke. It was a big bearish laugh that exposed the perfect teeth the wine shop had paid for. I knew there was a sales pitch coming next, so I waited for him to finish before moving on to ask about his trailer tenants.

"Listen, if I'm being too forward in asking, just tell me. Sometimes I get so caught up in a deal I can't help myself." He paused to take a breath and finish his glass of wine. "I wanted to ask you about your grandpa's ranch. I know you're a private detective and all. Hell, who doesn't? You even made the local paper. Hell of a thing, you shooting that politician. What was his name?"

"Marcus Lopez," I said. I hoped he wasn't going to ask me for any details. I was tired of talking about it and had told the story so many times it was starting to sound like an episode from *Gunsmoke*.

"That's right. Man, he could have been our governor. Hell of a thing. Goes to show, you never know about people. I didn't like him anyway. Everybody knew he was gonna push for a state income tax. I liked his highspeed rail idea, though. That might have brought in more customers." He paused and held up the reserva bottle. "You want more wine?"

I looked at Kelly. She shrugged.

"No thanks, Mike," we said together.

"Anyway, I know you're getting your grandpa's affairs in

order…" He poured the rest of the bottle into his glass, twirled the red liquid in the sunlight, and said: "I'd like to buy your place."

There it was. A bottle of wine and twenty minutes later, he finally got to the point.

"I know you're thinkin' it's not worth much since it's pretty far away from town, but I'm prepared to offer you a fair market price."

He was lying through his teeth, and Grandpa had turned down several generous offers.

"It's not for sale, Mike." I hadn't really made up my mind about what to do with the family land, but I wasn't ready to negotiate a price while Grandpa was still warm in his grave.

"Your mother said you were getting all the paperwork in order. I thought that meant you were getting ready to put it on the market."

"You talked to Helen?" The thought of her talking to Mike Bauer about the family ranch turned my stomach.

"I drove out yesterday to talk to you, but you weren't home. I thought that's why you were here. She said she thought you would sell out as soon as you recovered from your injuries. I told her y'all could stay in the old house as long as you wanted."

"Helen Jarvis doesn't have anything to do with my family ranch," I said a little louder than I should have. Kelly reached out and put her hand on my arm.

"Hey, I figured since she was living there…"

"She's not living there. She came for the funeral and is leaving soon. The ranch is not for sale." I checked my own emotions. His interest in the ranch had caught me off guard.

"Well, I was sure you'd be anxious to get back to San Antonio. You know, get back to work."

I set the remainder of my glass of Bauer Reserva wine on Mike's oak desk. Everybody I talked to seemed to think I was anxious to get back to San Antonio. Maybe I was. First, I had to find Maya Chavez.

"I am workin', Mike. Matter of fact, Helmut Geisler asked me to find his granddaughter, Maya." If there was any recognition in his eyes, I didn't notice it. "You know Helmut?"

"Yes, of course. Everybody knows Helmut. You say his granddaughter is missing?"

"The last time anybody saw her was at a party on the river. You know the place." This time he did know what I was talking about.

His smile vanished for the first time. "Damn kids. I own that property. I've been trying to keep them out of there so I can clean it up."

"You own it?" I asked.

"New business venture. Can't talk about it now. It's gonna be huge. The original owners moved to Houston in the sixties. Never came back. Hell, that's why everybody in high school partied out there. My class partied out there. I know yours did too."

"Your son was at the party along with one of your employees. I already talked to Owen. I'd like to talk to the employee. Big guy. Lots of tattoos."

"That'd be Russell Stevens. He's part of my security team."

"Security? In Fredericksburg?"

"Lot's changed since you lived here, Nick. I hired him to keep the kids off that Pedernales River property. Hate to have anyone get hurt down there. If he was on the river property, that's what he was doing."

"He lives in a trailer house near Palo Alto Creek?"

"Well, he doesn't exactly live there. I gave him permission to use it."

"I want your permission to talk to him at the trailer house."

He hesitated slightly. "Sure, but what for?"

"He may have seen Maya at the party."

He held my gaze without expression. His smile had vanished. "I'll give him a call," he said, and pulled a cell phone from his shirt pocket.

"That won't be necessary. If you don't mind, Kelly and I will just swing by."

"Be my guest," he said.

I extended my hand, and Mike shook it a little too vigorously. I tried not to show the pain I was still feeling from the bullet wound in my chest. He pulled Kelly close with his big right arm and gave her a side hug. He held her for an extra awkward moment.

"I can see that the climate in Lubbock is not only good for grapes," he said.

I thought Kelly might slap him. Instead she executed a quick step away from his bear grasp and slipped her hand into mine.

"Thank you," she said. "I've never been compared to a wine grape before."

Mike unleashed a forced laugh and slapped his own thigh. Mercifully, before he could think of a comeback, his cell phone rang. Mike looked at the caller ID and seemed to sober up.

"Gotta take this. Good seein' y'all. Let me know if you change your mind about the ranch. I know how much trouble and expensive a piece of land can be."

We left without buying a bottle of Bauer Reserva wine.

CHAPTER FIFTEEN

"I SHOULD HAVE WORN BOOTS FOR that meeting," Kelly said when we were back in my pickup.

"Whole Bauer family's full of BS," I said, waiting for the cars to clear so I could make a left turn back onto the highway. It was day two of the three-day festival, and the traffic was heavy.

"Mike and Zeller both pointed out that you are no longer a part of the good-ol'-boys club."

"And I thought I was the prodigal son." A dually pickup pulling a fifth-wheel travel trailer passed us in a hurry, probably trying to get to Lady Bird Johnson RV park before all the slots were taken. "He liked you, though."

"He's a perv. I'm pretty sure he's boinking the staff."

"Really? She's maybe twenty."

"Trust me. He thinks he's god's gift to women."

"He's full of shit about the ranch. Grandpa was offered a lot of money last summer."

"You can't sell the ranch." She said it as a statement of fact, as if she understood it better than I did.

"I'd never sell to Mike, but what am I gonna do with it? I could never make a living as a rancher. I mean, I know the basic operation and how to feed cows and horses, but I couldn't survive like that and keep the property."

"You'd never forgive yourself if you sold out. You love that place. By the way, you're supposed to be recuperating out there now, instead of driving around looking for a runaway teenager."

"Duly noted." I turned north on a gravel road that was a shortcut to the trailer on the Bauer property. I didn't want to argue about what I should or shouldn't be doing. I didn't want to talk about the ranch and whether I would sell it or keep it. Talking about it would bring up more immediate issues, like what to do with Helen. I was beginning to think that unless I threw her suitcase out on the highway, she would stay indefinitely.

"What's the plan of attack with Russell Stevens?" she asked.

"I thought I'd ask him about the party on the river. From what Lori described, he wasn't there as a security guard."

I drove past the point where Kelly and I had jumped the fence, and found the cattle guard leading to the trailer.

The gravel road wound through a thick cedar break. Kelly pointed to a surveillance camera mounted on a limb beside the road.

"Looks like they're monitoring our approach," she said.

I slowed down and checked my .45 magazine, then slipped the pistol back in my shoulder holster.

"Just remember that you're injured. If it comes to the rough stuff, let me do it." She smiled sweetly. Kelly wasn't what I would call petite. She had a strong jaw and an athletic figure. Anyone could tell she worked out on a regular basis. The charming smile was what fooled people. As a Marine Corps police officer, it was her best asset. Her smile could disarm even the most belligerent jarhead. She used it like a stun gun. While the perp's brain was registering beautiful lady, her boot was traveling at the speed of sound toward a vulnerable part of his body.

When we broke out of the trees, I saw one of the skinheads standing near the door and noticed one of the Super Duty pickups was missing. The black Jeep Cherokee with oversized tires was still there. I parked beside the Jeep, and Kelly and I got out.

"Howdy," I called to the skinhead. He was walking toward me with a sneer on his face.

"Remember me?" Kelly asked.

"This is private property," he said. "You're trespassing." He stopped about ten feet away and put his hands on his hips. He was probably six two or three and stocky. He looked older in the daylight, roughly my age, but he was a hard partier. Up close, I noticed a scar on this chin that was an angry purple color, visible through his week-old beard stubble.

"We've got permission. Mr. Bauer said it was okay. We came to talk to Russell."

He looked a little confused.

Kelly smiled and took a step sideways, giving her a better angle in case things got western. I liked the way she thought.

"I didn't hear nothin' about it," he said.

I took a step closer to him.

"That's 'cause it was need-to-know information. You didn't need to know."

"What?" He didn't get it.

"Never mind. Where's Russell?"

He was probably a dangerous man when he decided to hurt someone, but making decisions wasn't his strong point.

"Russell Stevens. Is he inside? Should I go in and take a look?" I took a step toward the trailer.

"Ain't nobody named Russell here," he said.

The trailer door opened, and Russell stepped out wearing tight jeans and square-toe cowboy boots with a sleeveless T-shirt that showed off his bulky prison-yard muscles.

"What's this about?" he asked. He was taller than his skinhead sidekick by at least an inch but weighed about the same. Every muscle in his body was coiled and ready to spring.

"Mike said you're working security for Bauer Farms. You a local?"

"What's that got to do with anything?" He walked toward my pickup like he was stepping into the cage for an MMA match, his movements fluid and powerful.

"Just curious," I said.

He sized me up and seemed to dismiss me as an unworthy opponent, then focused his attention on Kelly. His whole demeanor shifted like the surface of a lake on a windy day. "You came back. You wanna party?" he asked her like he was accustomed to getting his way.

Kelly flashed her badge. "Were here on business."

"I'm a private investigator." I held up my credentials.

Russell made no effort to look at it or read it. He stood with his arms crossed.

"Mr. Geisler's a local," I said. "He asked me to find his granddaughter, Maya Chavez. I thought maybe you saw her. She's a senior at the high school. Just turned eighteen. Dark hair about shoulder length. Five six or seven."

Russell responded without breaking eye contact with Kelly. "Don't know her."

"She was last seen at a party on the Pedernales River in August. Owen Bauer was there. Maya was there with another girl, Lori Kostoch. She's a blonde. Same age. A little shorter. Lori said you were there."

This caught Russell's attention. His demeanor shifted back to cage fighter. He looked at the skinhead then back at me. The skinhead backed away and went into the trailer.

"Part of my job is to keep the kids away from that place," Russell said.

"So, you were out there when the party was going on?"

"The land is private property. It's well posted. Mike don't want nobody out there. For insurance purposes. It's a liability. You should know that."

"Yeah, I get it," I said. "You went out there and told them to leave, is that it? You were just doing your job?"

He blew a sharp blast of air through his nose that sounded something like a snort from a buffalo. Russell was losing his patience. That was good. I wanted him a little off balance.

"You want answers, talk to Mike." He closed the gap between us and stuck his chest out like a silverback gorilla in the wild.

"We're just trying to find out what happened to the girl," I said.

He didn't speak. The expression on his face was blank. The prison stare. He inched closer expecting me to back away, but I held my ground. He was a big guy. If he started swinging, I wanted to be inside his wheelhouse where he couldn't get a full windup. He stood with his legs spread like fenceposts in the gravel driveway. On a good day, I knew I could land two punches to his one. My first would be to his throat. If that didn't connect, I'd go for the balls. Anything soft and vulnerable. The problem was, this wasn't one of my good days. I was still recovering from the bullet wound to my chest and upper arm, and I had lost my edge.

"Time for you to go," he said.

Kelly was closing on his right shoulder. She had her hand behind her back, no doubt resting on the P226. If Russell did take a swing at me, she would press the barrel into his temple.

"Sure, Russell, sure. No problem." I pulled out the yearbook picture I had of Maya and held it up. "Just to be certain. This is her. This is Maya. You've never seen her before?" I watched his dead eyes take in the picture without showing a hint of recognition. This was what Kelly had seen last night—his eyes were cold, dead, and unflinching. Evil.

I put the picture away. "Thanks for your time, Russell. Good luck with the security job." I turned and opened my pickup door.

Kelly jumped in the other side. "That went well," she said as I backed up and turned around.

"Yeah, we know he saw Maya at the party. The question is, why did he lie about it?"

"Why is everybody lying about her?"

"And where is Maya now?"

"I only hope she got as far away from the Dragon as possible."

CHAPTER SIXTEEN

HELEN'S CAR WAS PARKED BY the barn when Kelly and I rounded the edge of the spring-fed pond in front of the ranch house. There was something unsettling about knowing she was inside using things that belonged to a family she had abandoned many years ago. That, and her talking to Mike Bauer about the sale of the property without telling me put me in a foul mood.

"Maybe we should skip the ranch visit till she's gone," I said.

"Don't worry about it," she said.

"She's gettin' on my nerves."

"Maybe she doesn't have anyplace to go."

"She smells a payday."

"That's cynical."

"It's true."

Helen came out on the porch and waved at us. "I made some sandwiches," she called in a singsong voice.

"That's sweet," Kelly said.

I knew it was a setup, but I didn't say anything. We both got out and walked to the house.

"Come on inside," Helen said.

She acted as though she owned the place and was inviting us in for lunch. We followed her inside. She'd made roast beef sandwiches and cut them into diagonal portions, along with sliced pickles, coleslaw, and German potato salad.

"You didn't have to go to all this trouble," Kelly said.

"Oh, it wasn't any trouble," Helen said.

Kelly and I sat down.

"Why didn't you tell me Mike Bauer stopped by?" I asked.

She handed me one of my own Shiner Bocks in a longneck bottle and sat down in Grandma's place again.

"We haven't gotten a chance to talk. I know you've been busy with Kelly here and the Oktoberfest going on."

"You told him I was going to sell out?" I took a drink of beer and ignored the sandwich. I'd lost my appetite.

"I didn't say that. You know how Mike is. He's always trying to make a deal. He means well." She stood up quickly and grabbed a pitcher of sun tea from the counter. "Would you like some tea?" she asked Kelly. "If you'll excuse me, I want to get started on the bedroom. I bought the paint this morning, and I have everything covered."

"You're going to paint the bedroom?"

"Those rooms haven't been touched up in years," she said. "Oh, it's no bother. If we do decide to sell, the house will be ready. If we stay, it will be fixed up."

She hustled out of the kitchen before I could respond. She had said *we*, putting herself into the decision-making process.

"Look at it this way. You don't have to worry about doing housework while she's here," Kelly said helpfully.

It was small consolation. I reached across the table and kissed her. She tasted like roast beef. I pulled her closer.

Helen walked in on us. "Sorry," she said, smirking. "Came to get my paint rag. Don't mind me." She grabbed a rag from under the sink and hurried out.

I did mind her and the whole idea of her being there, but I couldn't come up with a plan to get rid of her.

We cleaned up the lunch dishes, and I took Kelly outside for a tour of the barn and the rest of the property. She'd been there before, but I had been in the early stages of recovery, and I wasn't able to get around very well.

The old barn door was mounted on a metal roller, which gave a rusty squeal when I shoved it open—a sound it never made when Grandpa was alive. I felt a sudden pang of guilt for neglecting my duties.

"This is where you killed the detective?" she asked when we were inside the limestone block barn. The temperature was ten degrees cooler inside the thick walls.

"Yeah, the son of a bitch had put Grandpa's shirt on and was hiding in plain sight. He had his back to me, and I thought he was Grandpa tied to the support beam. That's how he got the drop on me. Turns out, Grandpa was already dead. Shot through the heart that morning. Detective Peterson had been waiting for me to show up."

We walked up the steps to the hayloft. I pointed out the smudge marks on the wall where the fire had scorched the inside timbers the year after the Civil War and showed her the "new" steps Great-grandpa had built because he got too fat to climb the original narrower planks.

"He shot Skeeter from this window." We peered out the hayloft at the front yard. I could see the spring-fed pond and the hundred yards of gravel road that led to the front gate. I pointed to the line of cedar trees to the north of the house about fifty yards away. "I crawled to the edge of the trees. Skeeter parked out front, and when he got out, he left the shotgun I'd given him on the front seat. Peterson was waiting for him here in the window. I saw the rifle barrel and fired, but I was too late. Skeeter never saw it coming."

I pointed to the bullet holes in the window frame.

"You were both lucky," she said.

We walked back down the wooden steps to the ground floor. Grandpa's John Deere tractor was still there with the hay baler attached. He had left a hundred head of cattle, fifty or so goats, and a couple of horses that were both past their prime. I would have to decide what to do with them. Being a rancher was a full-time job that didn't pay full-time wages.

"Where did you find your grandpa?"

"In the last horse stall."

The smell of dried blood turned my stomach, but I knew it was only my memory playing cruel tricks. It had been six weeks since Grandpa's murder. I walked to the barn door for a breath of fresh air. White puffy mare's tails painted the blue sky. Kelly followed me.

"Grandpa used to say mare's tails in the sky meant rain was on its way," I said.

Kelly took my hand. I didn't need to say I missed him. She understood.

"There you are," Helen called from the front porch. "Would you help me move the furniture while you're here?" She was talking to Kelly. "I didn't want Nicky to do it. He's not supposed to lift anything heavy."

"Sure," Kelly said, unfolding herself from my arms.

I reluctantly let her go. "I'll wait for you out here," I said. "I need to call Skeeter anyway."

"Say hi from me," she said and followed Helen into the house.

I sat on the bench in front of the barn and called my partner in San Antonio.

"How's rehab coming?" Skeeter said when he answered the phone.

"I was just going to ask you the same thing," I said.

"I'm enjoying the peace and quiet," he said. He was staying at my house in King William while I was gone.

"Great," I said. "I have two houses, and I have to rent a motel room to be alone with my girlfriend."

Skeeter let out a deep baritone chuckle. He was six-foot-seven and weighed three hundred pounds. When he spoke, his voice originated from deep inside his massive body. I imagined him in my living room with his feet propped up on my desk, staring out at my yard and pecan tree.

"Did you at least mow the grass?" I asked.

More chuckling. "I'm not supposed to do any strenuous work," he said. "I let the neighborhood kid do it. I told him you'd pay him when you came back to town."

"Thanks. Run up the bill." I explained Helen's unspoken intention to stay at the ranch as long as she could find things to do. Which seemed like the next fifteen years.

"She's your mother. Give her a second chance. Maybe she just wants to help."

"Thank you, Oprah. Have you got anything on Maya?"

"The phone was a dead end. Your buddy Officer Zeller had already put her in the system. I posted her up on Facebook. No leads yet. I checked her account. No activity since August. Same for her Instagram and Snapchat."

"Dropped off the grid?"

"Apparently."

"Check out Lori Kostoch and Owen Bauer. See what's happening in their world. They're both seniors at the high school. They were with Maya the night she went missing. Also, I want you to do a background check on a thug named Russell Stevens, aka the Dragon. He's supposedly working security for Bauer Farms here in Gillespie County. See if he has a record anywhere."

"The Dragon, huh?"

"Yeah, he's got a really cute tattoo of one on his chest. Likes to show it off."

"My pleasure," he rumbled.

"Also, check the Greyhound bus records for the week following the tenth of August. I know the bus stops in town. There's no terminal, but she could have bought tickets online.

"Got it. And Nick..." He hesitated.

"What is it?" I asked.

"What's your gut feeling on this?"

"I don't like it. Too many people are lying. We're gonna have to move fast if we expect to catch up with her."

"That's what I was thinking. Nobody her age drops off of social media like that unless something's wrong."

Skeeter cleared his throat.

"What else?" I asked.

"It's good to be working again," he said, and disconnected.

CHAPTER SEVENTEEN

The Geisler ranch was ten miles north of Fredericksburg, tucked into the rolling limestone hills that were covered with live oaks, mesquite, and cactus. The grass was dead this time of year and colored the open spaces with an even tan.

I thought about Anna Metzger's story when we crossed the bridge at Palo Alto Creek. It was the same route the Kiowas would have ridden the night she was captured. Had Maya been kidnapped? Lori suspected foul play, but she hadn't seen anything happen. Either Owen or Russell Stevens had to know something. Maya couldn't have vanished into thin air.

"What are our options, Mr. Detective?" Kelly asked.

"Skeeter's working on the Dragon's background. He said Maya's social media accounts have gone dead."

"You wanna stake out the trailer?"

"If she was there, she's gone now."

"What about the girls and the weapons and drugs?"

"I'm not a policeman. That's Zeller's job and the sheriff."

I stopped in front of Helmut's front gate. He had replaced most of his family's original stone fence with hog wire years ago, and the wooden gate was now metal and decorated with a life-sized iron silhouette of a cowboy kneeling in front of a large cross. I didn't remember the gate from my high school days and wondered if the Christian theme had something to do with his wife surviving her fourth brush with death.

Kelly opened the gate, and we drove across a hayfield that was cut and plowed under, awaiting next year's crop. A herd of white-and-brown goats followed my pickup to the single-story, clapboard house with a wraparound porch.

The yard was tidy. The small patch of Bermuda-grass lawn was freshly mowed, and there was a row of peach trees beside the two-story limestone barn. Like grandpa's property, all the farm implements were in their proper place and looked oiled and ready for use. Fences were mended, and the lines on the corral boards were all straight and at right angles to the sturdy cedar posts. I parked near the house, and Helmut appeared in the open barn door holding a welding torch. Two border collies and a Labrador mix quickly dispersed the goats and stood barking.

"You need to get another dog," Kelly said.

"Yeah, I need a puppy right now to chew up my boots and crap all over the kitchen."

"What about hunting season?"

I couldn't argue with that. "All right, I need another dog." It was almost hunting season, and it would be the first one in a long time that I was without a dog.

Helmut shouted something at his dogs. They instantly retreated behind him. *"Guten Tag. Wie geht's?"* Helmut said as we got out.

The Lab mix snuck past Helmut and sniffed the cuff of Kelly's jeans. When she rewarded him with a scratch behind the ears, the jealous border collies rushed her. She laughed and tried to give them all some ranch-dog love.

"Sehr gut, danke," I said.

"Wer ist deine schöne Freundin." He said a lot more, but that's all my ear could catch up to before I held up my hand.

"This is my girlfriend, Kelly," I said. I gathered more from his expression than my understanding of German that he was asking about Kelly.

"Sitzen!" Helmut growled. The dogs quickly ran to his heels and sat down wagging their tails. He took Kelly's hand. "Glad to know you," he said. Helmut shook my hand too and thankfully switched back to English.

"It's good you have come." He looked up at the mare's tail clouds. "Going to be rain soon."

"We need it. Grandpa's spring is near dry," I said. I'd never talked to a farmer or rancher who didn't mention the weather in the first breath or two.

"What news?" he asked. He was anxious to hear about Maya.

"No luck yet. I was wondering if you could answer a few more questions. And maybe we could take a look in Maya's room. It might tell us something about where she went."

Helmut studied me for a moment and rubbed his aged fingers against the stubble on his chin.

"There's not much there," he said after careful consideration. "But you're welcome to look. We were only preparing for her to move in.

"I talked to her mother. She said you took her to court," I said.

A mixture of anger and regret flickered across his craggy face. "It was the only way to get her to act. Her brain is addled." He turned to Kelly. "I'm sorry," he said. "But my daughter's a drunk."

"Kelly is a police officer in Lubbock," I said helpfully.

He gave her an approving nod. "This is *gut*," he said. "We'll go into the house." He abruptly led the way. "I have cold beer."

The house was warm with no air conditioning but had obviously been designed to catch as much of the breeze as possible with the many windows. An older woman with her gray hair tightly pulled into a bun, wearing a blue cotton dress and a yellow apron, met us in the front room. The skin on her face and arms was paper-thin, and she couldn't have weighed more than ninety pounds.

"We have company, mother," Helmut said.

"Mrs. Geisler, it's good to see you up and around. This is Kelly Hoffman." I offered my hand. She reached past my hand and gave me a full hug.

"Oh, goodness gracious," she said. "Give me a hug. Just terrible what happened to your grandpa. How are you doing?" She had survived her fourth heart attack, and yet she wanted to know how I was doing.

"I'm fine, thank you," I said. "How are you feeling?"

She shrugged and crossed herself. "The Lord has given me one more life to live," she said, and held out her hand to Kelly. "I'm Elena, honey. Nice to meet you. Can I get you anything to drink? Supper's not quite ready."

"You have a lovely home," Kelly said. "I don't think we can stay for supper."

"They want to take a look at Maya's room," Helmut explained.

"If you don't mind," I said. "She might have left a clue. Something to tell us where she might have gone."

"You're welcome to look. I've looked a dozen times and haven't seen anything. She hadn't completely moved in," Elena said. "It's through here."

We followed her down a narrow hall and into a small bedroom that faced the barn.

"She only stayed with us for a few days. That poor girl's been through a lot."

"With the move?"

"That and her mother. She's gonna be a strong woman one day, if she ever gets the chance. She's hardheaded, that one."

"Which bathroom did she use?" I asked.

"The one at the end of the hall," she said, pointing. Elena walked back toward the kitchen and left us alone. I went in the small bathroom. There was an old-fashioned tub with legs and a simple cabinet and sink. Judging by the dark tinted age marks around the bottom edge of the mirror and the octagon brass hardware on the cabinets, I'd guess everything in the room was early nineteen hundred vintage. I found a toothbrush in the medicine cabinet along with a bottle of Tylenol and a tube of *extra-whitening* toothpaste. At least she took care of her teeth. The room was clean, and the old-fashioned tub seemed recently scrubbed. I doubted whether Mrs. Geisler would have had the strength or the energy to clean the bathroom. Helmut might have done it, but I had the idea that it was Maya's handiwork.

I walked back to the bedroom. Kelly was standing on a multicolor throw rug in the center of a small ten-by-ten room with hardwood floors.

"Her toothbrush is still there. What'd you find in here?" I asked.

"Not much."

There was a twin bed with a neat patchwork quilt in one corner and a small desk with a vanity mirror in the other. A matching dresser stood beside the door. There were no boy band posters on the walls or anything that gave the appearance of a teen girl's room, except the plastic appaloosa horse on the dresser.

"This was probably once her mother's room," I said.

Kelly opened the top drawer of the dresser and looked at a collection of underwear and socks. The next drawer contained jeans and shorts, all neatly folded and put in place.

I opened the drawer on the desk and found a small diary with a tiny lock.

"Here's something," I said.

We looked at the diary.

"It's locked."

Kelly smirked and quickly extracted a pin from her hair and jimmied the lock open. "I have two sisters," she said.

We sat on the bed and thumbed through the pages. The handwriting was easy to read. She had a looping style filled with hearts and exclamation points.

"Dear diary, I hate my life!!!!!!!!!" The first line read. I flipped to the last page and read the date. It was more than thirty years old. It was Maya's mother's diary. She probably still felt the same way.

The closet wasn't any more helpful. There were two pairs of Justin Roper boots and three pairs of tennis shoes that looked well used. There were a few modest dresses on hangers and a straw cowboy hat on the shelf. I also found a pink-camo backpack and a large red duffle bag.

"Why would she run away without taking her toothbrush or packing her suitcase or her backpack? You came for the weekend and you brought a suitcase and a backpack. And you're a Marine."

"I knew I'd be hanging out with you and likely get shot at or chased through the brush," she said.

"Good point," I said, hoping she was teasing me. "Can you imagine a teen girl out here by herself?"

"I didn't even see a TV. Did you?"

"No. It reminds me of growing up with my grandma and grandpa."

"How did you survive?"

"I got a job and bought a used pickup. They couldn't argue with work. I bought the things I thought I needed to keep up with the crowd. I made it through high school, then joined the Marine Corps. I heard they were looking for a few good men."

"And women." She laughed.

I heard steps in the hallway. Helmut opened the door.

"Find anything useful?" he asked.

"Are these clothes Maya's?" Kelly asked.

"Everything in the dresser is hers. I didn't keep any of my daughter's things."

We followed Helmut back to the front room, where he offered us both a beer. We took them and went outside to the porch. Kelly and I sat on the double-seat swing, and Helmut sat in a wooden rocking chair. He said Elena had gone to lie down. She could only stay up for a few hours a day. The herd dogs joined us and resumed their flirtation with Kelly.

"We don't have a lot of the things young people want out here. We never bothered with TV, and I wouldn't know what to do with a computer," Helmut told us.

"Was Maya worried about that?" Kelly asked.

"I gave her a horse to ride, and she had plenty of chores to do. She liked to help me feed the goats."

"Did she have any of her friends come out?" I asked.

"She said she hadn't been in town long enough to make friends."

We were getting a bleak picture of Maya's home life with her grandparents.

"Did she talk about going back to California?" Kelly asked.

"Never mentioned anything to us," Helmut said.

I drank some beer and thought about Maya. She had spent most of her life in California. Then she was suddenly forced to come back to rural Central Texas for her last year of high school. Maybe Les Zeller was right, and Maya had decided she would rather be in California. Still, it didn't explain her checking out of social media altogether.

"You know, Helmut," I said. "Maybe Maya decided Fredericksburg wasn't for her."

Helmut cleared his throat. I waited a long time for him to speak. I figured he was coming to grips with the idea that I might be right, and that Maya simply chose California over Central Texas.

"She was taken," he insisted.

"I know you've had a hard time with your daughter. I get that. She's an alcoholic. But is there anything else you're not telling me? I have to know everything if I'm going to find her."

Helmut stopped his rocking chair and stared out at his herd of goats. Had this been the nineteenth century, we would be gathering a posse of friends and neighbors to go after his granddaughter. Then, as now, local law enforcement had done little to keep settlers safe.

"I'm an old man, but by god if I didn't have my hands full with Elena, I'd go after Maya myself. Zeller's as worthless as tits on a bore hog." He challenged me with a watery cataract stare.

"I'll find her," I said. "I just need all the details."

He nodded. I went to my pickup and got the standard contract for him to sign that would cover my ass in case I had to explain why I was asking questions and requesting information. Helmut agreed to work out the fee later.

"I want you to call me if you think of anything else or if she gets in touch with you. Let me do the heavy lifting on this. That's why you hired me," I said.

"*Halt dich munter*," Helmut said, shaking my hand.

"*Halt dich munter*," I said.

CHAPTER EIGHTEEN

KELLY AND I DROVE IN silence for the first few miles. The sun was going down. The air was dry and had dropped ten degrees. I cut the a/c and rolled down the windows. The smell of cedars and fresh-mown hay filled the cab. We passed a fruit stand advertising fresh tomatoes and apples. Kelly's blond hair fluttered under her Texas Tech baseball cap. I appreciated the fact that she didn't feel the need to fill every moment we had together with conversation.

I wondered if Maya was watching the sun set and smelling the same smells or if she was somewhere nature couldn't reach her. That she had problems at home was obvious. Her mother couldn't or wouldn't provide for her. Helmut was trying his best. His heart was in the right place, but he had his hands full with a teenage girl. Maybe this wasn't a simple case of Maya running away or a direct kidnapping, but a combination of the two.

"Why didn't you tell Helmut about Russell Stevens?"

"Didn't want him to get worked up," I said.

"You think he'd do something?"

"Folks like Helmut and my grandpa are used to taking care of things on their own. If he thought Mike Bauer or Owen had anything to do with Maya's disappearance, he'd likely show up at Mike's house with a shotgun in his hand. Zeller be damned."

"You think he'd take on the Dragon?"

"In a heartbeat. Helmut's grandpa was fighting off Indian raids after the Civil War."

"Now you wanna form a posse and go after him?"

"Zeller won't do anything, and the raiding party is getting away."

"So, you're keeping the pioneer spirit alive or something? I'm not sure I buy that argument. We're not on the frontier."

"You don't think people should protect themselves?"

"I'm okay with that. The part about taking the law into your own hands is problematic. There is other law enforcement besides Officer Zeller."

"And they're all waiting for a crime to solve. I wanna find Maya before the crime happens. I just hope I'm not too late."

I stopped at a streetlight on Main Street. Traffic was still heavy. Oktoberfest was in full swing until midnight.

"What's next?" Kelly asked.

"I wanna know what the Dragon's really doing in Gillespie County and where he came from."

She smiled. "Relax. The raiding party isn't getting away. You can't do anything until you hear from Skeeter. I meant, tonight. It's my last night in town."

I took a deep breath and turned my attention back to her. "I can either turn right and go back to Oktoberfest—we can ask around about Maya, drink more beer, and dance the polka—or I can turn left and go back to the motel room. We could get naked, drink more beer, and make out to a polka band on YouTube."

"Why are Germans so romantic?" She leaned over and grazed her lips across mine.

"It's the hops," I said.

The light turned green. Someone behind me honked. My lips were glued to hers. They honked again.

"Turn left," she whispered.

I found the gas pedal and pulled into traffic with her in my lap. Probably not the safest driving maneuver, but we were cruising at under ten miles per hour. Main Street was crowded with tourists and locals on their way to and from the Marktplatz. All the shops and restaurants along Main Street were open for business, sponging the tourists for every dollar they could get. It was all I could do to keep my attention on the slow-moving vehicles in front of me and off Kelly's roving hand.

"I'm gonna miss you when you leave," I said.

"Liar. You'll be working the case. You won't even notice I'm gone." She moved her hand a little farther down. "I feel like the mistress. You're married to the job."

"That's harsh."

"The truth always is, mister. I'm a Marine, remember? I can take it." She traced the scars on my forehead with her finger.

"I promise to focus on you tonight," I said.

She smiled without speaking. By the time I parked near the staircase of our motel room, I had managed to work several of her shirt buttons loose, revealing a good portion of her red-lace bra. We both jumped out of the pickup. I caught her on the bottom step and wrapped my arms around her. Our lips locked together. I heard footsteps on the stairs. A couple in their late sixties dressed alike in white shorts, tennis shoes, and Hawaiian shirts passed us on the stairs. The woman frowned at Kelly. The man eyed her exposed red bra.

We giggled all the way to the top of the stairs. I dug the keycard out of my wallet and opened the door.

Inside, I finished undoing her buttons.

She let her shirt drop to the floor. The red-lace bra was next. I pulled at her belt, and she pulled at mine. Her bare skin glowed in the ambient light shining through window. I lifted her from below the waist and shuffled toward the bed with my Wranglers around my boots. I felt the sharp sourness in my chest from the bullet wound, but I was prepared to deal with the pain.

I looked over her shoulder for a soft landing spot.

There was a naked body on the bed.

"Oh, shit," I said, thinking we had somehow stumbled into the wrong room.

"What? What is it?" Kelly scrambled out of my grasp.

"It's a little crowded in here," I said.

Kelly saw the body. "Jesus. It's that girl. It's Lori."

I pulled my jeans up so I could get to the light switch without falling over.

Lori's body was lying naked and spread-eagle on the bed. From the marks on her throat, she'd been strangled. There were red abrasions on her upper arms and trauma to her wrists and ankles as if she'd been tied with rope at some point, but the restraints were missing. I put my finger on her neck, searching for a pulse. Nothing. Her skin was cold and chalky, her lips blue from lack of oxygen. The bed cover and the top sheet were on the floor, as were the pillows. We got dressed and stood staring at the body.

"Who would do this?" Kelly asked.

"A cold-blooded killer."

"The Dragon," she said.

My business card was on the nightstand. I picked it up by the edges and turned it over. Kelly's handwritten name and number were on the back. It was the card I'd given her that afternoon.

I'd seen death too many times to be completely overwhelmed with emotion, and so had Kelly, but the sight of a person so young and innocent dumped on the bed that we had shared was unsettling to say the least.

"You think she came here on her own?" Kelly asked.

"Maybe she had more to tell us." I checked my phone for messages, remembering I'd turned off the ringer when we went to visit

Helmut. There were two missed calls and two voice messages. I put the phone on speaker. Pressed play.

"Mr. Fischer?" Lori's voice sounded thin and scared and came in quick bursts. "This is Lori Kostoch. I thought of something else…" Then a pause and a sharp intake of breath. "Please, call me back." I could hear traffic noise as if she was still on Main Street where we left her that afternoon. The message had come at two thirty, roughly thirty minutes after we had dropped her off.

"She sounded desperate. Like someone was watching her," Kelly said.

"There's another message. This one came twenty minutes later. Almost three o'clock." I pressed play.

"Mr. Fischer, this is Lori again." Her voice came in a whisper, the phone pressed against her lips. "Can you please call me as soon as you get this?" There was a five-second pause. "You're probably at Oktoberfest," Lori continued. "There's something I need to tell you. I'll wait for you at your motel." She disconnected.

"Did she have a car?"

"She had to have a car. She had a job, and her mom lives at least five miles out of town. She said she drove Maya to the party on the river."

"You think someone followed her here?"

The door to the adjacent room was open.

"He got in from the next room," I said, pointing at the broken lock. "Check the front desk. See if they saw anything or if they have surveillance cameras. Ask who checked in next door."

Kelly dressed and left.

I checked my watch. It was six thirty. I searched the small room. Nothing under the bed or in the open closet. In the bathroom I found Lori's clothes in a pile by the tub. They were the same items she wore that afternoon. I also found three lengths of rope. It was cheap yellow-nylon cord, the kind they sold at every convenience store in Texas.

I walked through the broken door. The adjacent room was trashed. Clothes everywhere. Bathroom stuff scattered around the sink. Both queen beds had been slept in. I remembered hearing the two boys bouncing off the walls the night before. The occupants hadn't checked out.

I went back to our room and studied Lori's body. There were no bullet holes or knife wounds. There was no blood on the white sheet. I checked her fingernails and hands for signs of a struggle. There were no abrasions. She hadn't put up a fight. There was a lump on her forehead. Someone had put her lights out with a single powerful blow to the head. Someone with prison muscles and a dragon tattoo. I pulled the sheet over her body and left the room.

Kelly met me in the parking lot. The surveillance system was offline. Something about vandals breaking one of the cameras. It wouldn't be fixed until next week. The girl on duty in the lobby had talked to Lori. Lori told her she was going to wait for us to return.

"Did you tell her Lori was dead?" I asked.

"She didn't take it very well."

"What about the room next door?"

"Still occupied by the family with the teen boys. They went to the festival early this afternoon. Haven't been back. He could have stolen their key."

I found Les Zeller's number and hit dial. He picked up on the second ring. "Hey, Les," I said. "Sorry to bother you, but there's a dead body in my motel room. Her name's Lori Kostoch." I paused for him to respond. He didn't say anything. He probably didn't get too many calls like that working on a small-town police force. "Les, can you hear me? This is Nick Fischer. Lori Kostoch is dead. I found her in my motel room about ten minutes ago."

"Don't touch anything," he insisted, regaining his composure. "I'll be right there." He hung up without saying goodbye.

"Now we wait for the cavalry," I said.

CHAPTER NINETEEN

THE POLICE ARRIVED WITH SIRENS blaring and lights flashing as if an active shooter was on the scene. Six cruisers—every officer not working traffic on the Marktplatz for Oktoberfest—converged on the Best Western. The cavalry had arrived.

Zeller was the first one out of his car. For a big, well-fed guy in his forties, he was surprisingly quick on his feet. He shouted orders to his team and quickly spotted Kelly and me standing on the second-story landing.

"You'd think we were giving away free kolaches," I said.

Kelly rolled her eyes. "Hey, there was a murder."

"*Was* a murder. You don't think this is an exaggerated response? Zeller and the JP could have handled it."

"Not everybody is as jaded as you."

"I'm not jaded. I'm a realist."

She rolled her eyes.

Zeller hustled toward us with two officers in tow. The sun was already down, but they all still had on wraparound mirror sunglasses as if they expected the sun to reappear at any moment. They also had matching high-and-tight haircuts that must have been the latest in lawman hairstyle. I knew Zeller wasn't ex-military. I didn't know about the others.

Kelly and I met him at the bottom of the steps.

"Is this your motel?" he asked. He was as sharp as a razor.

"I think it belongs to Best Western."

"Are you gonna start shit, Fischer?"

"I called you, Les. There's a dead girl upstairs. We're not throwing a party. Lori's body is in my room. Number two thirty-six. Top of the stairs. It's open."

Zeller scowled, telegraphing his intent to throw me in jail, but he couldn't think of a reason yet, so he headed up the stairs.

"The adjoining room door was jimmied. Looks like he used a screwdriver or a crowbar," I called to him.

Zeller stopped and looked at me over his shoulder. "We'll do the investigating, Fischer. Don't leave. I'll need an official statement from both of you." Zeller yelled at the nearest officer. "Secure the premises. No one in or out." He turned to the younger one, who stood next to me. "Get their IDs," he said, then jogged up the steps.

"Were y'all at the festival?" I said to the young cop, trying to be friendly. His eyes were small and too close together, and he seemed a little nervous, like it was his first week on the job.

"Could I see some identification?" he said.

"Relax. I'm the guy who called you, Officer Markey," I said, reading his name from his name tag.

"Sorry, sir. It's part of the procedure."

I sighed and handed over my driver's license along with my private eye creds and my concealed carry permit, hoping the kid wouldn't freak out.

"I am armed, Officer," I said.

Kelly showed her ID, which included her police badge from Lubbock.

"We're both armed," she said.

He looked at our IDs as if he was not sure what to do next.

"Markey, get up here!" Zeller yelled down from the second floor.

Markey jumped. "Yes, sir," he said and ran up the stairs two at a time.

Zeller ordered him to secure the room, then stomped back down the stairs.

"All right, Nick. Why don't you start at the beginning?" Zeller pulled out his notebook.

I went over my meeting with Lori, starting at the beginning and including the fight with Owen. I added the part about my interview with Mike Bauer and Russell. Zeller seemed to dismiss all of them as suspects before I had even finished.

"When did you see her last?" Zeller asked.

"This afternoon. She tapped on my window while I was going through the drive-through at Whataburger," I said. "She said she drove Maya to the party on the river. Owen was there and so was Russell Stevens, Mike Bauer's security guard."

"She never said anything to me," he said.

"Scared, probably. She called again this afternoon. I didn't get the call because I'd turned my ringer off."

"Turned off your ringer," he repeated and made a note.

"We went to visit Helmut, and I didn't want to be disturbed."

He made another note. "Any other reason?"

"You think I'm a suspect?"

"I just wanna get everything straight. Did she leave a message?"

I got out my phone and played the messages. Lori sounded even more desperate than I remembered. "The last message came at two fifty-five. We got here at about six."

"And y'all were with Helmut all afternoon?"

"Call him if you want. We went to talk to him about Maya."

He looked at his watch. "I'll call him in the morning. It's past his bedtime. I don't wanna piss him off. Busiest weekend of the year…" Zeller let his sentence trail off.

"You have two obvious suspects," Kelly said.

He looked at her, still annoyed. "I get that you're a police officer in Lubbock, but we have our own procedure here."

"Just trying to help," she said, meeting his snarky response with a cold seriousness perfected from her years as an MP.

"This has everything to do with Maya's disappearance," I said.

Zeller bristled. "This isn't your case. I know you're working for old man Geisler, but this is a murder investigation."

"You're kidding me, right?"

"We're professionals," he said, implying that I wasn't.

"You don't think Maya's disappearance and Lori's murder are connected?"

"Maybe, maybe not. We have our own investigators. They'll be here soon, along with our CSI team and the JP. I'll need you both to come down to the station to sign a statement."

"Set up an appointment," I said. "Right now, we're tired, and our room is double-booked, so we need to find another place to stay on Oktoberfest weekend." I took out a business card and handed it to him. "Here's my number. I'm not hard to track down."

Zeller's jaw muscles clenched, but he didn't say anything.

"You gonna call Lori's mom?"

"Yeah, I'll take care of it," he said.

"I don't envy that job. First her husband, and now her only daughter."

"Her husband?" Kelly asked.

"KIA in Afghanistan. He was a Marine."

A moment of silence passed between us, then I took Kelly's hand, and we walked back to my pickup. Zeller seemed like he wanted to protest, but I didn't give him a chance.

"Does he really think we're suspects?" Kelly asked after we'd climbed into the cab.

"He just likes to give me shit. Been doin' it since the sixth grade."

I called Skeeter to get an update and fill him in on the new developments.

"What have you got for me?" I put my phone on speaker so Kelly could hear.

"Russell Stevens did five years for manslaughter. Convicted at seventeen for killing his stepdad. Since then he's kept his nose clean."

"That or he learned how to stay under the radar in prison," I said.

"He has some scary known associates," Skeeter added.

"Get me names and addresses. We need to track this guy down and find Maya before she ends up like Lori."

"I hope we ain't too late," he said.

CHAPTER TWENTY

The Dragon's trailer was abandoned. The front door was open, the lights were off, and the driveway was empty. I clipped my cap light onto my baseball hat, and Kelly and I searched the perimeter. Nothing. Inside, the trailer smelled like marijuana and sour milk. The only thing left was a half package of bologna Kelly found in the refrigerator. The plastic garbage sacks I'd seen through the back window were gone. Russell Stevens and his gang had moved out.

My phone rang. Skeeter.

"The Dragon's favorite hangout is a strip club in San Antonio," Skeeter said. "Out on Loop 410."

"I'll meet you there in two hours," I said.

"Ten four," Skeeter said. "No guarantee he's there."

"It's a start." I disconnected.

We got back in my pickup and drove over the cattle guard and turned south on the gravel road. "There won't be any rooms left in the county tonight. You can stay at the ranch."

"Don't even think about dropping me off. I'm coming with you."

"But you have to go to work tomorrow in Lubbock. I don't know how long this will take."

"I'm calling in sick. Besides, you and Skeeter are recovering from gunshot wounds. I'm the only one any good in a fight."

"You keep this up, I'm going to have to put you on the payroll."

"I was thinking more like a partner. *Hoffman and Fischer – Private Investigators.*"

"Why does your name come first?" I asked. "I'm the company founder."

"Obviously, I'm the brains of the operation," she said.

• • •

The strip club was located on the northwest side of San Antonio off Loop 410. I drove around the crowded parking lot until I found Skeeter's Dodge Ram 4x4 pickup. He was in the passenger seat with his head leaning against the glass.

"Looks like he's taking a nap," Kelly said.

"We're keepin' him out past his bedtime." I got out and tapped on his window. He didn't move. I tapped a little harder. Finally, he opened his eyes and unrolled the window.

"What's up?" he asked, and pulling off his headphones. Old-school rap music was pumping through tiny speakers. His bulk filled the open window.

"Nothin'. What's on the iPod?"

"The Fat Boys," he said.

I had no idea who that was and didn't want to ask. If I did, he'd lecture me on how rap was once great and how the new generation had ruined it. He could go on for hours.

"Hey, Clarence," Kelly called to him. She was the only one besides his mother that I ever heard call him by his real name.

Skeeter smiled and unfolded himself from his pickup seat. At six-foot-seven and three hundred pounds, he made Kelly and me look like sixth graders. The metal hook he wore as a prothesis was the only reason he wasn't playing in the NFL. He'd been in a car wreck the day he got drafted.

"Kelly!" His big baritone voice vibrated from somewhere deep in his chest. "What're you doin' here?" He grabbed her in a bear hug, and she kissed him on the cheek. It felt like a family reunion.

"Nick put me on the payroll," she said playfully.

Skeeter raised his eyebrow at me. "Sounds like we need to have a business meetin'."

"What business meetin'?" I laughed. "I'm the boss. It's Fischer Investigations. I'm Fischer."

"You're resisting the expansion?" Kelly said, taking my arm.

"This is more like a hostile takeover," I said.

"It's about time all our names were on the business cards," Kelly said.

"Yeah, Davis, Hoffman, and Fischer," Skeeter said. His baritone chuckle rumbled from deep down in his massive chest like a volcano before an eruption.

Kelly smiled and kissed me on the cheek. "I like it."

"So, now my name's last." I wasn't sure what had just happened. My new business had suddenly tripled its payroll without increasing its revenue.

"Does that mean I get a raise?" Skeeter asked.

"Sure, you can have half of my salary. Helmut agreed to pay with a hog and a goat."

"You kiddin' me?"

"Actually, we didn't talk numbers, but he is a pretty good butcher."

"You should have talked that over with your partners," Skeeter said.

"I didn't have any partners until a minute ago," I argued.

"Obviously, I will have to renegotiate our fee with Mr. Geisler," Kelly said. "I'm sure he'll understand."

"That will be a lot easier to do if we find Maya," I said. "Let's go see if Russell's home."

The three of us walked through the full parking lot toward the entrance. The music pulsed louder as we approached. It was a few degrees warmer in San Antonio, but still a pleasant sixty-five degrees. Not bad for fall in South Texas. The sky reflected city lights instead of stars, one of the things I missed most when I wasn't living in the country.

Two chunky bouncers wearing too-tight black T-shirts sat on barstools by the door. They were checking the IDs of two boys who looked like they were in high school. A row of Harley choppers lined the north wall of the building. The rest of the parking lot overflowed with pickups and utility trucks. The dress code was casual.

"You think Maya's here?" Kelly asked.

"Lori said something about that crowd on the river expecting them to dance," I said.

"You plannin' on goin' all Afghanistan and shit?" Skeeter asked.

"I wasn't planning on keeping a low profile. After Lori's murder, we don't have time to be discreet. Somebody upped the ante."

We waited behind the high school boys while the musclemen pretended to study their fake IDs. One of the boys passed a bill to the bouncer. The kid nudged his friend with his elbow. A moment later, the friend produced a bill that the bouncer quickly palmed. I checked the entrance for surveillance cameras and saw two on the corner of the building. One facing the parking lot and the other trained on the entrance. Either the cameras weren't working, or the two clowns didn't care they were being filmed. Maybe they were new on the job. The bouncers let the two teens pass.

I glanced at Kelly, who had her phone out with the video app recording. I stepped forward. Skeeter stayed a step behind us. Both bouncers focused on him.

"You really take bribes when the surveillance cameras are rollin'?" I asked. I was there to shake things up. That's what I did best.

The neck-tattooed bouncer smiled nervously and glanced at Skeeter. "He's with me," I added.

"What're you talkin', dude?" He managed to say.

"Those two boys were probably sixteen. You let 'em go in. I saw them slip you a bill. What's the price of admission for kids? Fifty? Or was it a hundred?"

"You a cop?" the other bouncer said. They were both standing now.

"Private investigator," I said. "These are my partners." I nodded toward Kelly and Skeeter and held up my credentials. "Do those cameras work?" I pointed to the two surveillance cameras.

"You're not a cop," Tattoo said. "We don't have to talk to you."

"Is that the way you wanna play it?"

"Yeah, fuck off." He reached behind his back, and I assumed he was going for a gun.

Kelly saw it too. She grabbed his thumb and twisted it up behind his back, then she pulled a pistol from his waistband and pointed it at the other bouncer. The move surprised me as much as the two bouncers. Skeeter let out a deep rumbling chuckle.

"You two new on the job? You're not very good at this game," I said.

"What the fuck do you want, man?"

"We wanna take a look at the surveillance tapes," I said.

"Fuck you," he said.

Kelly gave his arm a twist.

"Okay, bitch."

"Watch your language around the lady. You don't wanna really piss her off," I said. "Let's go inside."

Kelly pocketed his pistol, and we followed the tattooed bouncer inside the club. The music was throbbing loud enough to feel against my skin, limiting conversation to hand signals and facial expressions. The lighting was minimal except over the three stages. When my eyes adjusted, I could see the place was packed with a cross section of bikers, college students, and businessmen. There was a trio of topless girls gyrating on the mirrored main stage, each with a collection of bills tucked in their G-strings. We followed the bouncer to a door behind the bar. I stopped Skeeter before we went inside.

"Wait for us here," I shouted. "Don't let anybody else in." I waved my hand across the door.

He smiled and held up his thumb.

Kelly and I followed the bouncer into the back room.

A slightly-built man in his early forties with green hipster glasses and a shaved head sat behind a metal desk. He wore a blue velvet suit without a tie, and he had a tattoo of a cross on the back of his left hand.

"I'm Arnold Garza, the manager. What's this all about?" His voice was like sandpaper being pulled over a stick of wood.

"I'm Nick Fischer, and this is my partner Kelly. We're private investigators looking for this girl." I showed him the photo of Maya. His eyes flicked to the picture but quickly went back to me. "She went missing from Fredericksburg on August tenth."

"Never seen her before, man."

"Is Russell here?"

"Who's that?"

"Russell Stevens. Big guy, blond hair. Beautiful smile. Likes to wear tight jeans. We talked to him in Fredericksburg yesterday."

"That's the Dragon. No, he ain't here."

"We wanna see your surveillance tapes," I said.

Garza laughed. It was forced and awkward. His eyes were dull and dilated like he'd been high for most of the day.

"You're not cops. Get the fuck outta here."

"Here's what we already have," Kelly said and pulled out her cell phone. "Your bouncers on video taking a bribe from two underage kids. Let us look at the tapes, and we won't tell the cops what happened outside."

Garza stood up. He was about my height, six one, but skinny. He stepped in front of the bouncer.

"You stupid fuck!" He slapped him with an open hand. The bouncer outweighed him by fifty pounds, but he didn't make a move against the manager. "Did you take a bribe at the door?"

The bouncer shook his head. "No, boss. I swear."

The manager slapped him again. "Asshole! Get the fuck out of my sight."

"How about showing us the surveillance tapes?" I asked when the bouncer was gone.

"I'll have to check with the owners," Garza said and picked up his cell phone. I walked to the door marked Private. "You can't go in there." Garza moved to cut me off.

I opened the door and stuck my head in. I noticed a stack of electronic equipment and a back door.

"Did you hear me, fucker?" Garza shouted.

I shut the door and stepped back. "Take it easy, Arnold," I said. "Call the owner. We'll have a drink out front while we wait. Kelly followed me to the door. "Give 'em my name, Nick Fischer, private investigator."

We found a young dancer sitting at the bar beside Skeeter. She wore a sheer top and a gold G-string and had her tiny hand on his huge forearm. Skeeter's eyes were glued to her enhanced boobs.

"Enjoying yourself?" I shouted.

His head whipped in my direction. "This's Candy," he said.

I took a closer look at the girl. She looked about Maya's age, with heavy green eye makeup that sparkled in the light. Her eyes stopped at my forehead. She sucked her bottom lip between her teeth.

I smiled. "Hi, Candy."

She glanced at Kelly then back at me. "Y'all cops?"

"Private investigator," I said, leaning close to her ear. "Is there someplace we can talk?" I held a fifty folded to show the denomination.

Candy looked nervous but nodded and jumped down from the barstool. We followed her to a curtain that led to a private area behind the main stage. Another bored bouncer with a bald head slouched on a barstool beside the curtain. He looked up from his cell phone when Candy stopped beside him. She said something into his ear. He nodded. She held up her fingers in the universal sign for money. I was supposed to pay this guy to let us in. My expense account was getting low. I'd already broken my own number one rule, which was to not take on cases with zero money up front. I still had a mortgage on my fixer-upper in King William. Last time I checked, the bank didn't accept hog or goat meat as payment.

I pulled out another fifty. "Got change for a fifty?"

The bouncer smiled and tucked the bill in his sequined jeans. I turned back to Skeeter. He shrugged his massive shoulders.

"Again," he shouted over the noise.

I pointed to the main stage where the three dancers were doing a pole routine.

"Enjoy the show," I said. "I don't want any surprises coming through this curtain."

He nodded and then pulled a barstool from the edge of the stage and sat down opposite the bouncer. When you were his size, you sat wherever you wanted.

I followed Candy and Kelly to a private booth set up for close encounters. The only lights were from fake candles flickering on the tables and a few guide lights embedded in the floor so the servers could keep the overpriced drinks flowing. The music still vibrated off the walls but was quiet enough for conversation. I could hear a man in the opposite booth ask for another beer. I slid in beside Candy and held out the picture of Maya.

"Ever seen this girl?"

Candy took the picture and quickly slid it under the table. "You're gonna get me in trouble."

"Why, for answering a few questions?" Kelly asked.

"You swear you're not a cop?" she asked.

"I swear," I said.

Candy chewed her lip. A waitress stopped at our table. I wasn't going to get out of here for less than five hundred. Kelly and I ordered a ten-dollar Shiner Bock. Candy ordered something called a *Mad Mako* and waited until the waitress was gone before she continued.

"She was here last week," she said. "Dragon brought her in with two other new girls."

"What happened to her?" I asked.

"I don't know. Some girls only stay for one night."

"Where do they go?" Kelly said.

Candy squirmed out of the booth and stood up. "I've said too much already."

"What's the Dragon's connection here?"

There was a commotion at the door. The baldheaded bouncer was suddenly beside her along with Garza. "It's time for y'all to leave," he said. "I talked to the owner. He doesn't care what you have on video. He wants you gone."

"No surveillance tapes?" I asked.

"Get the fuck out of here."

The bald bouncer grabbed Kelly's arm. Big mistake.

Kelly grabbed his thumb and forced it up behind his back. Garza held his purple jacket open and showed me the butt of a Glock stuck in his waistband.

I stepped forward, grabbed the pistol, and shoved the barrel into his crotch. "Do you keep one in the chamber?"

Garza's brown skin turned gray.

I took that as a yes. “Bad habit to get into. You never know what might cause it to go off.”

He held up his hands. “Okay, man. Fuck.”

The waitress arrived with our drinks on a tray.

“The drinks are on the house,” he said.

“Rain check. We were just leaving,” I said. “Candy’s a great dancer. We enjoyed her company.”

“That’s right. She showed us a great time.” Kelly handed Candy a folded bill for her trouble.

“I’ll leave your Glock at the front door,” I said.

Skeeter had his eyes glued to a very well-endowed dancer who was shaking her sequined pasties an inch from his nose.

I tapped him on the shoulder. “What happened to guarding the door?”

“I didn’t know I was *guarding* the door. Besides, there were only two of them.”

“Let’s go.”

CHAPTER TWENTY-ONE

WE STOOD FOR A MOMENT beside my pickup in the strip club parking lot. My ears were still ringing from the noise. The city smelled like asphalt and exhaust fumes, a stark contrast to the sweet smell of hops and German sausage on the Marktplatz.

"You handled yourself pretty well in there," I said to Kelly.

"You keep forgetting I'm a Marine MP."

"Seeing you out of uniform plays with my memory."

"There'd be more of that if you weren't always working," she said.

Skeeter rolled his eyes. "You two love birds get any info, or were you makin' out in the dark?"

"Candy saw Maya," I said. "She didn't say where she went, but I'll bet she knows more than she let on."

"I think she wanted to talk," Kelly said.

"Yeah, if we can catch her away from work."

Kelly jumped in the passenger seat of my pickup, and I followed Skeeter to his Dodge Ram.

"I know that look," Skeeter said. "You're gonna asked me to break in and steal the surveillance tapes, aren't you?"

"No. We don't need to now. We have an eyewitness."

Skeeter got in his pickup and opened the window.

"When Candy comes out, follow her. We need to set up a private meeting. She knows more about Russell. She was just scared to talk inside. If we're lucky, she might lead us to Maya."

"Where you goin'?" Skeeter asked.

"This is Kelly's last night in town. If I spend it working the case, it'll be the last time I see her. Besides, you wanted to be a partner. Surveillance is part of the job."

"How are things… with Kelly? Is she *the one*?"

"After Sylvia I'm a little gun-shy. I don't trust my gut when it comes to women."

"You remember that old *Seinfeld* episode when Jerry starts dating a girl who's exactly like himself?"

"No. Did it work out?"

"Did it ever work out for Jerry?"

"You're comparing my life to a show that was about nothing?"

He flashed his pearly white teeth. "You're missing the point."

"Whatever."

"She a Marine. She likes to fight…" He let the sentence trail off.

"All right, I get it."

Kelly started my pickup. She saw us and waved while talking on her cell phone.

"You'll find a way to piss her off, or she'll decide you got too much baggage."

"Thanks for the warning. Call me if anything happens."

I opened my pickup door and heard Kelly say goodbye into the phone.

"That was my boss," she explained. "I told him I needed a little more time to help you through rehab. He gave me a three-day extension."

"You wanna help me find Maya?"

"And some other things," she said, smiling. "Our evening was kinda interrupted."

"With Skeeter on surveillance duty, we have my house here in town all to ourselves." I stepped on the gas and made it back to my fixer-upper in the King William neighborhood south of the Alamo in record time. The house was on the edge of the neighborhood near a high school and a Mennonite church. I bought it hoping to cash in on the gentrification. When I actually got around to fixing it up, I was sure it would pay off.

We pulled into the driveway beside the giant pecan tree. The porch covered the right side of the house supported with Greek columns. The left side held a large bay window that showcased a parlor I'd turned into an office. If it was nearer to one of the universities, it would have made a great frat house. Kelly climbed into my lap and unhooked the button on my shirt.

I looked out the window and saw my next-door neighbor, Rose Gustafson, peering through her front room window.

"We've got an audience," I said.

"Rose?" she asked.

I nodded. Kelly had met Mrs. Gustafson the week I was in the hospital. I had sent her to pick up extra clothes and a box of books. After the break-in that happened during my last case, Rose kept a sharp eye out when I wasn't home. It took a phone call from me to convince Rose that Kelly was entering the house with my permission.

Kelly and I hustled inside the house and up the stairs to my bedroom, dropping clothes along the way. I grabbed her around the waist, anxious to lift her onto the bed.

"Wait," she said and turned on the light. "I don't want any more surprises."

This time the bed was empty.

CHAPTER TWENTY-TWO

THE CELL PHONE WOKE ME up at a quarter to seven. My first thought was Skeeter. I'd left him at the strip club and hadn't heard from him all night. I checked the caller ID. Ochoa. That would be Detective Diana Ochoa from the SAPD. I let it go to voice mail.

I was normally an early riser, an old habit formed during my Marine Corps enlistment, but getting shot and spending time in the hospital had disrupted my routine. I searched the bed for Kelly but found it empty. I hadn't heard her get up. I stretched my sore muscles. Last night was the most exercise I'd gotten in a month. It was a good feeling, like maybe I'd turned the corner. Time and exercise, along with hard work, healed most wounds.

I smelled coffee and the warm scent of eggs and fresh pie crust. Two female voices drifted up from downstairs. I recognized the high-pitched laughter. Rose was here. Her curiosity had gotten the best of her, as usual. She couldn't stay away if she smelled a story.

My phone rang again. Ochoa. She wasn't going to be put off.

"Detective Ochoa," I said, answering. "Didn't expect to hear from you so soon."

"I thought you were going to take some time off," she said. I could hear the irritation in her voice.

"I am taking time off," I said. "Plenty of rest and lots of exercise."

"I'll bet. What's a young female corpse stuffed into the dumpster behind Walmart doing with your business card?"

"Do you have an ID?" I had the sinking feeling that it was Maya.

"Nothing on her, literally. That is, except for your card. The girl got the shit beat out of her. You wanna tell me what's going on?"

"Which Walmart," I said. She gave me the address. "I'll meet you there," I said and disconnected. A hollow feeling formed in the pit of my stomach. Had I let Maya down? Was she the Dragon's second victim? I slipped on a pair of clean Wranglers and a T-shirt and made my way downstairs.

Kelly and Rose were sipping coffee. A half-eaten egg pie cooled on the table in front of them. They both smiled like two teenagers caught spreading juicy rumors.

"Good morning," I said. "Morning, Rose. Y'all are up early."

"Oh, we've been cackling like two hens since dawn," Rose said. "I saw her go out jogging early, so I came over and invited myself inside."

"What's wrong?" Kelly asked, seeing the strain on my face.

"That was Detective Ochoa on the phone. A young woman turned up..." I hesitated, glancing at Rose.

"Don't mind me," she said, sensing the gravity of the situation.

"It'll be in the papers later anyway," I said. "Ochoa found a dead woman in a Walmart dumpster."

CHAPTER TWENTY-THREE

THE WALMART WAS OFF LOOP 410, not far from the strip club. It was Sunday morning and the traffic was light.

"Do you think it's Maya?" Kelly asked.

"I thought of that. I hope not."

"Second girl in twenty-four hours who died with your card."

"Yeah. I thought of that too. I'm gonna have to stop giving it out." I punched in Skeeter's number. He picked up on the first ring. I put the phone on speaker.

"I hope you're calling to say you're bringing me coffee and donuts," Skeeter said.

"That depends. Anything to report?"

"Yeah, I'm hungry and tired, and after a night of watching a strip club parking lot, I'm more convinced that the world is full of degenerates. Do you have any idea what goes on in a strip club parking lot?"

"I can guess."

"Did you enjoy your night off?" He tried to sound sarcastic, but he didn't have enough practice to pull it off.

"He slept like a baby," Kelly said.

"Good morning, Kelly. I'm sure you had something to do with that."

Kelly's cheeks turned red.

"What happened? Did you follow Candy?" I asked.

"I lost her," he said.

"How's that possible?"

"Russell showed up with six young girls. I could have sworn one of them was Maya. Same dark hair and facial features. Candy must have slipped away while I was taking a closer look."

"And?"

"It wasn't Maya. I never saw Candy again."

I told him about Ochoa's call and that we were going to check it out. He wanted to meet us there, but I gave him the morning off and told him to get breakfast and take a nap. I wanted to tap into his computer sleuth skills later, and I didn't want him to be dozing off.

If it was Maya in the dumpster, what would I tell Helmut? While I was busy entertaining my girlfriend, I let her get killed? I knew better than to blame myself for other people's evil actions. I'd been through that after my discharge. Still, I couldn't shake the feeling that I could have done more. Kelly sensed my mood.

"You couldn't have done anything."

"I should have been watching the parking lot."

She understood what I meant.

"I was just kidding about being a mistress to your work, but I'm beginning to think it wasn't a joke."

"I'm not blaming you for anything. Let's just see who it is." There was no point in discussing it with her. There was nothing either of us could do about it. I was disappointed in myself. Everything seemed to be happening at once—Grandpa's murder, Helen's return, Kelly, and now Helmut's granddaughter may be dead in a dumpster.

The parking lot behind Walmart was crawling with SAPD

squad cars and decorated with yellow crime scene tape. We parked and got out near the barrier and were immediately told to leave by a burly beat cop. I showed my PI creds, but he didn't care. He had a job to do. Kelly stayed in the pickup. I spotted Detective Ochoa standing by the dumpster. I shouted her name. She waved and walked toward us.

Detective Diana Ochoa was short, but I'd never seen her wear high heels. Her shoes were fashionable but practical, and she wore much less makeup than when I saw her last. She seemed more comfortable in her role as a detective in the department. Her legs were athletic and toned, extending from a formfitting black dress, and her shoulder-length raven hair was stylishly curled. It may have been an early Sunday morning call, but it hadn't caught her sleeping. She looked more like an actor on a cop show than the real thing. I wondered where she was when she got the call.

"It's okay, Officer," Ochoa said to the beat cop. "He's with me." I ducked under the yellow tape. "Good to see you're up and around. How're you feeling?"

"Never better."

She shook my hand, giving me a skeptical smile. Kelly got out of the pickup and crossed toward us.

"Thought you were still in Lubbock," Ochoa said when Kelly reached us.

"I came down for the Fredericksburg Oktoberfest."

Ochoa's smile vanished. "You're involved in this?" she asked Kelly.

Kelly held up her hands. "I'm just an observer."

"Did you ID the body?" I asked.

"Maybe you can help us out with that." She led us to the dumpster, where two ladders had been set up to form a scaffolding. "Take a look."

I climbed the scaffolding and stared at the frail, naked body of the dancer I'd met the night before. The long blond wig was gone, replaced by short dark hair, but the heavy green makeup was the same. She looked like a discarded mannequin from a sex shop window.

"I've never seen her before," I lied, still examining the body. It wasn't that I didn't trust Ochoa, but I didn't want police exposure to jeopardize my effort to find Maya before she ended up in a dumpster beside Candy. I had a good idea the Dragon was behind this, and I didn't want him to strike again before I caught up to him.

Ochoa turned to Kelly. "Does he pass his cards out on the street corner?" she asked, raising her eyebrows.

I glanced back to see Kelly shrug.

"It's not illegal, and it's free advertising," I deadpanned from the top of the ladder.

Ochoa frowned, sharpening the tiny wrinkles around her eyes. "Don't bullshit me, Fischer. I wanna know where this dead girl came from."

I turned back to the body. Candy had the same marks on her arms and throat as Lori had. There were bruises on her thighs that had a yellowish tint like they had been made days or weeks ago. Her wrists and ankles also showed signs of trauma like she'd been tied up before she was murdered.

"You wanna tell me what's going on?" Ochoa said when I jumped off the scaffolding.

"You're the detective," I said. "I can tell you that the card is definitely mine. How it got here, beats me. If I do find anything, I'll let you know."

"I have to ask you. Are you working on a case?"

"Right now, I'm trying to recover from my last case and settle the family estate," I said.

"That's good to know, because people seem to drop dead when you take a case," Ochoa said. She was baring her teeth when she said it, but she wasn't smiling. "And don't tell me you only take the cases we can't solve."

It was the last thing I'd said to her the week before I shot her ex-partner. He turned out to be a dirty cop working for a corrupt politician. I figured she was one of the cops who resented civilians seeing their dirty laundry aired in public and that was why she resented my being here.

"I want to help in any way I can," I said.

CHAPTER TWENTY-FOUR

"So, who was it?" Kelly asked after we climbed in my pickup.

I backed away from the crime scene tape, drove out of the parking lot, then headed south toward the Loop 410 entrance.

"Candy," I said. "Same marks on her neck and wrists as Lori Kostoch."

"And why are we withholding that from the police?" she asked.

"I'm gonna tell them. But I wanna find Maya first, before she ends up like Lori and Candy."

"You know she likes you."

"What're you talking about?"

"Did you see her reaction when I said I was with you in Fredericksburg?"

"I think she was checking my alibi and working suspects at a crime scene."

"That and she was jealous. Who dresses like that to work a murder scene at Walmart?"

"Maybe she was at church."

"Whatever. It's a mistake not to keep her informed."

"She has her priorities, and I have mine."

"Meaning?"

"Police priorities are set by the bureaucracy."

"Thank you for clearing that up." She turned away and looked out the window at the thick green canopy of trees that covered most of city.

"I'm not talking about you. I'm working for Helmut. My priority is to find Maya. Hopefully, alive."

"I get it," she said. "I'm starting to understand why you didn't make a career out of the military. You have a real problem with authority."

"I like to think I can get results when no one else can."

"I'm not disputing that. I've seen you in action. You also make a lot of enemies. One day that's gonna…" She stopped herself from saying it and spit between her fingers.

I saw the law as a gray area that sometimes helped and sometimes hindered me from gaining access to truth and justice. Kelly saw the law as an absolute. It was an issue we'd eventually have to deal with.

I called Skeeter to tell him we were on our way to his mother's house. A visit with Lola Davis could be an ordeal. She never let me forget that I saved her son from death row. I was the Saint Jude of private detectives according to her. She would have adopted me had I not talked her out of it. It was lunchtime, I was hungry, and she was a great cook.

Lola Davis lived in the far south side of San Antonio near Brooks City Base and Mission Espada, the southernmost of the four additional Spanish missions built in the eighteenth century. I turned in to the newer housing development and drove down the row of modest-sized single-story houses, each with a lawn and a collection of oak trees and ornamental laurel, and parked behind Skeeter's pickup. His mom didn't drive, and I didn't see any other cars parked near the house, which was a good sign. It meant Skeeter hadn't told his mother in advance we were coming. Had she known, family members from all over town would gather as if it were a Christmas party or a homecoming for a long-lost relative.

Kelly and I got out and made our way to the front door. I saw movement from the front window and heard Lola's voice shriek. Before I could touch the bell, the door flew open and Lola Davis filled the frame from top to bottom. It was easy to see where Skeeter got his size.

"Lord have mercy. Look at you. Skinny as a rail. Come in this house." She had to step back for us to enter. Her blue, flower-print muumuu flowed nearly to the floor. She had thick arms that looked and felt like they could squeeze a man in half. "Clarence!" she yelled toward the basement, then turned back to me. "Where have you been?" She wrapped her man-killer arms around me. "I can tell right now, you ain't gettin' enough to eat. Land's sakes, child. How you gonna recover if you don't eat?"

"Good to see you, Miz Davis. How are you?" I asked.

"Takin' care of Clarence takes all my strength."

"I heard that, Momma," Skeeter called from the basement.

"And this must be Kelly. Clarence never stops talking about you." Lola swept me aside and seemed to notice Kelly for the first time, as if she'd snuck in while no one was looking. "You are a pretty little thing." Lola's gaze seemed to peel back the normal layers of social armor that people put on when they met someone for the first time.

Kelly smiled at her. It wasn't forced, but I could see the discomfort on her face. She stood erect like the military officer she had been, as if she was being inspected. Which she was, but probably not like anything she'd ever experienced before. Lola Davis looked into your soul.

An awkward minute ticked by. Then Lola suddenly swept Kelly up in her big arms and squeezed her like she was a little girl. "My, my, my," she said. "This one's a keeper; I tell you what. She needs some meat on her bones, but I'll fix you both up right now."

"We don't want you to go to any trouble. We just came by to say hello and visit with Skeeter."

As if on cue, Skeeter stepped out of the stairwell. He saw Kelly smothered in his mother's arms and nodded knowingly toward me.

"Nick Fischer, you know better than that," Lola said. "You come with me, suga," she said to Kelly. "You can help me put together some lunch, and I'll tell you a few things about Nick you might not know yet." She took Kelly's arm and led her into the kitchen.

"Step into my office," Skeeter said.

I followed him down the stairs and into the basement room he used as a computer research laboratory. The room was twenty by thirty feet long and stuffed with electronic gear hooked together with bundles of wires and power cords that emitted a constant electric hum. I followed him to a large display monitor mounted on the back wall.

We sat in the two office chairs, and the screen sprang to life showing a mug shot of Russell Stevens, aka the Dragon, as a younger man. He was smiling for the police camera as if he had a secret he was dying to tell.

"This is one bad dude," Skeeter said. "A poster boy for prison reform. Turned eighteen in Huntsville prison doing five years for manslaughter. Strangled his stepfather with a coat hanger. The judge went easy on him because the defense attorney claimed years of abuse. Got his cute nickname on the inside. When he got out, he went underground. No convictions, but he's linked to drugs, prostitution, and auto theft. Must have learned how to stay under the radar from Convict U."

"Outstanding citizen."

"Lately he's been stepping up his game."

"Like what?"

"If you know who to talk to, the Dragon can get any kind of woman or man you want."

"Underage?"

"You name it. And he probably has cartel ties across the river. No one deals dope in SA without their permission."

"The question is, how did this character get mixed up with Mark Bauer in Fredericksburg?"

"No direct connection that I've found, but everything the Dragon does is under the table. Mr. Bauer has some interesting plans. His company has been buying up a lot of land in Gillespie County."

"Yeah, he wants to buy my grandpa's place. Said he wants to put in grape vines and make the house into a bed and breakfast."

"The biggest purchase seems to be a section along the Pedernales River. Some kind of convention center."

"That would include the beach where we used to party, the one Lori said she went to with Maya." The image shifted to a map of Gillespie County, outlining a large section of land along the river. "Any idea what he's planning?"

Skeeter smiled and touched a few keys on the keyboard. An architectural rendering appeared, showing a huge convention center complete with a thirty-six-hole golf course and condos facing the fairways. In the center was a luxury six-story hotel.

"That's a huge project," I said, marveling at the size and the complex design.

"Lots of money changing hands, which may explain what Russell is doing there. Could be he's looking for legit businesses to launder gangster money."

"It doesn't get us any closer to finding Maya."

He showed me the Facebook missing persons posting and the several dozen comments it had received—none offered more than moral support. The state and national hotlines were no better. It was frustrating, and unfortunately, all too familiar. If we didn't locate her soon, the chances of ever finding her were slim to none.

"Any luck with bus tickets out of Fredericksburg?"

"No one who fits her description."

"Everything points to the Dragon," I said.

Skeeter flashed Russell's younger smiling face back up on the screen. It was a ruggedly handsome face even at age eighteen, full of hope and intelligence.

"Looks more like a rock star than a gangster," Skeeter said.

"You ain't seen him lately," I said.

"Lunchtime," Kelly said, sticking her head into Skeeter's basement lair. The smell of fried chicken and cornbread followed her into the room. She studied the architectural rendering on the screen next to Russell's mug shot. "Who's the kid?"

"That's Russell Stevens before he became the Dragon."

"Wow, talk about contrast. He into real estate?" she asked.

"This is what Mike Bauer's building in Fredericksburg," I said.

"Clarence!" Lola Davis called from the top of the stairs in a voice that could have been heard at the local mission.

Skeeter immediately got to his feet. A lifetime of conditioning. "She don't like to call twice," he said and ducked through the door.

Kelly and I followed him up the stairs to the kitchen, where there was enough food laid out to feed the entire south side of San Antonio.

"You didn't have to go to all this trouble," I said.

Lola kissed me on the cheek and pointed to the place of honor at the head of the table. "You know better than to tell me that."

When we all sat down, Lola held out her hands and bowed her head. We joined hands around the table.

"Bless us, oh Lord, and these Thy gifts, which we are about to receive from Thy bounty," she chanted in a strong singsong voice. "And bless your son Nick Fischer. Guide him in all he do. Without him my son would not be with us today..."

As she continued to sing my praises to the Lord, Kelly squeezed my hand. Getting so much attention and praise made me nervous. I needed to find Maya, and the chances of finding her alive were fading quickly.

CHAPTER TWENTY-FIVE

AFTER EATING TOO MUCH CHICKEN and cornbread and saying our long goodbyes to Lola Davis, Kelly and I headed back to Fredericksburg. I was looking for the link between Russell Stevens and Mike Bauer. Talking to his son might generate a lead. At this point, there was nothing to do but keep asking questions and keep moving forward. Maya was out there somewhere. The only good news was that no one had found her body.

"What makes you think Owen Bauer will have more to say?"

"Lori's dead. I think Owen Bauer knows what's going on, and he's dying to tell somebody. Besides, he's more likely to talk than Russell Stevens."

"You going to call Zeller?" Kelly turned in her seat and faced me. As a former MP and current member of law enforcement, she was conditioned to go by the book. More issues with my unorthodox methods.

"I think time's running out for Maya. I don't wanna waste an afternoon talking to Zeller."

"Just remember Owen's a seventeen-year-old high school kid," she said. "If he won't talk, you have to let him go." I got the feeling she didn't trust me.

"The only thing I'll hurt are his feelings."

"I guess if I was missing, I'd want someone like you looking for me."

That seemed to settle the argument, but I knew it would come up again.

It was an October Sunday afternoon. The sky was clear, and the air felt crisp and dry. The fall season came late to Central Texas. When the people north of the Red River were experiencing their first snow, the Hill Country folks were just turning off their a/c. It felt like outdoor party weather.

When I was in high school, October Sunday afternoons were the perfect time to gather along the river for a swim and a cold beer before the new school week started. We didn't have football practice, deer season wouldn't start until November, and the hay was in the barn. I was counting on the fact that traditions die hard in rural Texas.

I followed the county road that wound along the river and found the dirt road that gave access to the swimming hole. It was the one where Lori had said she went with Maya and the last place anyone had seen her, not counting Candy.

Owen's pickup was parked on the road near the trail leading to the river.

"Looks like our boy is here," I said, pointing to his jacked-up four-by-four. I found a place to park, and Kelly and I got out. "Where did you hang out when you were in high school?" I asked.

"On Sunday afternoon, we'd go to the softball field behind the Catholic church. That is, when I could get out of doing chores. My dad was pretty strict about my sister and I doing our share of the work. We tried to get everything done early, right after we got home from church."

"I had the same problem. My grandpa didn't believe in kids having free time. Work was his answer to everything."

"Sounds like he and my father would have gotten along beautifully," she said.

We followed a couple of teenage boys toting an ice chest no doubt full of beer. They had on sunglasses and board shorts and still had tans from the long hot summer. The trail to the river was well worn from years of access. It was just like I remembered it from fifteen years ago, including the accumulation of trash. There were plenty of beer bottles and cans mixed in with potato chip bags and candy wrappers. We stopped when we came to the bluff overlooking the beach.

"So, this is where Mike Bauer's gonna build his resort?" Kelly asked.

"This is the spot. Gonna be a lot of disappointed high schoolers when that happens."

There were a couple dozen young people scattered along the river. Some in the water, others stretched out on beach towels. I spotted Owen Bauer sitting in a lawn chair wearing swim trunks and holding a longneck beer. He was surrounded by a couple of guys and a half dozen girls who were laughing it up and having a good time. A boom box was blaring one of those electric guitar country songs driven by a hard bass line. Reminded me a little of ZZ Top.

"There's Owen," I said.

"The one with the mirror shades and bushy hair?" Kelly asked.

"He's a stud."

Two boys from Owen's circle stood up when we approached, like they were some kind of security guards. They were tall and filled out with steroid-enhanced muscles but wore peach-fuzz beards that would scrub off with a washcloth. They were identical except one had dark hair and the other was blond. My guess was they were linemen or maybe linebackers. They stopped in front of us about twenty feet from where Owen sat with the girls.

"Private party, man," the darker one said.

"Coach V know you're drinking during the season?" I asked.

They both stood up a little straighter, not expecting to hear their coach's name. "He gave us the beer," the blond said, making a quick recovery.

His buddy laughed. I got the feeling the blond was used to covering for his friend. The girls around Owen were paying close attention, but Owen was trying his best to look nonchalant.

"No shit?" I said. I knew he was lying. "In that case, how 'bout givin' an old man a cold one?"

Kelly shot me a curious sideways glance.

I turned my head and winked so the boys couldn't see.

"Y'all defense or office?" I asked.

They looked at each other as if they weren't sure.

"I'll bet you're both linebackers."

"That's right. We're linebackers, man," the blond answered.

"No shit? That's what I played. I played tight end too. We played both sides of the ball in my day. I was on Coach V's team."

Both quickly lost the chip on their shoulders.

"You Nick Fischer?" the blond asked, taking a closer look.

"That's right, son."

"I seen your picture in the locker room," the dark-haired one said.

"You boys gonna take care of business this year?" I asked.

"Yes, sir," they replied in unison.

"How 'bout that beer?"

The dark-haired one beat feet over to the cooler and brought me a Shiner Bock longneck. Kelly cracked a smile but didn't say anything. I took a step so that I was standing between them. Kelly stayed where she was.

"Hey, Owen," I yelled over the music. "We need to talk."

The linebackers looked at each other then back at Owen as if waiting for instructions.

Owen stood up and reluctantly walked over to me.

"We already talked," Owen said.

"But we left so much unsaid." I smiled and took a drink of beer. It was cold and tasted good.

Owen stared at me like he had probably stared at most of his teachers during his academic career. I could relate. I had been clueless until I joined the Marine Corps.

"I'll make this easy for you. We'll go stand in the shade. I don't wanna get sunburned. Your friends don't have to listen."

"My dad's gonna nail you for this," Owen managed to say.

"Whatever. Let's go. We just wanna talk."

He studied my scarred face for a moment, then started walking toward the large cottonwood tree about fifty yards upstream. Kelly and I followed.

Owen leaned against the wide trunk and crossed his arms, determined not to tell us anything we wanted to know. I handed my beer to Kelly and snatched the mirror shades from his face.

"I like to see who I'm talking to," I said.

"Coach V's gonna hear about this. So's my father," he said, still throwing threats.

I turned to Kelly and raised my palms in mock surrender. "Wow, he's got us now."

Kelly cocked her eyebrow as a warning to me.

I moved a step closer to Owen. I knew the exertion and my temper made the scars on my forehead turn purple and more pronounced. "I remember when I was a high school football stud. I thought the sun rose and sat in my asshole. When I left town, I figured out I'd been a big fish in a very small pond."

"I'm a college prospect."

"Good for you. Let's start with Lori Kostoch," I said.

"What about her?"

"I noticed you're not in mourning," I said.

"Why should I be?"

"Because she's dead."

His lips parted, and his tan skin turned a shade lighter. He hadn't known. News usually travels fast in a small town. Somehow, news of her death last night hadn't hit his radar. Maybe Zeller had kept it quiet until after he'd made the call to Lori's mother. If he did, I'd have to give him credit for being a nice guy.

Owen unfolded his arms and looked at the river water churning downstream thirty yards away. His eyes filled with tears.

"Did you see her or talk to her yesterday?" Kelly asked.

"I—I don't know anything," he managed to stutter.

"That's not what she asked," I said. "She was strangled with a piece of rope and left naked in my motel room. Tell me if you talked to her."

"I don't know nothin'," he whispered.

"Oh, you know something. I followed you after our last conversation. You went straight to Lori. You met her behind the café. I watched you smack her around."

"It—it wasn't like that."

"Bullshit!" I raised my voice. "I followed you after you left the restaurant. You went to a trailer house on your dad's ranch and talked to Russell Stevens, aka the Dragon."

Owen looked down at his feet, hiding his tears.

"The police will get around to questioning you before long. You better have a better story to tell them, or you just might find yourself in jail. I don't care who your daddy is or how much pull he has. Murder is murder."

"You got it wrong. I didn't have anything to do with her murder."

"Why'd you slap her around?"

Owen stared at his group of friends who had all lost interest in him and were enjoying the cool river water and drinking beer. He seemed to wish he was with them.

"Whatever you're into, I can help, Owen," I said, lowering my voice to a friendly level.

"We know about the party," Kelly said. "Lori told us you asked her to bring Maya."

"You don't know this guy," Owen said, his voice slipping into a raspy whisper, as if someone might be listening. "He's fucking crazy."

"Who? The Dragon?"

He nodded.

"Right now, I wanna know where he took Maya."

"I was just supposed to bring a girl to the party. I swear."

"What did you get out of it?"

"The Dragon let us party here, man."

I slapped his face with my open palm. The skin on his cheek turned crimson. "Have you done it before?"

"No, man. Only Maya."

"You picked her 'cause you didn't think anybody would miss her?"

"Yeah, that's right. She said she was from Cali. We—we didn't know she was Mr. Geisler's granddaughter."

"You and Lori?"

He nodded.

"So, you used Lori to help you get Maya?" Kelly asked.

"I tried to warn her that he… that the Dragon was dangerous. She didn't understand."

"She understands now," I said.

The tears flowed down his suntanned cheeks. "I'm sorry, man… I…"

"Where's Maya now?" I asked.

He clenched his jaw.

Kelly grabbed my arm before I could crush his pathetic face. The kid deserved to get the shit kicked out of him, then to get thrown in jail. He was at the center of a murder and a kidnapping, but if he showed up with a shiner at the public school, I would be arrested or tarred and feathered and thrown out of town before lunchtime.

"Talk, Owen, or I'll turn him loose," Kelly said. "Tell us what you know."

"She left with him... with the Dragon. He didn't force her. She could have left with Lori. She didn't want to. She wanted to party."

"Were there drugs involved?" Kelly asked.

Owen looked down at his feet again.

"Were there drugs at the party?" I repeated.

"Yeah. Yeah, everybody was stoned."

"What was it?"

"Everything, man. Grass, pills, crystal... you name it."

"Are you dealing that shit to your classmates?" The idea hadn't dawned on me until that moment. This punk was a high school dealer.

Owen bit his bottom lip, all but admitting his involvement.

I slammed my hand against the cottonwood tree, inches from his face. "You little pissant! You're supposed to be the captain of the football team."

"Yeah, so what?" he asked. "I do my job on the field. I'm talkin' to college coaches. I got a career."

The kid really didn't get it. It had only been fifteen years since I'd left the high school gridiron, and the whole concept of high school sports had changed. Owen used the game to give himself celebrity status and a cover for dealing drugs on the side.

"What're you gonna do?" he asked hopefully.

"We're gonna find Maya and bring her home."

"But... are you gonna tell anybody about... about me? I don't push the shit on anybody. If they want it, they come to me. If they don't get it from me, they'll find another supplier." He had it all worked out.

"Forget about the football season—it's over for you. Forget the college coaches too. My advice: join the Marine Corps. I did. Best move I ever made."

Owen started to hyperventilate. "He—he threatened me. It—it was all the Dragon. I—I didn't have a choice."

"That's where you're wrong. You always have a choice."

CHAPTER TWENTY-SIX

Kelly and I left Owen standing under the cottonwood tree by the river. The teen crowd kept their distance from us as we walked toward the bluff. I noticed both linebackers were picking up their empty beer bottles. That was something new from when I was in high school. Maybe there was still hope for their generation. I finished my beer and tossed the empty to the blond linebacker.

"Do you believe him?" Kelly asked.

We retraced our steps along the path that wound through the prickly pear cactus and mesquite brush.

"I think he's covering his ass."

"So, what's next?"

"Keep stirring the pot till the Dragon stew starts to cook."

"You're gonna piss a lot of people off."

"I'm not in this to make friends."

"Why then?" she asked.

She waited for an answer, but I didn't have a snappy comeback. I started my pickup and took a last look at the dark-green canopy of cottonwood trees that marked the river's meandering path. Mike Bauer's convention center may be good for the local economy, but it would sure mess up a hell of a pretty place in the country.

"Skeeter says you're an adrenaline junky. Is that it? Do you just like to fight?"

She was searching for answers and analyzing my motivations as if she were checking a section of my resume, trying to decide if I was long-term boyfriend material. We'd said a lot of things over the weekend. We'd made love, held hands, and even talked about the future, but now she wanted to know if I was someone she could hang with for the long haul.

"What do you think?" I asked.

"I think he's right. I also think you still feel guilty."

"Guilty for what?"

"For coming home alive. I know you left brothers on the battlefield. If you're trying to make up for that by putting yourself in danger, it will never work."

"Maybe finding Maya is just me doin' a favor for an old family friend?"

"Maybe you're full of shit," she said.

We passed the quaint *Willkommen* to Fredericksburg sign, and a police cruiser lit us up. Officer Zeller was on my bumper with his lights on and siren blaring. I pulled to the side of the road near the liquor store and started to get out of the car. Les beat me to it.

"Stay put, Fischer!" he yelled through my open window. "Put your hands on the wheel." He was out of breath from jogging to my door.

"Les, what the hell's wrong with you? Was I speeding?" I asked.

He poked his Pillsbury Doughboy face in the window, close enough that I could smell the cheeseburger with onions he had for lunch. "I just got a call from a very angry parent. He said you assaulted his son by the river."

I could see my own pissed off reflection in his mirror shades.

"Did Mike call you?" I asked.

"You were trespassing on private property."

"Come on, Les. Half the high school football team's down there drinking beer."

"I'm going to have to take you down to the station."

"That's bullshit, Les," I said. "You know what goes on at the river, and you don't do anything."

"Mike hired private security to handle that."

"Sure, a gangster named the Dragon."

"Just doing my job, Nick," he said. a flicker of a smile on his lips. He was enjoying this a little too much. "Step out of the car, please."

I saw Officer Crowley in the side mirror, approaching at a crouch with his hand on his weapon. I took my phone from the console and looked up Rocky's number in my contacts. "Call Rocky Velosic." I showed Kelly the number, and she tapped it into her phone.

"What can he do?" she asked.

"You're from a small town. You know how much pull the head football coach has. Besides, all those guys were on his team. Tell him what we know and how Owen's involved. If nothing else, he'll want to protect his quarterback. If he doesn't answer the phone, drive over to the stadium. He's probably watching game film in the field house."

"Never a dull moment with you."

She was more concerned than she was letting on. She leaned over the console and kissed me. I took advantage of the move to slip off my ankle holster and slide my .38 pistol under the seat. My .45 was in the console, and I didn't want either to end up in a police storage locker.

"Okay, Fischer. Let's go," Les barked.

I got out of my pickup and glanced at the dozen lookie-loos slowing down to stare at the convict.

"Hands on the hood." Crowley took a step back, keeping his hand on his pistol.

"You're gonna cuff me, Les? What the fuck's wrong with you?"

"Look, Nick. I know you, and I knew your family. But this is my job."

I put my hands on the hood and looked through the windshield at Kelly. She had a smile on her face. At least she was enjoying herself. I probably should have kept my mouth shut, but just because you've known someone for a long time doesn't make them a good person. He was an asshole in high school, and age hadn't change him.

"Do you give blowjobs to all the city council members or just Mike Bauer?"

Crowley snickered under his breath.

"You're such a nice guy, Nick," Les said.

Officer Crowley slipped on a pair of blue plastic gloves. He was nervous and started to pat me down a little harder than necessary.

"There's a bandage on my chest. It's a bullet wound, and it's sore as hell. If you cause me any pain, I will kick your ass," I said.

Crowley eased off on the pressure, found my pocketknife in my back pocket and tossed it on the hood.

"He's clean," Crowley said.

I put my hands behind my back and let him slip the handcuffs on. He opened the rear door of the cruiser and guided me into the back seat.

I'd been to the local police station many times as a kid when my dad was still alive. The last four years of his life he had been the county sheriff. I used to stop by the station on my way home from football practice. He had even locked me in a holding cell once just to show me what it was like. The closest I'd ever come to actually getting arrested was the summer after he was murdered. Rocky and I thought it'd be fun to tie one of his uncle's rodeo bulls to the front door of the courthouse. It was Les's father who had kept me out of trouble and made me work all summer to pay for the new door.

When Zeller pulled into the station parking lot, Rocky was already there, leaning against his pickup.

"Lester, have you lost your marbles?" Rocky shouted.

Les pulled his bulky frame out of the cruiser. "Rocky, you stay out of this. I'm takin' Nick inside. You can talk to him later if you want."

Crowley hustled around to open the back door.

"We need to talk, Les," Rocky said.

Crowley left the door closed and me locked inside while Rocky led Les toward the opposite side of his pickup. I could hear some sharp exchanges but couldn't make out what they were saying. Rocky was doing most of the taking. Les's chubby cheeks were getting redder and redder. Finally, the two walked back toward the cruiser.

"Let him out," Zeller said. "Turn him loose."

"But…" Crowley started to protest.

"Get out of here, Fischer," Les said. "This is my town now. I don't care if you're a private dick. I don't need help solvin' crime around here. You got that?"

Crowley opened the door and took the cuffs off.

"Sure, anything you say, Lester," I said. "Have a nice day."

Les took a step toward me, his right fist clenched. If he could get momentum and put even half his weight behind a punch, he could take out a good-sized bull. His trouble was, he was slow and telegraphed his move like the trailer for a blockbuster movie.

"Drop it, Les," Rocky said.

Les's forward motion stopped. His eyes said he wanted to hit me. He thought he had what it took to take me out. Maybe he did. We wouldn't find out today.

"Good choice, Les. I'll take my pocketknife," I said.

He held my gaze for a full minute before he spoke. "Watch your step, Nick," he finally said and walked to the station door.

Crowley handed me my knife and followed his boss inside.

Rocky waited until they were gone before he spoke. "You're still the same cocky bastard. Les was itching to take a swing at you."

I followed him to his pickup.

"Why'd you stop him?"

"'Cause he was lookin' for an excuse to lock you up. You almost gave him one."

We got in and he cranked the engine.

"What'd you tell him to get him to let me go?"

Rocky chuckled. "I called Mike. Told him I would suspend Owen for drinking."

"Your linebackers said you bought them the beer."

"Those little bastards'll pay for that. Didn't I ask you not to harass my star quarterback?"

"Come on, Rocky. I can't do that. A girl's missin'. Another one's dead. Owen Bauer is involved. I don't give a shit about your football season."

Rocky turned off the engine, irritated. "Goddamnit!"

"Owen's not just involved in some silly prank. He's dealing drugs, Rocky. His supplier works for Mike. He and Lori took Maya to the party. I'm not the bad guy in all this."

His top lip closed over his buckteeth. "You're right, you son of a bitch. I don't know what I was thinkin'. I guess I was too caught up in my season to see it." He slammed his open palm on the steering wheel. "Sheeit!" He looked out the window at the row of oak trees lining the parking lot. "We would have had a hell of a year." He shook his head as if he'd just lost his mother.

"It's just football, Rocky."

He laughed. "You've been away a long time."

"Do you know of any reason Mike would hire a gangster as a security guard?"

"None whatsoever."

My phone rang. I hit accept.

"Hello, jailbird," Kelly said.

"Come and get me, darlin'. I'm at the station."

"Am I breaking you out?"

"They let me go. Something to do with my being German."

She laughed. "In this town, it wouldn't surprise me."

CHAPTER TWENTY-SEVEN

KELLY PICKED ME UP AND we drove back to the ranch house. I told her about my conversation with Rocky and how he convinced Officer Zeller to let me go.

"Why do you think Bauer hired a guy like Russell Stevens?" she asked.

"That's what I asked Rocky. He didn't know. Mike's a businessman and a shrewd operator. He's donated a lot of time and money to local events over the years. I don't know why he would jeopardize all of that to go into business with a gangster."

"Maybe the Dragon made him an offer he couldn't refuse."

"Blackmail?"

"It would explain a lot."

"Yeah, but for what?"

There was a light on in the house when I got out to open the front gate, and I remembered that Helen was still in residence. So much for getting a good night's sleep. I drove past the pond and saw two vehicles instead of one. Beside Helen's white Chevy Tahoe was a black Suburban with Bauer Farms stenciled on the door.

"Looks like your mom's got company," Kelly said.

"What the hell is Mike Bauer doing here?" I parked by the barn, and Kelly and I got out. The temperature had dropped into the high sixties. The wind had shifted to the north. A dark line of clouds obscured the harvest moon. A norther was coming.

As we walked toward the porch, I heard laughter from inside. My muscles tensed. Kelly took my hand.

"Take it easy," she said. "Maybe he came to talk about Owen."

"At least he saved us a trip to Bauer Farms."

Mike and Helen were seated at the kitchen table when we walked inside. Helen stood, obviously surprised. There were empty dinner plates showing the remains of spaghetti and red sauce and an empty bottle of Bauer's reserva wine between them.

"Entertaining guests?" I asked Helen.

"Nick, come on in. Have a glass of wine. I brought an extra bottle," Mike said.

"I didn't think you'd be back tonight, Nicky," Helen said.

"Where else would I go? It's my damn house."

Mike finished his glass of wine and stood up. "Now, Nick. Your mother and I were just having a little dinner."

They looked like two teens caught in the high school janitor's closet after school. The two of them were on some kind of date.

"I-I wanted to talk to her about the property," Mike stuttered.

"Helen has nothing to do with my family ranch," I said.

"I was looking out for your interests," she said. "Mike has made a very generous offer that I think we should consider."

"There is no *we*," I said. "What I do with this ranch is none of your business."

"Nicky, don't get all worked up," she said.

Kelly sat in the chair by the window wearing a neutral expression and nodding like a family counseling therapist.

"Helen might have a legitimate claim to the ranch. I've been checking the county records," Mike said. His cheeks were flushed from the wine.

"Helen has no rights to the Fischer family ranch. If she ever had any, she gave them up twenty years ago. And what the hell were you doing digging into the county records?"

"Nicky, he was just—"

I cut her off before she could finish and turned to Mike. "You were trying to come up with a way around me to get your hands on the ranch."

"Now, it's not like that."

"Skip the crap, Mike. I'll let you know my answer right now. The Fischer ranch is not for sale. Not now. Not ever. Not at any price. It stays in the family."

"We don't have to make a decision tonight," Helen said.

I turned to Helen. "You have worn out your welcome. I asked you to leave nicely. Now I'm making it official. You're out."

Her eyes brimmed with tears. "You don't have to be cruel." She wiped her eyes with the back of her hand. "I thought we could have this conversation in private." She glanced at Kelly for support.

"We did have this conversation in private, several times. It didn't do any good."

"I only want what's best for you," she said.

"Bullshit. If you wanna stay in Fredericksburg, I can't stop you. But I want you gone. Now. Tonight. In the next five minutes. Get your stuff and go." I pointed up the stairs.

Helen slowly backed away from me and retreated up the stairs.

"You didn't have to do that," Mike said.

"You stay out of this. We still have unfinished business. Russell Stevens is into a lot more shit than you know, or maybe you do know and you're not talking. Somehow he's behind Maya Chavez's disappearance and Lori's death."

"That's preposterous. You can't prove any of that." His wine-flushed cheeks turned a shade redder.

"Russell Stevens is on your payroll. If you're protecting him, that makes you an accessory to murder and kidnapping."

"How could he be involved? Those are ridiculous charges," Mike said. A tiny bead of sweat broke out on his forehead.

"If anything happens to Maya, Russell's a dead man. And if I find out you have closer ties to Russell than you're letting on, I will bury you right beside him."

"Now wait just a goddamn minute! You can't threaten me."

"What's he got on you?" I asked.

"Russell Stevens is legitimate. He works for me. There's nothing illegal going on," Mike insisted.

"He's got a record. You gonna tell me you didn't know that?"

Mike let out a deep breath and seemed to get himself under control. "You can't hold that against him."

Helen dragged her suitcase to the top of the stairs. "Can I come back for my other things later, Nicky?" she asked sweetly.

"Fine. I'll put everything by the front gate," I said.

"Oh, be serious!" she huffed.

"They said your last deployment made you a little crazy," Mike said. "That when you got home you were never quite right in the head." A trace of a smile formed under his beard.

I stepped to within a few inches of Mike's face. "Then you better not be hiding anything from me, Mike, 'cause I might just go psycho on your ass. I wanna find Maya, before your friend the Dragon ties a rope around her neck."

His smile disappeared.

Helen stomped down the stairs with her suitcase in her hand. "I hope he listens to you," she said to Kelly.

Kelly tactfully kept her mouth shut.

Helen hesitated at the door, waiting for a nod or a gesture of reconciliation—a sign that I would change my mind. I didn't give her one.

Mike picked up Helen's suitcase, and the two walked out the front door.

"Tell Russell to produce Maya, alive, and we can make a deal," I called after him.

"You'll hear from my lawyer," he hollered from the porch.

Kelly put her arm around me. We listened to both vehicles start and the tires crunch on the gravel driveway.

She wrapped her arms around me. "I do think you should give her another chance. Maybe not right now, but after we get Maya back. I think that's all she wants, not part of the ranch."

"You don't know her like I do." My muscles were tense. The bullet wound in my chest throbbed.

Kelly felt the tension and began to rub my shoulders. "How close is the nearest neighbor?" she asked.

"The house is a mile away, but the owner lives in Dallas. He only comes in the summer."

"So, we can make as much noise as we want?"

"That's right. If Comanches attack, we're screwed. But if you scream with pleasure, no one will hear you but me."

She pulled my T-shirt over my head and let me undo her buttons. I slipped off her shirt and draped it over the back of the kitchen chair.

CHAPTER TWENTY-EIGHT

By the time we reached the top of the stairs, the amorous moment had dissipated, like sugar melting in hot coffee, only without the sweet aftertaste. We both tried to go through the mechanical motions of lovemaking, but every time she pressed against me the pain in my chest interfered. If that wasn't enough, when my primal instincts should have been taking over, all I could think of was Maya. *Is she safe, or is she dead in a dumpster? What can I do to bring her home safely?*

We finally gave up. Kelly put on one of my T-shirts and wrapped herself in a quilt. I started to explain, but she put a finger to my lips and said goodnight. The north wind had picked up. The cold front was in full swing, dropping the temperature inside and out twenty degrees.

At some point, I drifted off to sleep. When my phone rang, it sounded muffled and distant. I searched the cold wooden floor first, then followed the noise downstairs and into the front room. I found the phone where I'd left it in my jeans pocket on the floor and checked the caller ID. Skeeter.

"Talk to me," I said.

"I found Maya."

"Where?" I suddenly woke up.

"West side flophouse. I followed one of the bouncers. He had two of the dancers from the strip club when he left. They didn't look happy to be going anywhere. It's an old two-story house. He took the two girls upstairs. That's where I saw Maya."

"Is Russell there?" I asked.

"Didn't see him."

"How many people in the house?"

"Looks like four thugs. Three downstairs and one upstairs. The one upstairs is a customer, if you know what I mean."

"I hear you. Stay on the house. I'll be there in an hour." I hung up and struggled into my jeans. I heard Kelly's footsteps on the stairs.

"Everything all right?" she called to me in the dark. I saw her naked silhouette draped in my loose-fitting T-shirt. She held her SIG Sauer pistol at the ready position, pointed down and tucked close to her chest.

"That was Skeeter," I said.

"And?" she asked, lowering her weapon.

"He found Maya."

"Is she safe?" she asked.

"She's alive."

"Thank god," she said and relaxed. "It's freezing in here."

"The norther finally made it." I found my socks and shirt. "We have to go."

"Let me change the bandage on your chest first," she said.

"No time."

"At least put on a clean T-shirt," she said. "You've got to take care of that wound or it will never get better."

"Okay, you're right." I followed her upstairs to the bathroom.

"I can see how this goes. While you're on a case, I'm always gonna have to take a backseat."

I couldn't argue with her. It was true. Maybe it was hardwired into my system. Maybe I didn't want anyone to get too close. Kelly applied a fresh bandage on my chest. Right now, I didn't want to worry about anything but getting Maya home safe.

• • •

By the time we hit the edge of San Antonio, traffic was already starting to pick up. It was four a.m. Monday morning, and the area military bases were open for business by four thirty. Skeeter had sent the address to my phone. It wasn't completely unfamiliar territory. The house was located on the west side near Lucky's gym.

I took the Vance Jackson Road exit off Interstate 10 and cut over to Zarzamora Street. The plan was to meet Skeeter at the gas station a block from the flophouse, then work out the details. The street was lined with car repair shops and Hispanic markets. The only new business in the last twenty years seemed to be the Dollar General store.

I found a taco truck open for business and pulled in to grab some breakfast. I didn't want to break into a flophouse on an empty stomach.

"You hungry?" I asked.

Kelly studied the mobile food truck and the string of Christmas lights that illuminated three worn picnic benches and a collection of rusty metal chairs. There was one other customer standing by the open side of the van who looked like he'd partied most of the night away. I hoped he didn't have far to go.

"Too early for me," she said.

"Suit yourself." I got out and smelled the grilled meat mixed with onions and freshly scorched flour tortillas. This was my kind of place. An older woman stood on a wooden box behind the grill, her face a roadmap for the many places she'd cooked early morning breakfasts. A younger man appeared by the window.

"*Buenos días*," he said.

"*Tengo hambre*," I said. He smiled. I knew my accent was a little too white, but he understood.

"Good," he said. "How many?" The older woman was watching and listening.

"*Dos huevos y barbacoa*," I said.

She checked with him for clarification. Evidently my Spanish wasn't clear enough for her to understand. He repeated my order in a rapid-fire version that she immediately understood.

"*Bueno*," she said and laughed at my expense.

While she cooked my breakfast, I called Skeeter. The status hadn't changed. No one had been in or out in the last thirty minutes. I told him to meet me at the taco stand.

Kelly got out to stretch her legs.

By the time my tacos were done, Skeeter pulled in beside my pickup.

"You're takin' your life in your hands eatin' here," he said.

Kelly laughed. "That's what I was thinking."

"Y'all don't know what you're missin'," I said.

"What have you got," Kelly said, anxious to get to work.

"It's a two story with a front porch. Kind of like your place, but better maintained."

"Thanks a lot," I said. I didn't think my fixer-upper was in that bad of shape, but Skeeter was always encouraging me to get started with the fix and repair part.

"You have a leak in the upstairs bathroom, and the kitchen sink is backed up," he said.

"I haven't been home in a month."

"Can we talk about that later?" Kelly asked.

I bit into my fresh breakfast taco. The barbacoa flavor mixed with grilled onions and cilantro were in perfect proportion. There were just enough jalapeños to make my tongue tingle and my eyes water.

"This is what tacos are supposed to taste like," I gushed.

She rolled her eyes, turned to Skeeter. "What about the house? Is there a door upstairs?"

"There're steps leading to an upstairs deck off the back of the house," Skeeter said. "I wouldn't trust them, but they would probably hold you."

"That's the plan then," I said and pointed at Skeeter. "You take the front door. If anyone is awake, you detain them long enough for us to slip up the back stairs and get Maya."

I finished my second glorious taco and tipped grandma an extra five. We piled in my pickup and drove to the house. It was a corner lot in a row of similar houses built in the late forties and early fifties after World War II. Some were falling down. Some were in a state of repair. Some were simply abandoned. Most of the yards were enclosed in hurricane fencing. The lights were on in the downstairs area. I parked across the street and studied the windows for any sign of movement. Rap music blared from inside the house. With any luck, the thugs had all passed out and left the music playing. The sound would mask our movements in the house.

"That's the kind of noise that ruined rap," Skeeter said, listening to the music.

"Whatever," I said. I didn't share his taste in music.

Skeeter checked the loads in his 12-gauge shotgun. It was a model 870 with a pistol grip. The pump action was a challenge to operate using his metal hook, but he had worked out a system that made it look easy and natural. He looked like a cyborg soldier sent from the future to kill John Connor.

"Give us two minutes to clear the top floor," I said to Skeeter. "If you have any trouble, use that shotgun." I checked my watch. Four twenty. With any luck, we would get Maya and be gone by four thirty.

The streetlight on the corner had long since been shot out, and the yard was dark except for the light bleeding through the windows. Several dogs barked from the neighbor's yard, announcing our arrival. The full force of the north wind had not reached San Antonio. The trees were quiet and still, as if holding their breath waiting for the storm.

CHAPTER TWENTY-NINE

I FOLLOWED KELLY TO THE STAIRS that led to the second story. Light poured through gaps in the rotten house boards, and nails protruded an inch higher than flush on the steps. I pulled my .45 and pointed out the flaws in the stairs to Kelly before leading the way. The wooden frame squawked and pulled away from the house several inches but held firm. The noise was covered by the loud rap music mixed with electronic blasts from video game gunshots. Whoever was inside wasn't listening for intruders.

We stopped at the second-story landing. I signaled a thumbs-up to Skeeter in the front yard and watched him point the 870 toward the front door and climb the porch steps.

The back door to the second story was locked. The deadbolt above the knob was completely rusted, and the wooden doorframe suffered from years of neglect.

I stepped back and lifted my leg, preparing to give the lock a blast from my boot heel. The small three-by-three wooden landing wobbled like a two-legged chair.

Kelly stopped me with a hand on my shoulder and produced a Marine Corps issue Ka-Bar knife, known in the military's distinct parlance as, *Knife, Fighting Utility*—a lethal weapon with a sturdy seven-inch fixed blade honed to a needle point. She slipped it between the door and the jamb near the deadbolt and gently popped the door open.

We found ourselves in a dark hallway that ran the distance of the second story. There were three doors on the right facing open windows. The stagnant air smelled like cheap perfume and marijuana and clung to my skin like a damp paper towel. At the end of the hall, a staircase descended to the first floor.

The downstairs music abruptly stopped. Skeeter's baritone voice rumbled up the staircase, barking out orders.

Kelly and I flattened out on either side of the first door. I reached for the knob. Locked. Kelly reached for her Ka-Bar.

A female voice came from inside the room. "Stop it," the voice insisted.

I brushed Kelly aside and kicked in the door.

A man in his late twenties with no shirt and a collection of random tattoos held a naked girl by her long dark hair, his shorts around his ankles. The girl was on her knees. It was too dark to see her facial features, but judging by her slight build, she couldn't have been more than sixteen.

Random Tatts kept his hand on the girl and turned to me. "What the fuck, dude. I'm not finished."

I hit him with the barrel of my .45. He dropped like a wet bath towel. "You are now."

Kelly pulled the soiled sheet around the girl and sat down beside her.

I flipped on the lights. The room was bare except for the mattress and a powder-blue backpack that looked like it belonged to a third grader.

"It's okay," Kelly assured the terrified girl. "We're here to help you."

The blonde's pupils were dilated, and her lids rested at half-mast.

There was a discarded syringe on the floor. I produced Maya's yearbook picture from my pocket and showed it to her.

"Have you seen this girl?" I asked.

She seemed to not understand.

The john came to with a red face and an angry attitude. "You fucking hit me," he said. The guy was a genius. "I paid for that shit." He pulled up his shorts and stood up.

I shoved my pistol under his chin and flipped open my private investigator license. "What do ya think's goin' on here, Ace? That girl's underage. You know what that means?"

His eyes swiveled toward the girl. In the harsh glare of the single 100-watt bulb dangling from the broken ceiling fixture, she looked even younger. The heavy makeup around her eyes and dark red lipstick couldn't mask her youth.

"I didn't know, man," he said.

"Bullshit." I kept my pistol jammed under his chin while I yanked the chain on his belt that was attached to his black leather wallet. He had a stack of bills with a hundred on top. I didn't count it.

"Here," I said, handing the money to the girl. "Find some clothes and get out of here."

"You can't do that," he protested.

"Just did. The only reason I don't shoot you is I don't wanna traumatize this girl any more than she already is by splattering your brains all over the wall." I leaned close to his face. "Take a good look. If you ever see my face again, you better be running the other way. Understand?"

The man stumbled backward toward the door.

"Take the back stairs," I yelled, then tuned back to Kelly. "Leave her. I'll call the police. Let's find Maya."

Kelly's look said she didn't like it. "Help is on the way," she told the girl.

The next door was open. I flipped on the light. Empty. It had the same drab layout. A dirty mattress on the floor, bare walls with mildew around the edges of the window. There was a worn carry-on suitcase with wheels and an extension handle. Whoever parked it there hadn't been here long or was planning a trip.

The last room was locked. I paused to listen. I heard voices behind the door. The video game still played downstairs. Skeeter must have been keeping himself entertained. The neighborhood was quiet. No police on the way. The dogs next door had gotten bored and gone back to bed. I checked my watch. Four thirty. If Skeeter was right, one of those voices belonged to Maya.

I kicked in the door.

Two girls gasped when they saw me step into the room with my .45 held at the ready. One sat on the mattress. The other was on the floor leaning against the wall. Both had dark shoulder-length hair and wore shorts and T-shirts. The air was cool, but damp and sticky, and smelled like weed. I quickly stashed the weapon in my shoulder holster.

"It's okay. I'm Nick Fischer." The girl on the floor matched my picture of Maya. Her hair wasn't combed, and she looked like she'd skipped a few meals, but it was definitely her. I knelt beside her, extremely relieved that I found her alive.

"Maya Chavez?" I asked.

She nodded. "What'd you want?" She was instantly on the defensive.

"You a cop?" the girl on the bed asked. "We ain't done nothin'."

"I'm not a cop. Maya's grandpa hired me to find her and bring her home."

Maya pushed herself up from the floor and sat down next to the girl on the bed.

"What if I don't wanna go?" She took the other girl's hand and waited for my response.

I didn't know what to say. This wasn't what I expected.

"Do you understand what's goin' on here?" I asked.

"I'm not going back. Nobody in F-burg gives a fuck about me." She sounded bitter.

"That's not true. Your grandfather loves you," Kelly said.

"Two people have died already. Your friend Lori, and Candy from the strip club. I think you better come with us, before that happens to you."

"You're lying. Russell wouldn't do that. He—he wouldn't do that to me."

"You're friends?"

"He loves me."

A loud bang shook the old house. The noise came from downstairs. No more time for conversation. I threw Maya over my shoulder. She felt like a ten-year-old girl.

"You can't do this," Maya shouted.

Kelly grabbed a small backpack from the floor. "This yours?" she asked Maya.

Maya didn't respond, but the girl on the bed nodded. Kelly tossed the bag over her shoulder and followed me down the stairs.

Maya pounded my back with her fists, but there was little strength behind the blows. Three thugs in their twenties wearing T-shirts and baggy shorts were lounging on a threadbare couch on the first floor. Two held video game controllers and were focused on the cartoon thugs being chased by the cops on a fifty-inch screen. The third had a glass bong in his hands and was in the middle of taking a huge hit.

Skeeter stood to the side of the screen with his 870 shotgun leveled toward the couch.

"That our girl?" Skeeter asked.

"Meet Maya Chavez," I said.

"She don't look too happy," he said.

"Let me go!" Maya shouted.

I put her down and turned to Kelly. "Can you talk some sense into her?"

"Take it easy," Kelly said, taking Maya's hand. "We wanna help you."

"I don't need any fucking help." Maya tried to jerk her hand away, but Kelly was too strong for her and had done this kind of thing before.

"Put her in the pickup. We'll sort it out when we get her away from here," I said.

Kelly led Maya out the front door.

I turned my attention back to the game on the big screen. "What is that," I asked. "Grand Theft four or five?"

The thug on the right with a neck tatt acknowledged my presence. "One," he said, putting down the controller and reaching under the couch cushion.

"Wow, that's old-school." I hit him in the temple with the barrel my .45, then caught his head and pushed it back against the armrest. I found a Glock 9mm under the cushion and stuck it behind my belt.

The thug in the middle made a move to stand.

"Sit tight," I said, raising my pistol.

He sat back down.

"We don't want any trouble," I said. "We came for the girl. I'm taking her home."

The thug who had the bong squirmed in his seat. He was older than the other two and had probably been left in charge.

"You fucked up, dude," he said.

"I know, I know. You're the baddest of the bad and you're gonna kill me."

"You know it, fucker. This house belongs to the Dragon, man. Maya's his girl." He said it like a threat.

"Now I'm shaking in my boots. I'll bet he's not on the property deed." I reached for a cell phone that was plugged into a speaker. "This your phone?" I asked and unplugged it.

The thugs didn't respond.

During my time in the sandbox, cell phones were a gold mine of intel. I tossed it to Skeeter. "This might come in handy." The phone bounced off his chest and hit the floor. He picked it up with his prosthetic hook and shoved it in his back pocket.

"You can't take that," Neck Tatt said.

I pulled a handful of zip ties from my back pocket. "Show me your hands," I said. "I don't wanna get followed, and you better pray to god I don't ever have to come back."

CHAPTER THIRTY

THE NEIGHBORHOOD WAS AS QUIET as a city neighborhood ever gets. The dogs next door were barking again. A few houses down, an engine cranked and didn't start. Cranked again. Somebody was going to be late for work. The mixture of oak and pecan trees that covered the street remained motionless, anticipating the cold front. I checked my watch. Four forty. We were only ten minutes behind schedule.

"No doubt, Mr. Dragon will be pissed off," Skeeter said.

"He won't miss one teenage girl," I said, walking toward my pickup. The cab light was on, and Kelly was sitting in the back seat beside Maya.

"That punk said Maya was his girl."

"I read somewhere that ownership was illegal," I said.

"You think this is over, smart ass?" he said.

I opened my door. "We got what we came for." I climbed in and started the engine.

Skeeter got in the passenger side and stared at my profile.

"What?" I asked.

"You're turning into an optimist," he said.

"We have a problem," Kelly said.

"You're kidnapping me!" Maya shouted from the back seat.

I put the pickup in gear, made a U-turn, and drove back toward Commerce Street. The first stop was going to be my house in King William. I figured we could all use some rest.

"Did you hear me?" Maya shouted again.

"Look, Maya, calm down," I said.

"Don't tell me to calm down! Let me out." She reached for the door handle.

Kelly grabbed her wrist. "We're trying to help you, Maya."

"I don't need help," she protested.

I sped up to avoid a red light. "Just keep her in the truck till we get home," I said to Kelly.

"I know my rights. I'm eighteen. I can do what I want." Maya spat the words across the seat.

Rose was at her kitchen window when I pulled into the driveway. She waved to me. There would be plenty to gossip about today. I hoped she wouldn't come over for breakfast.

Kelly helped Maya out of the back seat while Skeeter stood beside the door. Both expected her to bolt at any minute.

"You can't do this," Maya screamed defiantly.

"Take her in the house," I said. That warm fuzzy feeling I had for finding her alive now felt more like I'd stepped off the trail and walked into a prickly pear cactus.

Kelly and Skeeter escorted Maya into the house and sat her down on the leather chair in my office. I went to the kitchen and put on a pot of coffee. None of this was making any sense. I was hoping a jolt of caffeine would help.

While the coffee brewed, I walked back to my front office, where Maya sat with her arms crossed and a scowl on her face. She was thinner than she appeared in the high school photo. Her hair wasn't shiny or curled and covered her face. She made no attempt to brush it out of the way.

"Are you hungry?" I asked.

She didn't speak.

I glanced at Kelly and Skeeter. They both shrugged.

"How about something to drink?"

She let out a breath of air like a three-year-old throwing a tantrum.

Kelly followed me into the kitchen and watched me pour two cups of coffee. I handed her one. We both took a sip.

"What do you think?" I asked her under my breath.

"We should all get some rest. She's scared right now and probably still high. Maybe she'll feel differently in the morning when she's rested and sober."

We walked back out to my office. Maya's position hadn't changed. She clenched her jaw, challenging me. Kelly sat down next to Skeeter on the couch. I knelt in front of Maya.

"Your granddad asked me to find you. He's worried sick. We all were. Why don't you want to go home?"

She blew steam out of her nose. Her eyes were red and starting to well up with tears. "That's not my home."

Kelly knelt beside me. Maya let her brush the hair from her eyes. "Tell us what happened." She took Maya's hand.

For the first time since we'd met her, Maya let go of her anger. Her shoulders relaxed. The tears began to flow. "He doesn't want me," she sobbed.

"Did you have an argument?" Kelly asked.

"Y-yes," she stuttered.

I knew Helmut could be a little rough around the edges. He was a tough-as-boot-leather Central Texas rancher whose track record with young female family members wasn't exactly stellar. His daughter had turned to drink in high school and had run off with her boyfriend as soon as she graduated.

"What about your mother? She's worried about you too," Kelly said.

"Have you met my mother? She don't give a shit about me."

"What about school?" I said. "Don't you want to finish your senior year?"

"Not in Fredericksburg. The people suck. That town's a joke."

I thought about bringing up the two girls who died in the aftermath of her disappearance, but I didn't want to argue with her or upset her even more. Her mind was made up. I wasn't a counselor, and I got the feeling that the more I talked, the worse I made it. I checked my watch. Five o'clock in the morning. Not the best time for a therapy session.

"Let's get some sleep," I said. "I promised your granddad I'd find you and bring you home. That's what I'm gonna do. What you do after that is your own business. I know Helmut. He's a good man. Maybe you can work out your differences."

Maya's jaw was clenched.

"Maya, you can sleep in the spare bedroom upstairs," I said. "Skeeter, you can have the couch."

Kelly escorted Maya upstairs, and I followed. The spare room had a bed and a separate bathroom. I used it for storage, but the bed was made, and the sheets were clean. I let Kelly take Maya in and get her settled. Hopefully, she would go to sleep so that we could all get some rest. I thought about cuffing her to the bed, but there was only a small window that opened to a twenty-foot drop, and to get to the stairs, she had to walk past my open bedroom door.

When Kelly came into my room, she looked exhausted. "What do you think?" she said.

"I think Helmut has some explaining to do. He didn't tell me about his argument with Maya."

"What about the Dragon? Do you think he'll come after her?" She took off her shoes and lay down on the bed.

"He's not gonna be happy, but then I don't really care what he thinks." I slipped my .45 from my shoulder holster and placed it on the nightstand.

"What are we gonna do? She's eighteen. Legally, she can do whatever she wants. You can't force her to go back to Fredericksburg."

"She's a scared little kid. I don't care if she's eighteen. She doesn't know what she wants."

She pulled the cover up to her chin. "It's like a refrigerator in here."

"I'll put the heater on," I said and walked downstairs.

Skeeter was already sawing logs. I found the thermostat, flipped it to heat. I hadn't used the central heating since last January. When the blower kicked in, I waited by the vent near the front window for signs of warm air. The pecan tree in the front yard was just beginning to move in response to the brisk north wind. The leading edge of the storm had finally hit the city. After a few minutes, a steady stream of warm air escaped the vent, but it was overwhelmed by the cold air seeping under the windowsill. If I ever got a break, replacing the windows was at the top of my fixer-upper list.

I checked the deadbolts on the front and the back door. If Maya wanted to escape, she'd have to have a key.

CHAPTER THIRTY-ONE

"SHE'S GONE!" KELLY SAID FROM the bedroom doorway.

My head cleared, and I reached for my Wranglers. "Gone?" My throat was dry and sore from breathing dry air from the central heating unit. I slipped on a sweatshirt and followed Kelly into the spare bedroom.

"She went out the window," she said.

I went to the open window. She would have had to creep along a two-inch gutter to the porch roof and jump ten feet to the yard.

"You check downstairs?"

"I checked the backyard, everywhere."

"Outsmarted by a teenager," I said.

A knock came from the front door. Kelly and I hustled downstairs. Skeeter was still sleeping on the couch.

"I guess he didn't see anything," I said, pointing to Skeeter.

"No, and he snores like a diesel engine. It sounded like my dad was plowing the cotton field down here last night."

The knocking got more insistent.

I opened the front door.

Rose Gustafson stood holding a pie pan covered with tinfoil.

"Thought you could use some breakfast with all the extra mouths to feed," she said, peering around me into the front room.

"Hi, Rose. Now's not a good time," I said.

She ignored me and smiled at Kelly. "Well, hello, sweetie. I brought y'all some breakfast." She walked into the kitchen.

Skeeter sat up on the couch, aroused from slumber by the smell of Rose's quiche.

"What's that wonderful smell?" he asked, knowing full well what it was. While I was staying at the ranch, he had been the recipient of many of Rose's delicious meals.

"That was quite a racket y'all put up last night," Rose said, setting the dish on the kitchen table and removing the foil.

"Sorry if we woke you up," I said.

"I was awake when you came home. You know I can't sleep. My hip's been bothering me lately something fierce." She looked around the room. "Where's the little girl you brought home?"

"That's what we're trying to figure out. She ran off last night," I said. "Did you see anything unusual?"

Rose kept a diary of the people who came and went in the neighborhood to keep her busy on nights she couldn't sleep. "I saw a black Jeep parked on the corner about an hour ago. I'd never seen it around here before."

"Russell Stevens drives a black Jeep Grand Cherokee," Kelly said.

"That son of a bitch," I said. "Excuse my language, Rose."

"I'm almost eighty. I've heard every cuss word there is. I'm not easily offended."

I ran up the stairs and put on my socks and boots. She must have had a phone in her pocket. I kicked myself for not searching her. If she bought one burner phone, she knew how to buy another one. Or more likely, Russell gave her one to keep in touch.

I slipped on my shoulder holster and strapped my .38 S&W above my boot.

Kelly joined me in the bedroom and laced up her running shoes. "Where do you think they went?" she asked.

"The strip club and the flophouse are the only two places I know."

"He wouldn't take her back there. He knows you'll look for her."

"What do you suggest?" I asked.

Neither of us had an answer. Downstairs, Skeeter was enjoying an extra-large slice of quiche, and Rose was pouring him another cup of coffee. He held his fork with his metal hook prosthetic like Poseidon holding a trident.

"Why not call him?" He held up the thug's phone with a smug look. "You were right. It had a wealth of intel. I found the Dragon's number."

Skeeter dialed the number and put the phone on speaker.

We listened to the phone ring several times. Finally, a tired voice came on the line.

"Yeah," the voice said. It was Russell.

"Where you at?" I said, trying to sound like a thug.

"Who's this?"

"Who you think, dog?"

"Nick Fucking Fischer," he said, fully awake now.

"Middle name's Lee, after my dad, but close enough. Should I call you Russell, or do you prefer the Dragon?"

"I don't want you to call me at all. I want you to disappear, along with your cute bitch and that big fucking one-armed nigger."

"Now, let's not get personal, Russell. I'll leave you alone if you give me Maya."

"She's with me. Don't you get that? She made her choice."

"She's a kid, Russell. She doesn't know what she wants. Turn her loose or I'll take you apart."

"Fuck off. You can't do jack. You ain't the police."

"Let me talk to Maya," I said, but the line went dead. I hit redial and got the *not-in-service* message.

"No doubt who has Maya," Skeeter said.

"What do we do now?" Rose asked. She had listened to the whole conversation and felt she was part of the team. "I've got my shotgun."

"Leave it in the closet and stand by the phone," I told her.

She looked disappointed. I'd seen her shotgun. Another weapon handed down from her father. I had no doubt she could and would use it if she had to. I also knew her reaction time wasn't what it used to be, and her cataracts limited her vision.

"We're gonna need some lunch," I said.

That got her attention. "I'll have it ready by noon," she said and hurried off to start cooking.

I turned to Skeeter, who was finishing the last of Rose's quiche. "I need names and addresses for anything that has to do with Russell Stevens."

He nodded without speaking. He knew what to do and what I was going to do with the information. We had been together long enough to communicate without the need for explicit instructions.

Kelly listened to our exchange and raised her eyebrow. "What's that for?"

I let the silence stretch for an uncomfortable moment.

"You gonna let me know what's going on?" She was irritated.

"You heard the Dragon. He's not going to give up Maya. He's got her brainwashed."

"So, you're gonna do what, target Russell Stevens?"

Skeeter excused himself. "I'll be outside," he said and walked out the front door.

"Got a better idea?"

"Yeah, let's go to the police. We talk to Ochoa and tell her what's going on. Then we make our case to Zeller."

"And they'll do what? Maya's eighteen, remember. She left on her own. What can they do?"

Kelly chewed on her bottom lip. She saw the reality of the

situation without me having to explain. It wasn't a crime for Maya to be with him. I knew what was going on, and we both knew he was behind two murders, besides trafficking girls. Getting the police to legally put Russell behind bars would take time. Something Maya didn't have.

"We need to tie Russell Stevens to Candy's murder and Lori's," Kelly insisted. "We need to build a case." Her lips pinched shut and her eyes narrowed.

"If I were a cop, that's what I'd do. But I'm not, so I'm gonna get Maya back before it's too late."

"Targeting Russell makes you a vigilante."

"You know what's gonna happen to her if she stays with him."

She stood her ground in the middle of the room.

I knew it would take time for Skeeter to get the information I needed to take Russell Stevens down. "Fine," I said. "Let's go talk to the police."

CHAPTER THIRTY-TWO

I PARKED IN THE PARKING GARAGE across the street from the downtown police station. Kelly zipped up the bomber jacket she borrowed from me, and I flipped the collar up on my jean jacket. The north wind was a welcome change from the long, hot, sticky summer.

Kelly and I walked past the odd public art display that consisted of thirty-foot-tall metal beams painted white and standing on end like unstable teepee poles in a gale force wind. We went through the glass door and found Sergeant Hugo Vera on duty at the front desk. He nodded at me and smiled at Kelly.

"I see you're keepin' better company these days," he said and winked.

"What's the good word," I asked. We shook hands over the desk.

Vera was an old-timer who had retired from SAPD once but came back to work part-time because he said his wife got tired of seeing him around the house all day. He also had a history with my father when he was sheriff of Gillespie County, but he'd never shared the details. When the subject came up, his only comment was, "*Lee Fischer could walk on water.*"

"Every day above ground is a good day. I see the PI business is attracting some very beautiful company." He'd always been a shameless flirt.

She held out her hand. "Kelly Hoffman," she said, rewarding him with a smile.

Vera stood and shook her hand. "I hope you can keep this upstart in line."

"That's a full-time job," she said.

"You look up to the task." He sat back behind his desk and turned his attention to me. "Who'd you come to harass today?"

"Detective Ochoa," I said.

Vera shook his head. "Diana ain't very happy with you."

"We have some info that might lift her spirits."

"I hope so. She brings me donuts when she's havin' a good day. I haven't had any this week."

"Then you ought to thank me for helping you manage your weight."

He ignored me and turned to Kelly. "Good luck with this guy. He's stubborn as a barn-sour mule. Just like his father." Vera made the call upstairs. Detective Ochoa agreed to meet us.

Kelly and I took the elevator.

"Will you agree to do what she says?" Kelly asked when we were alone.

"Let's talk to her first."

We got off the elevator and found Detective Ochoa standing by her corner desk. She didn't look happy to see us.

"What brings you down here, Fischer?" she said, not bothering to offer her hand. She glanced at Kelly and seemed to size her up as if they were wearing four-ounce gloves and about to get it on in an MMA cage match.

"Truce," I said. "Mind if we sit down?"

Ochoa shrugged and plopped herself behind her desk. There was a picture of a five- or six-year-old boy with an angelic smile and dark hair. It was a new picture. The boy's hair was colored dark purple in the last picture I'd seen.

"How's your son?" I asked, trying to thaw her chilly mood.

A flicker of a smile crossed her face, but she quickly pursed her lips. "He's fine. With his father this weekend."

"That must be touchy," Kelly interjected.

"Yeah, well, it is what it is. One day Aaron will realize what an A-hole his father really is. Until then I won't interfere with their relationship."

"Is he a cop?" I asked.

She sat back in her padded office chair. "Did you come down here to ask me about my personal life?"

"Sorry, just curious." I cleared my throat. "Candy."

"I'm fresh out," she said. "Aaron steals it out of my desk drawer whenever he's here."

"No. Candy was the name of the dead girl in the dumpster."

"You suddenly remembered that obscure name while eating your morning protein bar?"

"I had quiche, but yes that's what happened," I said.

"Didn't figure you for a quiche kind of guy." She smirked.

I let that pass and started at the beginning and explained how I'd gotten involved with Maya's case and what we'd found so far. I also explained that I only withheld the name because I was certain that Maya was going to be the next victim and I needed to get to her fast, before that happened.

"Now you're bringing it to me?"

"We found Maya," I said. "She ran away from us."

"She's eighteen, right?" Ochoa asked.

I nodded, knowing where this was going.

"I have to treat this as a voluntary missing person."

I shared a glance with Kelly and shook my head.

"Look, we know about Russell Stevens, aka the Dragon. He's on our radar. He's into more than prostitution. He's a big-time dealer and plugged into the big dogs across the border. Runs distribution from San Antonio."

"Now he's branching out to Fredericksburg," I said.

"We suspected that too." She stood up and walked around the front of her desk. "You wanna know why I'm pissed?"

I kept my mouth shut for a change. I figured she was dying to tell me anyway.

She leaned back against the edge of her desk and crossed her arms under her breasts. She wore black slacks and a cream-colored silk button-down blouse. The matching jacket was slung over the back of her office chair. Her shoes were classy but sturdy—the kind that would hold up in a footrace.

"I'm pissed 'cause somebody took down a flophouse on the west side that we were watching. We suspected it was run by Russell Stevens. Because a group of vigilantes broke into the house and rousted the inhabitants, including the girls we suspected of being trafficked, we can't make the connection or an arrest. In fact, citizen Stevens called 911 last night and claimed his girlfriend Maya Chavez was kidnapped by someone named Nick Fischer."

"That piece of shit," I said.

"Technically, he's right. It was a kidnapping."

"You just said it was a flophouse. She was there against her will."

"Then why did she run away from you?"

"You know that happens all the time," I said. "The victim gets attached—"

Ochoa cut me off, annoyed. "I know that. The problem here is you ruined my chance of linking a crime to the Dragon. I don't have a money trail. I don't have shit. You helped Russell Stevens give SAPD the royal shaft."

"What about Candy?" I asked. "She was gonna tell us about Maya."

"We already ID'd the girl. Kim Lucey, from Portland, Texas.

Ex-cheerleader. We also have the time of death. The Dragon has an alibi. The strip club surveillance cameras put him at the club at the time she was killed."

I stood up. I didn't need to hear any more.

"I know he's a thug. I know he's dealing drugs to strippers and probably pimping them out. But until I have evidence, my hands are tied," she said. "I have to follow the law."

I walked toward the door. "Thanks for your time."

Kelly scrambled to follow.

Ochoa put a hand on her arm. "You're a cop. You know what I'm talking about. Do him a favor and convince him to stay away from the Dragon. I'm building a case, and I don't want him to interfere."

I turned in the doorway. "Where does that leave Maya? By the time you build a case, she'll be dead in a dumpster." I walked out without waiting for an answer. I knew she didn't have one.

CHAPTER THIRTY-THREE

I waved to Sergeant Vera on my way out of the building. He was answering questions from an older couple that seemed to be lost. I wasn't in the mood to chat. Kelly hustled to keep up as I crossed the street to the parking garage.

"So, what's next?" she asked, catching up to me as we entered the lower level.

"Lock and load," I said.

"You heard what Ochoa said."

I found my pickup and we both got in. "Maya's in danger whether she knows it or not. I can't stand by and wait for her to get killed. I made a promise to Helmut." I drove out of the garage and turned north. I was angry at the Dragon for getting away with murder, and I was angry at Maya for falling for his line of BS.

"Maya said she had a fight with her grandfather."

"Yeah, I know. He can be a crusty old fart. I've known him all my life."

"Why don't we go and ask him what the fight was about? Maybe we can get him to reach out to Maya. It could change her mind about returning home."

She had a point. Reconciling with her grandpa might tip the scales in favor of returning to Fredericksburg. Besides, at the moment, I had not heard from Skeeter. He was making the connections I needed to take down the Dragon. I needed to know where he did business, and more importantly, who handled his money.

It was close to lunchtime, so we stopped at Chris Madrid's for burgers and fries. The line was usually long, but the cheeseburger was worth it. We took our burgers outside and joined a half dozen businessmen in suits, a street crew in uniform, and a handful of students from nearby Trinity University.

I tried calling ahead to see if I could catch Helmut at home and tell him we needed to talk, but like my grandpa, Helmut didn't have a cell phone and didn't have an answering machine. Calling him was like sending a sound wave message into outer space—you know the aliens are out there somewhere, but they never answer the phone.

The drive out from San Antonio was quiet. Kelly was absorbed in her own thoughts, and I tried to clear my head by focusing on the countryside. There were signs of fall everywhere. Central Texas didn't get the dense fall color like New England. Here the signs were more subtle—barns full of hay, crops harvested, fields plowed under, and farmers selling pumpkins and gourds of all shapes and sizes along the highway. When I reached the turn to Helmut's ranch, I unrolled my window. The smell of damp fresh-cut hay helped clear my head. The rain had stopped, and the sun was peeking through a line of clouds. The air felt cold and crisp like it always does after a norther blows through Central Texas, as if Mother Nature was apologizing for the damage created by the storm.

"You think he's home?" Kelly asked when I stopped at the ranch gate and stared at the metal works. The repentant cowboy still knelt with his hat in his hand before the iron cross.

"Monday afternoon. If he's not here, I don't expect he's gone very far. The livestock auction's on Thursday. Sunday is church. Friday night's the fish fry at the VFW. He might be at the grocery store, but other than that, where's he gonna go?"

"Hard to believe people still live like that."

"It's not such a bad life when you think about it. You don't have to worry about social media updates. All your friends and family already know where you are."

Kelly laughed for the first time since our last polka dance on the Marktplatz. I didn't know how many more times I would hear it. It wouldn't be the first time a case had interfered with my love life.

I got out and opened the gate. Helmut's pack of dogs started barking as soon as I rattled the chain. When I parked by the barn, they waited at the passenger door wagging their tails. Kelly had wrapped the uneaten half of her huge Chris Madrid's cheeseburger in a napkin. The Lab mix took charge and pushed the two border collies out of the way.

"Sit," she commanded when she got out. They obeyed immediately. She tore the burger into three equal parts and gave each dog a portion.

"You made three friends for life," Helmut said as he came out of the barn.

I held out my hand. "*Guten Tag*, Helmut."

He shook hands with me then Kelly. There was apprehension on his grizzled face.

"We found Maya."

His thin lips twitched.

"But she ran away again."

He scratched the gray stubble on his chin with a leathery hand. His lips twitched again. He was like my grandpa and most of the Central Texas ranchers I knew. They took the good news and the bad with a stoic acceptance. It was something bred into the people in this part of the country, especially those families who had been here since the beginning when death and misfortune were constant companions.

"Want some coffee?" he said. "Elena's gone to town. Won't be back till suppertime. She's does the grocery shopping on Monday and visits her sister to catch up on the gossip. Takes her six days to recover. You're welcome to wait and have supper with us."

We followed him inside and sat down at the hundred-year-old kitchen table while Helmut lit the gas burner on the stove and slid the metal coffee percolator over the flame.

"Just made this fresh for lunch," he said.

"We found Maya staying at a house in San Antonio. We believe she was coerced into going there by a man named Russell Stevens, who she met at a party on the river." I explained Russell's connection with Mike Bauer and the events that had taken place so far.

Helmut absorbed the information. The only visible sign that he was upset was when he didn't get up to get the percolator when it began to boil.

"I'll get that," Kelly said. She grabbed a dish towel and used it to pull the steaming pot off the fire, then poured black coffee into the three wide-mouth mugs. It smelled fresh and strong enough to float a horseshoe.

"She said y'all had a fight," I said. "She doesn't think you want her to come home." I waited for him to respond.

Kelly put the cups of coffee in front of us, and we all sat staring at the steam rising to the ancient ceiling.

"Why would she say that, Helmut?"

"There's milk in the icebox," Helmut said. "Don't use it myself. Never got the taste for it. Elena uses it because she says I make the coffee too strong." After sixty years of marriage, they had worked out their differences. It was the same way when I was growing up. Grandpa made the coffee because he didn't trust Grandma to make it strong enough. Grandma compromised and drank her coffee with milk.

Kelly found the small can of condensed milk in the refrigerator. She filled her cup to the brim and stirred until her beverage resembled chocolate milk.

"She's eighteen, Helmut. If she doesn't want to come home, there's not much anybody can do about it," I said.

The old man took a sip of coffee. His chair faced the front window, which looked out over the freshly mowed hayfield that stretched for a hundred acres down to the county road. He seemed to be looking beyond that, to Cross Mountain or Enchanted Rock. The country surrounding his ranch was as unchanging as he was.

"I told Maya that if she was going to live here with Elena and me, she had to abide by our rules. No smoking or drinking. No staying out after ten. And she had to go to church every Sunday. She also had a trunkload of clothes from California that made her look like a two-bit hussy."

Kelly suppressed a smile. "She is a teenaged girl. The dress codes are different in California, Helmut."

"That don't mean she needs to show off her teats like a nanny goat for every young billy in the county to see. Excuse my language, but that's how I see it."

Helmut lived in the nineteenth century untouched by the modern world who obsessed over the Kardashians. Maya had grown up in Southern California, where nothing seemed real unless it showed up on Facebook or Instagram. I wasn't sure they would ever get along.

"Did you tell her that?" I asked, trying to get to the bottom of Maya's argument with her granddad.

"For her own good." Helmut took another sip of coffee and turned his attention to me. "I raised one drunken daughter. I'll not do it again."

"You told her to shape up or ship out?" I asked.

"That's about the size of it."

Kelly shook her head but didn't say anything.

I had known and respected Helmut Geisler all my life. I remembered watching and listening to him tell stories about pioneer days in Gillespie County. But his tough love approach with Maya had backfired.

"Goddamnit, Helmut. What did you expect? She spent most of her life in Southern California doing whatever the hell she wanted. Did you think she was gonna settle down and live on a ranch ten miles from town just because you said so?"

Helmut raised both eyebrows. It was more facial expression than I'd ever seen him use. "Rules are rules," he said.

"No, they aren't. Not when it comes to your own family. Maya's not a cowhand. You can't toss her out of the bunkhouse because she don't pull her own weight. Now she's living with a damn drug dealer in a flophouse in San Antonio. Is that what you want?"

Helmut stood up and walked to the stove. His back was to us. I figured he would turn and point at the front door and tell us to leave. Ten years ago, he might have socked me in the jaw. Twenty years ago, he'd have whipped my butt with his belt for raising my voice to him. I wondered if I'd wasted my breath, if it was too late for the old man to change or accept any advice. He reminded me of the iron cowboy on his front gate, only his head wasn't bowed and he wasn't kneeling.

Then he took the percolator from the back burner and poured his cup full. He raised the cup to his lips and tested the temperature. Satisfied, he turned back to the kitchen table.

"Y'all want more coffee?" he said.

"I'm fine, thanks," Kelly said.

A shaft of sunlight shot through the kitchen window, and dust filtered through the light. One of the dogs barked.

"What have I done?" he asked. For the first time in his life he was completely unsure of his next move.

"Do you want her back?" I asked. "Even if it's on her own terms?"

Helmut set his cup down and steadied himself with the back of the kitchen chair. "I'd give anything to have her back."

Maybe it was his age or having to deal with his wife's illness that had changed him, but the tough-as-nails rancher was willing to meet Maya halfway.

"I'll see what I can do."

CHAPTER THIRTY-FOUR

We crossed the Palo Alto Creek and headed south toward Fredericksburg.

"What're you thinking?" she asked.

"I was thinking about another kidnapped girl, not Maya or Anna Metzger, but Cynthia Ann Parker. She was the most famous. She was the model for that John Wayne movie."

"*The Searchers*? I loved that movie," she said.

"Her story happened like in the movie, only it took a lot longer to find her. Twenty-one years longer. Comanches slaughtered her family and took her captive when she was ten years old. She was adopted into the tribe and later bore three children. Her son became the last war chief of the Comanche tribe."

"I never heard that."

"When they did finally find her, she didn't want to come home."

"Did it happen near here?"

"It was closer to Dallas and thirty years before Anna Metzger's ordeal."

"In the movie, she seems happy to be home."

"They kinda glossed that part over. When the real Cynthia Ann was reunited with her family, she no longer spoke their language.

She tried to escape several times and return to her tribe and her two sons."

We both looked out the window at the harsh Hill Country terrain full of cactus, mesquite, and live oak trees. If you avoided looking at the powerlines and barbed wire fences, it was easy to imagine Comanches riding on the horizon or cowboys chasing a herd of cattle up the limestone canyon. Not much had changed in a hundred and fifty years.

"Maybe living with her grandfather isn't the best thing for Maya," Kelly said.

"You'd rather have her stay with the Dragon?"

"She did make a choice."

"You really think that?"

"You're going after her, even if it means breaking the law?"

She knew my answer. I parked in front of the Fredericksburg police station. We had been to see Detective Ochoa and Helmut, and now I was going to extend an olive branch to local law enforcement. I knew it was a waste of time, but I was willing to make an effort. Besides, I was still waiting for Skeeter to gather the intel I needed to start plan B.

Kelly noticed that blood had seeped through the bandage on my chest and formed a red line under my shirt pocket. "You're bleeding," she said, alarmed. She reached across and unbuttoned my shirt. "Why didn't you say something?" She found a paper towel in the console and wiped the blood from my skin.

"I didn't notice," I lied. All the activity the last two days was not good for the healing process. I couldn't take sick leave. Maya was still out there. So was the Dragon.

"You should be home in bed," she scolded. "When we're finished here, I'm taking you back to the ranch. We can take the rest of the day off."

We found Officer Zeller at this desk, busy with paperwork for a change. The remains of a barbecue sandwich rested in his inbox.

"Where do you get good barbecue in this town?" I asked.

"Frank's," he said. "It's first rate."

Kelly and I helped ourselves to a couple of folding chairs while Zeller finished his paperwork.

"Hear you been causin' trouble," he said, wiping his hands on a paper towel.

The good-ol'-boy law enforcement network was working overtime. I suspected Sergeant Vera might have spread the word. He was an old family friend, but he had ties to Fredericksburg, and he loved to gossip.

"I like to stir things up, especially when I'm on a case. Maya is still missing."

"I heard you found her and let her go. We may not be as sophisticated as the SAPD, but we still follow the law. Maya is eighteen. She can do whatever she wants. The fact that she don't wanna live with her granddaddy don't surprise me in the least. Helmut is a cranky old bastard."

"We just talked to Helmut. He agreed to work out a deal if Maya comes home," Kelly said.

"Ha!" Zeller snorted a fake laugh. "I arrested his daughter Helen yesterday for public intoxication. She was wandering down Main Street cussing out the tourists after Oktoberfest. I called Geisler as a courtesy. You know what he told me?" He looked at Kelly and then me, waiting for an answer.

I shook my head and let him continue.

"He said he didn't have a daughter. The drunk woman I had in jail could stay overnight and for the rest of the year for all he cared. Said that it would probably do her some good."

"He might be right," I said.

"The problem is, he told me the same thing before she left for California."

"You arrested her ten years ago?"

"Several times. Not once did her father ever come bail her out."

"Well, I think he realized his mistake with Maya. I just have to find her again and bring her home. That's why I came down here. The person who took her works for Mike Bauer."

"You're talkin' about Russell Stevens?"

"That's right," I said. "Maya was with him the night she disappeared. Lori Kostoch was going to tell me that right before she was killed."

"If you're accusing Russell of murder, you're barking up the wrong tree. We have nothing to link him to the Kostoch girl. He's got an alibi for the time of the killing."

"Did Mike provide the alibi?"

"He's an employee of Bauer Farms. We asked Mike about him. Our detectives interviewed him. Everything checks out."

"Did you do a background check on Russell Stevens? The guy's a gangster. Ask yourself why he's in town? Why the hell does Mike need a gangster for head of security?"

"Trespassing is a problem," Zeller said.

"Then what's your theory on Lori's murder?"

"We don't have any leads yet. More than likely a drifter passing through town. We get our share of those. Or a migrant worker. We've had problems with them in the past. We'll find him. You can be sure of that."

I stood up. Kelly was watching me. I wanted to reach across the desk and grab Zeller by his greasy shirt collar, but I didn't want to give him an excuse to toss me in a jail cell.

"Thanks for your help, Les."

"We'll catch Lori's killer, and find Maya. Don't y'all worry. If you get any specific info, be sure to let us know."

"Sure thing, Les. I'll give you a heads-up."

Kelly followed me out to the parking lot. "That was different," she said.

I opened the passenger side door for her. "What?" I pretended innocence.

"You know what."

"Les isn't a bad guy or a bad cop. He's just a dumbass."

CHAPTER THIRTY-FIVE

KELLY WAS QUIET ON THE drive out to the ranch house. We both knew what was coming next. I had followed her advice and reached out to Detective Ochoa and Officer Zeller. Neither one was going to do Maya any good. The law enforcement arm of the legal system worked great once a crime had been committed. Every cop I knew had his favorite story of how he tracked down the bad guy and took him off the streets. I admired their hard work and dedication. I'd grown up listening to my dad tell the same kind of stories.

What they weren't good at was preventing the crime before it happened. It wasn't necessarily their fault. Once you joined the law enforcement community, you agreed to follow a set of strict rules. There was a science fiction movie about a police division called pre-crime. The officers got information about a future crime from a trio of vegetative humans who lived in a pool of water in the basement of the headquarters building. The unit was shut down in the end because there was a flaw in the system. Humans have free will. We can choose to do something else besides commit a crime. That may be true on a theoretical level, and it made a good premise for a sci-fi movie, but Russell Stevens, aka the Dragon, was going to commit a crime. He was going to kill Maya or do something worse.

If Maya stayed with the Dragon, her life would be over before it had a chance to begin.

Kelly got out and opened the ranch gate. A pair of mallard ducks were enjoying the afternoon in the spring-fed pond before continuing their migration south for the winter.

"Why does it have to be you?" Kelly asked.

"Who else is gonna go after her, Helmut? Russell would kill him."

"What if he kills you?"

We got out and made our way into the house. The evening temperature was forty-five and dropping quickly. It would get down to the low thirties by sunrise. I turned on the lights and took off my shirt. Blood had soaked through the bandage and the paper towel Kelly had tucked under my shirt.

"Will you at least give this hole in your chest a few more days to heal?" She helped me off with my shirt and guided me to a kitchen chair while she stripped the blood-crusted bandage from my chest.

"There's no time. Russell knows we're after Maya. He'll move her. If that happens, we'll never find her."

She took a bottle of rubbing alcohol and used a dishtowel to clean my wound. The skin was red and felt hot and sore.

"You go up against the Dragon with this hole in your chest, you'll lose."

"Thanks for the vote of confidence."

"It's the truth. Your mother could land a punch on your chest and you'd go down." She tapped my chest, and I winced in pain. "You see," she said, satisfied she'd made her point. She put the bloody towel in the sink and washed her hands with dish soap.

"I'll keep that in mind."

Kelly applied a new gauze patch. I got up from the table, and she stood behind me and wrapped her arms around my waist. Her hands were warm from the hot water.

"It feels like you're being deployed," she said, pressing her face into the center of my back.

"Maya deserves another chance," I said. I felt her breath on my skin.

"Even if she doesn't want one?"

I turned to face her. She knew my answer.

She lifted her face. A tear formed in the corner of her eye. I kissed her and held her tight against me.

"I can't do this," she said. "You never stop. One day you'll… I can't even say it. It's bad luck."

"I know."

My phone rang.

"You don't have to answer it," she said.

I looked at the caller ID. Skeeter.

"'Bout time," I said, pushing connect.

Kelly turned away.

"You always underestimate the difficulty of what I do," he said.

"Come on, you're sittin' on your ass hacking computers. How hard could it be?"

"If it was that easy, you'd be doin' it for yourself."

"Fair enough. You wanna raise?"

"That would be nice."

"I made you a full partner. What more do you want?"

"How 'bout an actual paycheck?"

"The meat's on the way. What have you got?"

"The Dragon's an entrepreneur."

"That means he's got a soft spot."

"Is Kelly there, or did you run her off?"

I put the phone on speaker. "She's right here."

"Hi, Clarence," she said without enthusiasm.

"What's wrong?" he asked.

"I'm going back to Lubbock. You boys are on your own."

"What did he say to you?"

She laughed, but only out of habit. "I'm going back to work before I lose my day job."

"Good for you," Skeeter said. He understood as well as I did why she had to go.

"You take care," she said.

I took the phone off speaker and listened to Skeeter's report. He had what I needed. He was good at his job. It was time for plan B.

Kelly gathered her clothes from upstairs and packed her duffle bag. When she came back downstairs, I followed her out to her pickup.

"I'm going after—" I started to tell her my plan, but she cut me off.

"I don't want to know the details."

She climbed in her pickup, and I shut her door.

She started the engine and rolled down the window. "When it's over, give me call. I'd like to know you're safe. I don't wanna read about you online." She started to close the window but stopped. "This isn't all about your job, you know. One day you're gonna have to deal with your mother. She really did a number on you."

I felt my cheeks and neck turning red.

"Don't get all bent out of shape. It's just my observation. You should talk to her."

I nodded. I didn't have anything to say.

She finished rolling the window up and drove to the front gate.

There was no moon. The Milky Way provided a blanket of cold stars. The north wind had died, but the air was still and cold and crisp. I pulled the collar of my jean jacket tight around my neck. Maybe she was right, but right now I needed to clear my head of distractions and focus on finding Maya.

CHAPTER THIRTY-SIX

LUCKY'S GYM WAS LOCATED ON the west side of San Antonio in a working-class neighborhood—a mixture of neglected track houses, auto shops, and taco stands. I stopped at the stand I'd visited with Kelly and found grandma still hard at work, standing on her wooden box behind a sizzling grill. She recognized me and flashed a toothless smile.

"*Buenos días*," she called to me.

"*Tengo hambre*," I said.

She laughed and rubbed her own stomach. I didn't understand what she said after that, but I guessed it was something like, *you've come to the right place.*

"*Donde está su hijo?*" I asked, not seeing the younger man that was there the night before.

"*La universidad,*" she said. She was obviously very proud. She was putting her son through college by dishing out tacos to hungry gringos.

"*Muy bien*," I said. "*Dos huevos y barbacoa.*"

She plopped a scoop of lard on the hot griddle and went to work cracking eggs in a plastic bowl with her right hand while she sliced the barbacoa with her left, movements she could do in her sleep. I gave her a five-dollar tip when she bagged my breakfast. Her eyes lit up. I was becoming a regular customer.

Lucky's gym was the anchor business for a strip mall that also housed a Mexican restaurant, a tattoo and massage parlor, and a mom-and-pop gas station. It was a big two-story building that had once been a furniture store. Caesar Hernandez, or "Lucky," had retired from an impressive welterweight professional career and used his winnings to open a boxing gym as a way to give back to the community.

I parked on the street and tossed my taco wrapper and paper bag in the trash on my way through the front door. In the afternoon, after the local school let out, the ground floor looked like a high school gym. Lucky let the kids work out for free as long as they showed him a report card each session to prove they were in school and keeping up their grades. The mornings were reserved for serious training and guys like me who were trying to stay in shape.

Lucky's partner, Jerry Muth, aka Sarge, had taken over the upstairs. Sarge was an ex-Army Ranger who offered classes in mixed martial arts. He was cashing in on wannabe tough guys who were watching MMA on TV thinking they should get in on the action. Sarge was the quiet type who looked like Chuck Norris with a gray ponytail and could kick your ass before you knew he was pissed.

I found Lucky leaning on the center ring ropes watching two middleweights pound away on each other. Before I took a bullet in my arm and shoulder, I came in three times a week and sometimes sparred with his heavyweights. I wasn't a natural boxer, but Lucky liked the fact that I could take a punch. I considered that a compliment.

When the bell rang to signal the end of the round, Lucky jumped down and shook my hand. "What you doin' here? Figured you was still recuperatin'?" He grinned, exposing his missing front teeth. He had two gold replacements, but he kept them in his pocket when he was at the gym.

"I still have to put food on the table. You know how it is when you work for yourself."

"I got a sparring partner waitin' for you when you're ready."

I missed my normal routine. Before my last case tossed my life into a tailspin, I did my roadwork at night along the River Walk trail. Whatever time I got home, from ten p.m. to three a.m., my Lab, Sam would be ready at the back door, wagging his tail and barking. Three times a week, I was at Lucky's working his collection of free weights for strength, the speedbag, focus mitts, and finishing in the ring with a sparring partner. It was usually an up-and-comer Lucky was tuning up for a fight or a young kid auditioning for club membership.

I did three sets of squats with three quarters of my max weight. I needed to ease back into the routine after taking a couple of months off. By the last rep, my leg muscles were complaining loudly. I switched from weights to lunges and let the muscles scream a little louder. I was one of those guys who enjoyed the workout pain. It gave me a little more confidence that the muscles would be there when I needed them. The lower-body work wasn't what I was concerned about. The real question was the bullet wound in my chest. Kelly had proved it wasn't ready.

After six rounds with the speedbag, I was feeling more confident. I checked under my shirt. The bandage was still in place and didn't show any sign of leaking. I switched to the heavy bag. I imagined the bag was the Dragon. The more I thought about him, the harder my punches got. I slammed my fist into the canvas with everything I had. My head moved with my shoulders and torso. My feet followed the rhythm, but my movements were rusty. I pushed myself harder.

Russell Stevens's smiling mugshot danced with the bag. I wondered if prison had changed him or simply revealed his true nature.

What did he say to Maya to make her want to stay with him? When I found her again and told her what her granddad had said, would she still choose Russell? I believed she wanted to be free. I believed she wanted a second chance. That's what kept me going. I didn't want this to end like Cynthia Ann Parker, after a twenty-one-year chase.

Lucky tapped me on the shoulder, and the image disappeared.

"You trainin' for a fight?" he asked.

It took a moment to clear the image of Russell Stevens and Maya escaping on horseback from my mind. Lucky had been watching me the whole time. He knew fighters and fighting better than most. He knew me and my fighting style. He could tell when I was playing around and when I was focused on a specific opponent.

"You need some time in the ring. Let's see if you're ready." He gestured toward the center ring, where a big black guy in his early twenties was shadowboxing in the corner.

He was right. Working a bag was great for stress relief and to build confidence, but nothing took the place of stepping into the ring with an opponent who could punch back.

I slipped on the headgear and switched to a pair of sixteen-ounce sparring gloves. The black kid was heavy, almost the same size and weight as the Dragon, and quick on his feet. He danced back and forth while I climbed into the ring. His hands were quick. He showed off a lethal jab/hook combination that had probably taken out more than a few opponents.

We met Lucky in the center of the ring and touched gloves.

"Nick Fischer meet Darnell Green. He's trying out for a spot on my team."

I nodded.

Lucky turned to Darnell. "Mr. Fischer's got a fight coming up. He needs a little tune-up."

Darnell showed his white teeth through his mouth guard. I

knew he thought Lucky was joking. Lucky never joked. Not about fighting or boxing.

The bell rang, and Darnell came on fast. I blocked his first combination and landed a right hand to his left ear guard. It didn't faze him. He could take a punch. We traded several more punches. I didn't have what Lucky would call "style." I usually planted my feet, blocked incoming punches, and waited for my opponent to drop his guard.

Darnell had style and footwork. He had more to prove and was definitely trying to show off for Lucky. He landed a good left to my chin that set me back on my heels. I countered with an overhand right that jolted his confidence. Until that punch, he had been thinking of me as an old man getting in a workout—he wanted to show off, but he didn't want to knock me out. After that punch, all bets were off.

By the end of the round, my legs were shaking, and my lungs were on fire—the result of a month of inactivity. I leaned against the ropes and noticed Darnell staring at my chest from across the ring. I looked down and saw blood. Lucky was beside me before I could grab a towel from the corner and cover it up. The bell rang, but Lucky waved Darnell off.

"Enough for today," he said.

Darnell walked over to my corner. "You okay, man?" He looked concerned, like he'd hit me a little too hard. His heart was in the right place.

"I'm good," I told him. "It's from an older wound."

Lucky stripped off my gloves, and I pulled my T-shirt over my head. The bandage had come off, and blood was leaking from the broken scab. Darnell shook his head and climbed out of the ring.

Jerry Muth had come down from the second floor to watch the sparring match. He handed me a clean towel, and I pressed it over the wound.

"You should probably take another month off," he said.

Lucky helped me take off my headgear, studying me like a trainer. "Whatever you got planned, you ain't ready," he said.

"You know how it goes. Trouble don't wait for you to get ready," I said, climbing out of the ring. I checked the clock on the wall. It was almost time for Skeeter to show up. I started for the locker room, but Lucky and Sarge blocked my path.

"What trouble?" Lucky asked.

Both of them had helped me out of a jam on my last case. Four thugs had shown up at the gym with the intent of doing me harm. They were young and cocky and working for the lawyer who was trying to keep me from interfering in his political ambitions. Lucky and Sarge had stood at the top of the stairs, accepted the thugs' insults and amused banter about their advanced age, and then calmly kicked their asses.

I was reluctant to get them involved with Russell Stevens. They had proved that they were both tough fighters, even though they were both pushing seventy, but things were going to get western, and I didn't want to be responsible for them getting hurt or worse. I wasn't going to play games or give any warnings. This was a strictly S&D mission—search and destroy.

"Let's have it, jarhead," Sarge said. He was a retired Army master sergeant and had earned the right to call me jarhead.

"All right. Let me get cleaned up," I said.

Lucky was waiting for me with rubbing alcohol, a fresh gauze pad, and surgical tape when I came out of the shower. He was a good corner man.

While Lucky worked on my shoulder wound, I told them Maya's story starting with the party on the Pedernales River. By the time I got to the part about finding her in the flophouse and her running away, Skeeter had joined us. He took the story from there while I finished getting dressed. He explained the Dragon's connection to the strip club and added his new findings. Russell was running drugs out of two used tire stores on the south side. I didn't ask him how he found out. I didn't want to know.

"I can't ask y'all to get involved," I said.

"You don't have to ask," Sarge said. "That young girl's in danger."

CHAPTER THIRTY-SEVEN

It was Tuesday afternoon. The sky was clear. The temperature was a crisp, dry sixty-four degrees, and the shit was about to hit the fan. My plan B was simple—rattle the Dragon's chain until he made a mistake, then nail him and take Maya back where she belongs.

The first stop was the strip club. The parking lot was mostly empty. There were two pickups out front and a City of San Antonio work truck parked near the back door, out of sight of the street. A black jacked-up Dodge Ram pickup occupied the reserved space near the back door.

I checked the magazine in my Springfield .45 and strapped the S&W .38 on my ankle. Skeeter loaded the pistol-grip 870 shotgun. Lucky and Sarge watched from the back seat.

"You can wait in the pickup," I said to Skeeter. Of the four of us, he was the least prepared for this kind of operation. Skeeter was a gridiron tough guy. Grew up playing football. He'd weighed in at over two hundred and fifty pounds since ninth grade and didn't get into many street fights. His training consisted of a YouTube video on how to operate a model 870. That and watching me.

"I'm in," Skeeter said. "You made me a full partner, remember? Let's find Maya."

Sarge tucked a Glock 9mm in his waistband and followed us to the back door. I knew I didn't have to worry about Lucky or Sarge. Lucky grew up on the mean streets across the border in Nuevo Laredo. He knew the kind of people we were dealing with. Sarge was like me, a combat veteran, trained to neutralize the enemy. We weren't here to negotiate a surrender or read anybody their rights.

The back door was open. It was a VIP entrance used by local celebrities and members of the resident pro basketball team. We slipped into the darkness. There were crates of booze and cases of beer stacked to the ceiling. An AC/DC song drifted in from the main floor. I held up my hand. We all stopped and waited for our eyes to adjust to the darkness.

"Follow my lead," I said, pulling my Springfield and stepping through the curtain. Only the main stage was occupied. A young dancer worked the chrome dance pole in a drug-fueled haze to "*You Shook Me All Night Long*."

The beefy bouncer with the shaved head slouched against the back wall watching the performance. He turned just in time to see the barrel of my Springfield approaching his left ear. He crumpled into a pile on the floor. The dancer kept humping chrome, oblivious. Her focus was on the greenbacks in the city worker's hand.

There was movement near the front entrance. I pointed in that direction, and Sarge and Lucky took off. Skeeter followed me between the tables toward the bar. The bouncer with the neck tattoo glanced up from behind the bar. He dropped the beer he was holding and reached under the counter. I aimed my .45 at this head.

"Hands on the bar," I yelled over AC/DC.

Neck Tatt slowly put his hands on the bar. Skeeter sank onto a stool and pointed the 870 at the guy's chest.

"Be cool. Stay put and you won't get hurt," I told him.

His eyes were on the barrel of the shotgun. A twelve gauge always looks bigger when it's pointing at you at short range.

"You fucked up, man," he said. He wasn't scared, but he respected Skeeter's weapon.

"You're gonna tell me where the Dragon is."

"He'll kill you."

"Where is he? Let's get the party started. I know he's pimping girls. I know he's dealing drugs in here. He can't do that without your permission. You must have a really cozy relationship. How does it work? You need new meat on stage, you give him a call, and he shows up with the girls and passes out the drug candy? Is that it?"

Neck Tatt's eyes darted to the office door, like he expected someone to come out. The brass knob turned, and the door moved. I took a step and kicked the door just as Arnold Garza shoved his pistol through the opening. The gun exploded, sending a stab of flame into the dark room, followed by the young dancer's scream. The city worker scrambled for the door, taking his fist full of dollars with him.

I brought the Springfield down hard on Arnold's wrist. His pistol dropped to the floor. I grabbed his hand and yanked him out the door. He went to his knees still wearing the blue velvet suit he'd had on when we first met. His hipster glasses flew to the carpet. I kicked him onto his back and aimed my pistol at his mouth.

"Howdy, Arnold. Long time no see." The music suddenly stopped, and the house lights came on. Sarge and Skeeter had taken care of the other employees.

"What the fuck do you want?" Arnold said. "I told you I'd never seen that girl."

"You lied. We're past that. I found the girl I was lookin' for. Puff the Magic Dragon took her back. Where is he?"

"He'll kill you."

"I'm sure he'll want to. But when he finds out he's got a lot to lose, I think he'll want to negotiate."

"You ain't got nothin' he wants."

I holstered my pistol, grabbed Arnold by the velvet jacket, and hauled him to his feet. The surprise and initial fear on his face turned to anger and contempt.

"I'm sending a message to anybody who does business with Russell Stevens."

"We got rights, man. You can't come in here and fuck with us," he said.

He'd either heard that line in a movie or it had worked for him before, because he smiled when he said it like he was holding up a magic shield.

"You want me to honor your rights?" I picked up his glasses and handed them to him. "Put these on. I don't want you to miss anything." I took the 870 from Skeeter, pointed it at the mirror behind the bar, and pulled the trigger. Glass showered down like confetti on Neck Tatt's head and shoulders.

"What the fuck're you doin', man?" Arnold screamed.

"You gave up your rights when you shook hands with the Dragon."

I pumped another shell in the chamber, pointed at the liquor shelf, and pulled the trigger. Another shower of glass mixed with spirits rained down on the bar. I pumped the action again. Boom! The mirror behind the back stage shattered.

"Okay, okay! What do you want?" Arnold pleaded.

Sarge and Lucky pushed the two bouncers from the front door into the room. Sarge had them covered with his Glock. The bald guy I had clocked near the back entrance stirred and started to stand. Lucky stepped in front of him.

"Stay down," Lucky said.

The guy should have listened. Instead, he lunged forward and caught an uppercut from Lucky that put him down for the count.

"I want Maya," I shouted and pumped another round in the chamber, looking for another target.

"She ain't here, man. I told you that," Arnold said.

Boom!

I took out the mirror behind the main stage. At the very least, it would take them a couple of days to clean up before they could open again. The owner of the club would get the clear message that dealing with Russell Stevens was bad for business.

Boom!

I put another load in the bar. A scream came from the dancers' dressing room. There was more than one girl back there. I motioned for Lucky to check it out in case there was another bouncer not accounted for. Arnold hopped from one foot to the other. He wasn't sure what I was going to do next. It was the reaction I was looking for.

"Tell Mr. Dragon I will keep going until he brings me Maya, safe and sound. When I'm through, no one will do business with him."

"You're a dead man," he said.

I shoved the barrel of the 870 into his chest. Arnold fell backward on the floor. I called to Skeeter: "How many shells does this model 870 tactical pump shotgun hold?"

"The model 870 express tactical pump shotgun packs a full seven rounds of three-inch 12-guage firepower with the factory installed two-shot extension," Skeeter recited. He'd memorized the manual when I gave him the weapon.

I looked at the manager. "Seven rounds. Did you keep count?" I pressed the barrel under his chin.

"You're fuckin' crazy."

There was fear in his eyes. I was getting through to him.

"Convey the message to Russell. He knows my number. I'll keep going until he gives up Maya. Is that clear?"

I pointed the 870 at the ceiling and pulled the trigger. The pistol grip jerked in my hand, sending a load of buckshot into the ceiling and showering us both with drywall plaster.

"Guess I had one more round," I said.

A dark wet stain expanded around the crotch of his velvet suit.

Lucky walked out of the dressing room. "All clear."

"Good. We're done here." I handed the 870 back to Skeeter and walked toward the back door.

CHAPTER THIRTY-EIGHT

I BACKED ACROSS THE PARKING LOT toward my pickup, keeping my Springfield level with the strip club VIP door. Once Arnold realized the extent of the damage, he would come after me. He knew the repair would come out of his pocket. I opened my pickup door, found a cheap pair of sunglasses on the dashboard, and slipped them on to cut the harsh afternoon glare. I waited while Lucky and Sarge climbed in the back seat and Skeeter settled into the passenger seat.

"Wait," Skeeter said. He opened the small black backpack he was never without and took out a black box about the size of a USB wall adaptor. "GPS tracker. In case they come after us or go visit Russell."

Skeeter fitted the device to the four-by-four parked in the reserved space. I checked my watch. It was almost five o'clock.

"You don't mess around," Lucky said.

"Thanks for your help," I said.

"You didn't really need us," Sarge said. "But it was fun."

I checked the rearview mirror. Sarge had a smile on his face.

The only other time I'd seen him smile was after he and Lucky kicked ass on the four thugs who were after me in the gym.

When Skeeter was finished, he booted up his laptop and checked the connection. We would have a heads-up if Arnold came to visit, and we might be able to track him to Russell.

I drove out of the parking lot. "Now that we got the Dragon's attention, it won't be as easy the next time."

"You don't think he'll hand Maya over?" Skeeter asked.

"He'll do what Low Ball did," I said.

"Come after you?"

"Who's Low Ball?" Lucky asked.

"The dude who framed me for murder," Skeeter said.

"That apartment fire on the east side? I remember that," Sarge said.

"Nick saved my ass."

"What happened to Low Ball?" Lucky asked.

"He took my place on death row," Skeeter said.

Lucky leaned over the back seat and pointed to the damp spot on my chest. Blood had soaked my T-shirt. In all the excitement, I hadn't noticed that the bandage had come loose and the scab had broken open again.

"Maybe you should skip town for a couple of days," Lucky said. "That dragon dude knows you mean business. If he don't give up Maya, we'll hit him again."

Skeeter used his metal hook to hand me a paper towel. "That sounds like the voice of reason."

Now that the adrenaline rush was wearing off, the muscles in my chest were on fire, and I felt lightheaded from the loss of blood. "One problem. The Dragon's already killed Lori and Candy. Nothing is stopping him from doing it again."

I took the towel from Skeeter and pressed it over the wet spot on my T-shirt. The muscle tissue was on fire. I drove under the 410

Loop and went south on San Pedro hoping to avoid rush hour traffic. No such luck. San Antonio suffered from traffic as much as any big city. It wasn't as bad as Houston, but that was hardly any consolation.

It was past six when I parked across the street from the two-story house where we'd found Maya. I shut the engine off and checked my phone. No missed calls or messages from Russell. I wasn't surprised. He would wait for my next move. He would probably send a couple of thugs to my house in King William. My only concern was my neighbor, Rose. If she happened to see someone on my property, she wouldn't hesitate to confront them. They wouldn't hesitate to kill her.

"Looks like they stepped up security," I said, looking at an overfed gangbanger lounging on the front steps. He had a black silk do-rag and a wife-beater T-shirt despite the cooler weather.

"He'll be packing," Lucky said.

"Noted," I said. I knew Wife-Beater would have a pistol stuck in his shorts. I didn't think he could get to it in time to protect himself. Several rolls of fat obscured his waistband. I pointed out the staircase that led to the upstairs and sent Lucky and Sarge through the alley to get there. I hoped the occupants hadn't added another lock. I was counting on the element of surprise.

Skeeter reloaded the 870. I waited until I thought Lucky and Sarge had had enough time to climb the back steps before stepping into the street. Skeeter followed me across the dirt lawn that was strewn with fast food wrappers and cigarette butts. I could hear the pounding rap music coming from inside the house. I picked up a three-foot length of galvanized metal pipe lying in the neglected flower garden.

Wife-Beater shifted his massive weight forward but didn't get up. He probably weighed in at three eighty and, like all fat tough guys, expected his looks to scare people away. I stopped six inches from his black LeBron Nike basketball shoes. They were new and expensive and had never seen a basketball court.

"Give me a pound of crank and a couple of underage girls for me and my friend here," I said.

He smiled big, stretching the size of his double chin into a full dewlap. He looked like a bulldog waiting for supper. "I know you, *guero*," he said.

"I'm flattered." I hit him in the head with the metal pipe.

"You are a man of few words," Skeeter said.

Wife-Beater slumped forward, a trickle of blood oozing from the edge of his silk do-rag.

"This ain't really a social call," I said, walking to the front door.

The same three junior thugs were on the couch, playing the same video game, as we came through the front door. I pulled my Springfield and fired at the fifty-inch screen. The TV exploded in a shower of glass and plastic. They jumped off the couch like a covey of quail from a brush pile.

The thug nearest Skeeter pulled a pistol from the couch. Skeeter hit him in the side of head with the barrel of the shotgun. He dropped the pistol and collapsed on the floor.

I leveled off on the other two. One of them held a pistol pointed at the floor.

"Drop it," I yelled. He let it fall to the floor. "Cover them," I said to Skeeter, then kicked in the door to the back room. A skinny girl wearing a black bra and panties was scooping stacks of money into a plastic garbage bag. She kept working while I searched the room for more bodies.

"What d'ya want?" she asked, not caring about my pistol and not the least self-conscious of being seen in her underwear.

"Just keep working," I said. "Fill up the sack."

She tossed in the rest of the money. There were four kilo bags of meth or coke on a shelf behind her. She'd been mixing and filling smaller plastic bags for sale.

"Throw in the drugs too," I said.

When she was finished, I motioned her toward the front room.

The stairs creaked, and three women hustled down the wooden steps followed by Sarge and Lucky. One was in her mid-forties with dyed-blond hair and a tank top that didn't quite cover her protruding belly. She must have been the house mother for the younger girls. Her face was twisted into an angry scowl.

"You ain't cops," she shouted at me. "You can't come in here."

I ignored her. "Upstairs clear?" I asked Sarge.

He nodded. "All clear."

"Check the kitchen and the pantry," I said.

He disappeared through a swinging door.

"Do you hear me? You don't have a warrant. You can't come up in here. We got rights," the big woman screamed. She'd seen the same movie as the strip club manager.

"Everybody's got rights. What about their rights?" I pointed to the young girls. "Who's lookin' after their rights?"

"We do business here. Ain't nobody get hurt."

Sarge reappeared. "All clear."

"We're done here. Everybody out." I heard a commotion on the porch. The door burst open, and Wife-Beater came through with a 9mm in his hand.

I fired first and hit him in the left leg. The .45 slug splattered blood on the wall. Wife-Beater screamed and did a four-hundred-pound faceplant on the hardwood floor.

"Everybody out," I yelled again. "Take fatso with you."

The thug Skeeter cold-cocked came to and staggered out the front door. His two companions helped Wife-Beater to his feet. I took a closer look. The bullet had grazed his outer thigh. He would live. I didn't want to leave any bodies lying around.

I found a lighter on the coffee table. The house was a 1940s vintage wood-frame construction. With a little help, it would go up in smoke like a stack of last year's hay. I fired the lighter and held it to a couch cushion. When it caught fire, I tossed it into the kitchen and grabbed another. By the time I walked out on the porch, smoke was already billowing from the front windows.

"What're we supposed to do?" House Mamma screamed.

"Find a job that doesn't involve drugs or underage girls," I said. She wasn't going to convince me she was a victim. "I would get the hell out of here if I were you." I pulled out my cell phone and dialed 911. The local fire department had a great response time and would have this fire out before it did damage to the neighborhood.

We hustled back to my pickup. The neighbor's dogs barked. An older couple across the street came out on their lawn.

"It's about time," the older woman yelled.

House Mamma gave her the middle finger.

"You're a disgrace to the neighborhood," the old man yelled.

I cranked the engine and drove away. The neighbors wouldn't complain about me removing the resident flophouse, even if I had trampled on a few civil rights to do it.

CHAPTER THIRTY-NINE

WE PASSED THE FIRST FIRETRUCK speeding toward the blaze as I made the turn onto Zarzamora Street. Russell would get my message. Now he knew how I played the game and what the stakes were.

His next move would be to retaliate. I didn't expect him to give up or turn Maya over. I wanted him pissed off enough to make a mistake, to give up his location or challenge me himself. That's when I would nail him.

I felt the dampness on my chest. Blood had soaked the folded paper towel I'd tucked under my shirt. The only flaw in my plan was that I was operating with a hole in my chest.

Before I got to my King William neighborhood, I explained to Sarge and Lucky what I had in mind. They protested at first, but when I told them that Rose was an excellent cook, they agreed to stay and guard both our houses.

The setting sun shot streaks of pink and orange over the green canopy that covered most of the city. Rose appeared in her kitchen window when I pulled into the driveway. I waved.

"I'll let Rose know what's going on," I told them. "Skeeter will show you the gun safe. Pick out what you're comfortable with and double the ammo you think you'll need."

"You think he'll hit us hard?" Sarge asked.

"He'll want to even the score," I said.

Sarge smiled again. The second time in two days.

Rose met me in the front yard. Her gray hair, as usual, was braided and wound in tight coils, like a Viking queen welcoming home the fleet from Britain. "I trust you've gotten yourself into a pickle," she said.

"Nothing I can't handle," I said.

She scrutinized the men getting out of my pickup. "Where's Kelly?"

"She's gone back to Lubbock."

She waited for me to fill in the details, but I stayed silent.

"You're a hard man to get along with," she said.

I explained briefly that we had not been able to find Maya and that I was taking things in a different direction than Kelly thought we should go. "There may be trouble."

She pointed a boney finger at me. "You're the trouble."

"I didn't ask her to leave."

She was a retired university biology professor and treated everybody like one of her freshman students. "I don't blame her. You're about as friendly as a ground hornet when you're working a case."

"She had to go back to work, that's all."

"I know you better than you think, Nick Fischer. Once you're on a case, nothing and no one gets in your way. Girlfriends, friends, the law… nothing. If I wanted answers or justice, I would come to you in a heartbeat. I know you're not going to stop till you get one or the other. But if I were a young woman looking for a husband, I'd drop you like a red-hot coal."

"So, there's no hope for us?" I asked.

That brought a twinkle to her eye. "You've got issues, Nick Fischer. God help you; you've got issues. One of these days, you're going to have to face that fact."

I conceded her point. She loved to argue, and I didn't have time to get into it with her. Instead, I explained to her that Sarge and Lucky were going to stay in my house just in case the thugs I was after showed up wanting to wreak havoc. I told her that if she saw anything to stay out of sight and let them handle it.

"I keep my dad's revolver in the kitchen drawer, and I've got my shotgun," she said.

She'd shown me the weapon before. It was a .38 Special police model that her dad purchased in the thirties. She kept it well-oiled and loaded, but I didn't think she'd fired it in twenty years.

"Keep it there. Let Lucky and Sarge do any shooting if it's necessary. They have more practice."

"What about the police?" she asked.

"What about them?"

"Shouldn't they be involved?"

"They will be. But right now, they would slow me down. A young girl's life's at stake."

She clenched her jaw like she was going to protest, before slowly nodding in agreement.

"I'll make them some dinner," she said after a moment and hurried toward her back door. She was excited to be in on the action.

I found Sarge and Lucky taking inventory of my arsenal. Skeeter had been living at my place while I was at the ranch, and I had given him the combo to my gun safe so he could bring me ammo and a spare pistol while I was recuperating.

"I think we can hold off the Dragon's gang with this stuff," Sarge said, inspecting an AR-10. I had a dozen spare twenty-round magazines and enough ammo to fill them all a few times over. I told them Rose would stop by with supper. If she didn't, I asked Sarge to check on her. I didn't want to take any chances.

Skeeter was sitting at the kitchen table glued to his laptop. He could type faster with one hand than most people could with two.

"Anything new?" I asked, pulling a Shiner Bock out of the fridge.

"That Dodge Ram from the strip club is on the move."

"Headed our way?"

"Not at the moment."

I drank my beer and watched Sarge finish his inspection of the Colt AR-10 and load a full twenty-round clip. Lucky chose a Colt 1911 .45 to supplement his 9mm. It was well used but could still get the job done. I was confident that they would protect the house and Rose without much trouble. Keeping them all at my house would also be safer for them. I wouldn't have to worry about putting them in a situation where they might take a bullet or worse. I had put Skeeter in harm's way on my last case, and I didn't want that to happen again. I also worked better alone. It didn't matter how much training or experience Sarge had or how many street fights Lucky had been in, if they were with me, I would always be looking over my shoulder to protect them.

"What're you gonna do?" Skeeter asked.

I took another drink of beer, then checked my phone. No messages. It was eight thirty and full dark outside. "Send me the addresses for his tire shops."

I pulled an AR-15 from the safe. I had another AR-10, but the 15 was smaller and better suited for close combat work. I had a Surefire suppressor for the AR-15, and the reduction of noise might come in handy. It could also take a thirty-round clip in case I needed more firepower. I loaded the rifle, extra magazines, and two spare boxes of .223 ammo in a black duffle bag. The last thing

I tossed in was a Mossberg shotgun. If Russell Stevens wanted to go to war, I was ready.

"Stay in contact. I wanna know if they come to the house." I pulled my Kevlar bulletproof vest over my head and slipped on a button-down shirt to cover it.

"Be careful," Skeeter said as I picked up the duffle bag and walked out the door.

CHAPTER FORTY

THE TIRE SHOP SKEETER LINKED to Russell Stevens's criminal enterprise was located past the air force base on I-90. It wasn't the kind of place you'd take the family minivan to have a flat fixed. There were old tires stacked outside and piles of accumulated trash mixed into the weeds and dead grass along the base of the neglected fence. The building used to be a gas station, but the pumps had been removed and sealed with metal covers. The only thing new on the property was the soda pop machine near the front door.

I pulled in behind the stack of used tires and looked for signs of life. There was a vintage Chevy Impala in car-show condition parked in front of the service garage entrance. It was painted deep purple and had a lowrider hydraulic lift package. The business on the east side was a mom-and-pop Mexican food restaurant that had served its last meal in the seventies. On the west side was a pawnshop featuring a sign that welcomed active duty military. They were already advertising a Veteran's Day sale. It was no accident that the Dragon set up near a military base. Every place I'd ever been stationed had scum just like him who preyed on young servicemen looking for an escape from the long duty hours and lonely down time miles away from home.

A late-model Chevy Tahoe with a base parking sticker pulled in beside the Impala. The driver hit the car horn twice. I could see the side of the driver's face through the open window. He was young, probably eighteen or nineteen, with a bootcamp haircut and a clean shave. Two identical young men sat in the back seat.

The front door of the station opened. A kid of maybe twenty-five appeared. He was not much older than the young airmen in the Tahoe. He was white with an array of tats on his arms and neck. He wore red high-top basketball shoes and a black silk do-rag that hung to his shoulders. His jean shorts sagged below his waist, cinched there by a white cotton belt. The kid was a *GQ* fashion icon.

He glanced up and down the mostly empty feeder road, then walked to the passenger side of the Tahoe. I couldn't see the exchange, but I didn't have to guess what was going on.

The Tahoe sped away, and GQ shuffled back inside the garage. I waited a few more minutes to see if there would be any more traffic. When the coast was clear, I slipped out of my pickup and grabbed my spare gas can from the back. The rap music coming from inside was loud enough to mask any sound I made. I had no doubt the men inside were dangerous, but mainly to themselves and servicemen buying their shit.

I searched the plywood-covered windows for an opening and found a hole in the back window large enough to see into the garage. Stacks of boxes took up most of the space. This place hadn't seen a tire customer for a long time. GQ and his twin were lounging in the corner watching a porn video. They probably weren't related but wore the same T-shirt and black-silk do-rag like a uniform. An older thug wearing designer jeans walked out of the restroom zipping his fly. There was a Glock tucked behind his back.

He opened a beer and stood behind the younger men staring at the naked woman with impossibly large breasts on the widescreen TV. I waited for ten minutes, but nobody else was in the building.

I found a length of rusty chain and hooked it around the handles on the double doors. My plan was to give them only one way out. Then I circled back to the front entrance.

It was a shame to trash such a sleek ride, but I knew how they paid for it and didn't feel guilty. I opened the gas can and sloshed fuel on the plastic upholstery. The gas soaked in for a few minutes, then I lit a match. The explosion was instantaneous. I retreated to the stack of old tires near my pickup and pulled out my Mossberg shotgun.

The fire quickly engulfed the Impala. Tongues of flame licked the rusty service station overhang. I waited for the heat or the noise from the fire to get their attention.

The door sprang open. A hand holding a chrome-plated pistol appeared. Flame spit from the barrel. Shots rang out over the roar of the fire. The pistol bucked four more times, randomly blasting the night air.

A voice shouted: "Who's out there?"

"I'm looking for the Dragon!"

The pistol bucked again, this time in my general direction. The bullets made hollow plunking sounds hitting the old steel-belted radials.

GQ appeared in the doorway.

I pulled the trigger. The shotgun blast hit him in the chest. Blood spread quickly across his white T-shirt before he collapsed on the driveway.

"I'm looking for the Dragon," I shouted again.

Two hands grabbed GQ and pulled him back inside.

"Did you hear me? Where is he?"

"Fuck you!" someone shouted back. The barrel of a rifle appeared. They were upping the ante. A pistol couldn't penetrate the tires from this distance, but a .223 or a .308 might do some damage.

I fired the Mossberg at the door.

"Don't shoot, man. I'm coming out!" a voice shouted.

GQ's twin dove through the open door and landed on his stomach, firing the AR-15 blindly in my direction. The bullets cut through the tires and hit the side of my pickup.

I pulled the trigger.

The twin screamed in pain. He rolled onto his back and put his hands in the hair. "You fucking shot me!"

"Toss the weapon," I shouted.

He dropped the AR and rolled away from the fire.

"I'm coming out!" the older voice shouted from behind the door. A hand appeared holding a Glock pistol. "I'm coming out. Don't shoot." The hand tossed the pistol on the concrete driveway. The car fire roared like a bonfire.

The man with the designer jeans walked out with his hands up. He had shoulder-length dark hair and enough lines on his face to be in his late thirties or early forties.

"Get down on your knees," I yelled.

"The car's gonna explode, man!"

The GQ kid yelled for help, but the man ignored him.

I walked forward, keeping the shotgun level with his waist. "Then you better talk. Where's the Dragon?"

"Nobody knows where he is."

"Down on your knees," I yelled.

He got down on his knees, turning his face away from the flames. "Who're you? What d'you want, man?"

Something popped over the roar of the fire. The purple paint bubbled, and the upholstery gave off a thick black smoke. The fire jumped to the plywood covering the front door of the garage.

I took another step forward. The heat was intense.

"There's money inside. Let me go. I'll get you twenty grand," he begged.

"Where does the money go? Who collects it?"

"Come on, man. Dragon will kill me."

"You think I give a shit? I know you sell to the kids on base."

"I'm just trying to make a living."

I aimed at the burning Impala and pulled the trigger. The blast blew the trunk open, exposing a pile of melting black plastic bags.

"Who picks up the money?" I repeated. "Tell me and I let you go."

He glanced at the burning car. Sweat poured down his face.

"Tell him, Manny," the GQ kid yelled. "Get me outta here!" He tried to drag himself away from the flames.

"Leo, man. Leo the jeweler," Manny said.

"Where can I find him?"

"He runs a pawnshop on Culebra."

An explosion rocked the Impala, sending sparks flying in all directions. The man jumped to his feet. His right hand went behind his back.

I pulled the trigger.

The shotgun blast hit him in the legs, forcing him backward into the flames. He screamed and dropped the pistol.

I ran to my pickup. Sirens raced toward the scene. Red flashing emergency lights appeared on the I-90 freeway. I grabbed a blanket from behind the seat and ran back to the flames. I threw the blanket over the man and pulled him out of the fire. I grabbed GQ next and dragged him beside Manny. They would live but would always remember what happened here.

"I'm Nick Fischer," I said. "Call the Dragon and tell him what happened here. Tell him I want Maya Chavez back."

CHAPTER FORTY-ONE

IT WAS AFTER MIDNIGHT BY the time I returned to my house in King William. I parked on the corner and spent fifteen minutes studying the other cars on the street, looking for anything out of place. I was under no illusions that Russell Stevens would suddenly do the right thing and hand over Maya. He had shaken hands with the devil when he killed his stepfather and never looked back, and he would kill me in a heartbeat. He didn't play by the same rules as everybody else. To get Maya back, I had to think like him.

The pawnshop on Culebra was near St. Mary's University, where I'd spent a year and a half in law school. If I didn't hear from Russell by morning, Leo the jeweler was next on my list. Between now and then, I could use a couple hours of sleep.

The lights were off inside my house. I approached the front door with my hands in plain sight. I knew Sarge and Lucky were watching the yard. The door was open.

Sarge was waiting in the living room with the AR-10 strapped to his left shoulder. He had on a dark-green T-shirt and a black watch cap and was ready for anything that walked through the door.

"Any trouble?" I asked.

"Skeeter tracked the manager's pickup. It cruised past the house about two hours ago. We had the lights off. He didn't stop."

"How was the pot roast?" I asked. The smell of cooked meat and gravy lingered in the air.

"We left you a plate in the fridge, unless Skeeter ate it."

"That wouldn't surprise me."

"How'd you make out? You smell like smoke."

"I had a bonfire. The tire shop was a front for his drug operation. I shut it down."

"Still no word from the man?"

"Nothing."

"You sure you're all right? You don't look too good."

"I just need some pot roast and a few hours' sleep." I wandered into the kitchen and found the plate of food where Rose had left it in the fridge covered in foil. There was a thick slice of beef smothered in gravy with new potatoes and carrots on the side. After a few minutes in the microwave, the meal smelled like heaven. The last couple of days had reminded me of being on deployment, but this meal beat the hell out of the vacuum-packed military MREs.

I finished the glorious pot roast and rinsed the plate for Rose, then I left Sarge on watch and made my way upstairs. It felt good to strip off the bloody T-shirt and rinse the wound. I taped a new gauze pad in place and stumbled to my mattress. Before my eyes closed, the phone rang. I was hoping it was the Dragon, but the caller ID showed Detective Ochoa.

"Tell me why I shouldn't arrest you right now?" she asked when I accepted her call.

"Good to hear from you, Detective."

"Don't give me any of your shit, Fischer. I've got calls from all over town."

"Somebody's doing your dirty work for you."

"So, you're a vigilante now? When you can't get what you want, you start shooting up clubs and burning down gas stations? Tell me why I shouldn't have your license revoked right now?

"You know who they belong to. If you don't, you're not doing your job."

"I am doing my job, which is why I'm calling you in the middle of the night. Don't you care about law and order?"

"Give me forty-eight hours and I'll bring you enough evidence to take down Russell Stevens."

"You're in a very dangerous place right now. I don't know whether you're my new hero or just another gangster. Either way, if you keep going, you'll be dead by morning."

"I'm just trying to do the right thing."

There was a pause on the other end of the line. Ochoa took a deep breath. Her voice shifted from anger to concern. "If you have something, give it to me now."

"I need to find Maya first."

"Tell me what you got. Let me help. You think I don't want the bad guys off the streets as much as you do?"

"Look, you're good, and I trust you. But you'd only slow me down."

"Goddamn you, Fischer." She took a long moment to collect herself. I listened to her steady breathing through the phone. "You got twenty-four hours. Get me that evidence or I will arrest you, hero or not."

CHAPTER FORTY-TWO

THE PAWN SHOP WAS STILL closed when I arrived at eight thirty the next morning. It opened at nine, and I wanted to be in the parking lot before Leo arrived. Skeeter had done some digging and found a picture of the owner in an old online advertisement. Everybody had a digital footprint. His full name was Leonidas Kostopoulos. The headshot showed a man in his fifties with a trimmed goatee, bushy sideburns, and red designer eyeglasses. His chubby cheeks and double chin gave him the look of someone who spent more time behind a glass counter than out in the sunlight. He definitely didn't resemble his namesake warrior from ancient Greek history.

At eighty forty-five a new silver Lexus LX pulled into the reserved parking place beside the back door. The man who got out had on a tan suit with a seventies-style dark blue button-down shirt. A thick gold chain hung across a chest full of gray hair. He'd put on a few pounds, but it was the same guy from the picture, and he still wore the same designer eyewear.

While he fumbled with a set of janitor keys hooked to a chain on his belt, I pulled my Springfield and got out of my pickup. He put the key in the lock, and I pressed the barrel of my pistol to the back of his thick neck.

"Good morning, Leonidas."

He raised his hands to shoulder height, giving me a good view of the diamond studded pinky ring on his left hand.

"I don't have any money," he said. His voice had a singsong quality that emphasized his Greek accent.

"You're lying, Leo. Let's go inside."

I followed him through the door and into a cluttered back office. There were stacks of papers on a cheap metal desk and boxes on the floor covered with dust. I turned on the light and frisked Leo for weapons. He had a S&W .40 stuck inside his elastic waistband.

"Turn around," I said.

Leo kept his hands up and slowly pivoted. His face was pale, and he was sweating despite the morning chill.

"You're him."

"Expecting someone?"

"Nick Fischer. You burned down the tire shop. Y-you don't have to do this," he stuttered.

"Do what?"

"Kill me."

I let him sweat while I examined the pictures on his desk. One showed a teen girl in a white school uniform dress, her dark hair tucked over her shoulders. She had a shy, intelligent smile. Another showed a boy near the same age, maybe a year older, with ironed khaki pants and a white Oxford shirt with a dark blue tie.

"Those your kids?" I asked.

Leo nodded nervously.

"They go to private school?"

"St. Mary's Hall."

"Business must be good."

"I do all right."

I tapped him hard in the chest with the barrel of my .45. He took a quick step back to keep from falling over. "You're the worst kind of scum. You think your hands are clean, but your money is covered in blood."

"I don't know what you're talking about."

"Russell took a girl your daughter's age from Fredericksburg. She's the granddaughter of on old friend. I want her back."

"You're gonna kill me?"

"Not unless you get in my way. I want the Dragon's money. Where is it?"

He walked to a closet and opened the door. A metal safe filled the space with a keypad lock. He punched in the numbers and turned the handle. Stacks of bills covered the bottom three shelves. Two trays of jewelry occupied the top shelf. I pulled the empty plastic garbage sack from the trash can and handed it to Leo.

"Take the money. All of it."

He filled the sack with more money than I would see in ten years of investigations. The Dragon was doing a very lucrative business.

I made Leo carry the sack to his Lexus. The parking lot was still empty when he popped the trunk. He moved a bag of soccer balls and orange cones out of the way and lifted the money into the back.

"Your kids play soccer?" I asked.

"Football. My girl plays. I'm the coach."

I raised my eyebrow. He didn't look like the athletic type.

"Back in the day, I used to play for a club team in Athens," he said, smiling for the first time.

I unhooked the key ring from his beltloop. "You drive," I told him. I opened his door and checked under the seat and the door's side pocket. I didn't want Leo to surprise me with a spare pistol. I didn't come up with anything, except a pink scrunchy and a plastic squirt bottle of lavender-scented hand sanitizer. There was no doubt Leo had a teenage daughter.

The soft leather bucket seats in the Lexus LX fit like a glove against my back, a far cry from the worn cloth seats in my dated F-150. Leo pressed the start button. The engine buzzed to life, and the seat automatically adjusted to my weight. A female voice with a British accent said, *Welcome back, Leo. Where would you like to go?*

Leo looked at me. Car and driver were waiting for my answer.

"Southcross," I told him.

"You're going to hit all my stores?"

"That's the idea. Unless Russell turns over the girl."

"It won't work. The money comes from all over. The Dragon answers to the higher-ups."

"Then he'll want to make a deal before the boss finds out he's losing money."

"He won't negotiate. That's not what he does. He can't afford to."

"What would you do, Leo? What would you do if someone took your daughter?"

He didn't answer. He twisted the transmission knob to reverse. The rearview camera popped up on the screen. The friendly British woman said, *Be careful backing up. Where should I route the GPS?*

Leo spoke to his car. "We go to Southcross Pawn."

Thank you, Leo. Routing to Southcross Pawn. Head east on Culebra.

"Can we turn that off," I said.

Leo touched a switch on the padded steering wheel. He clicked the transmission knob to drive and pulled out into morning traffic. A gold Saint Jude medallion dangling from the rearview mirror caught the sunlight. The patron saint of lost causes.

"I'll never get used driving without a key and a handle to shift gears," I said. We stopped at a stoplight, and I watched the morning traffic pile up behind us. "I learned how to drive on a stick shift."

"So did I," Leo said. The light turned green, and he pulled into the left lane to get around a slow-moving city bus. "Americans are spoiled. In Greece, everybody drives a stick."

He was still sweating despite the cool air, and he kept tapping his pinky ring on the dashboard while he drove.

I thought about the Volkswagen I'd rented for a week in Germany. It was after I'd been discharged from the Landstuhl Regional Medical Center following the IED I'd hit in Afghanistan that ended my military career. I needed to get away from men in uniforms recovering from their battle wounds, so I rented a car and drove around in the back country. South of Heidelberg, I searched for the tiny town on the Rhine River that the Fischer family was supposed to have come from. Driving the stick and seeing the road signs in German had made me homesick for Fredericksburg, Texas.

Forty-five minutes later, Leo pulled into the pawnshop and jewelry store on Southcross Boulevard. There were a few cars in the parking lot, and the doors were open for business.

"Pull around to the back," I said.

"I'm just an accountant," he said, as if that justified his association with the Dragon.

"Do everything you normally do, and you won't get hurt," I said.

I followed Leo in through the back door and tucked my pistol behind my belt. This time it opened into the main room behind the glass counter. Two women in their forties turned to greet us. Both eyed me suspiciously.

"You're early," one of the women said. She had on an orange dress that was too tight and sky-blue makeup that didn't match.

"My daughter's soccer game is this afternoon," Leo told her. I've got to be back on the north side by four o'clock."

The woman smiled. She was looking at me, waiting for an introduction. I didn't offer one. Her eyes lingered on the scars on my forehead. All her pawnshop customers probably had scars of some kind.

Leo led the way to the back office. I didn't have to ask this time. There was a similar layout—a closet hiding the money safe. I handed him his janitor key ring and a plastic trash bag. He opened the door and the safe, and I watched him strip the money off the shelves. The Dragon and whoever he worked for were doing a very lucrative business. Again, I told Leo to leave the jewels.

I followed Leo back to the Lexus and opened the trunk. He hoisted the money bag into the back. It was quite a haul.

"Where to?" he asked.

"You know where," I said. "Houston Street."

"You did your homework."

We climbed back in the front seat. Leo hit the start button and flipped the transmission indicator to drive. I could feel the dampness under the Kevlar vest and knew it was a mixture of sweat and blood. Luckily, following Leo the Greek around hadn't been physically taxing, but I was worried about the final stop. Leo had started to tap his pinky ring on the dashboard again, like he knew something was coming.

When he made the turn onto Houston Street, I made him keep driving past the pawnshop and pull into the minimart on the corner. I scanned the street and the nearby buildings for anything suspicious. His employees knew the schedule. They knew who was part of the team and who wasn't. It was their business to know. Their livelihood depended on being aware of who was in charge and who might cause them harm.

Leo tapped a steady beat with his pinky ring. I watched two women enter the front of the pawnshop. Fifteen minutes later, the same women came out.

"How many employees work here?" I asked.

"Only two."

"Male or female?"

"A husband and wife. They've been with me for fifteen years. They're good people. Please, don't hurt them."

"Cooperate and no one gets hurt. Does your daughter really have a soccer game this afternoon?"

"Yes. Her team plays St. Pious."

"What position does she play?"

"Midfielder. She's tough like her father. I played the same position when I was younger."

"I played football in high school."

"Ah, American football is no good. Is not a real sport."

"We're gonna disagree on that point."

He laughed. I told him to start the car and pull around to the back door.

"This girl you're looking for, is she a relative?" he asked while he was waiting for the light to change so he could cross the street to the pawnshop parking lot.

I didn't see any reason to hold back. I told Leo the story of how I'd gotten involved with Maya and her grandfather's relationship to my own grandpa. I also told him how I'd found Maya in the flophouse and how she'd run away again.

"I'm no saint," Leo confessed. "But I'm just the accountant."

"You said that once. That's no excuse. You're helping keep the Dragon in business."

"You don't understand. I don't have anything to do with his business. I came to this country thirty years ago. My soccer career was over. I injured my left knee. I had an operation, but I would never be the same on the field. So, I left. I put my life savings into my business. I built it up over all this time. I got married and had two beautiful children. I opened two new locations and was living the American dream. Then three years ago, the Dragon came to me and said take this money. At first, I refused, but he threatened my family. He is an animal."

"Why didn't you go to the police?"

Leo kept quiet. He pulled the Lexus across the street and around to the back door of the pawnshop. There were two other cars in the lot. Next door, the Jack in the Box restaurant parking lot was overflowing with a lunch crowd. The odor of cooked meat and hot grease made me hungry. I hadn't eaten anything since Rose's quiche for breakfast.

Leo cut the engine and turned to me. He wanted to explain his life. "I didn't have a choice—" he started to say. I cut him off.

"We all have a choice." I didn't want to hear Leo's sad tale. "The only victim here is Maya Chavez and the other girls whose lives the Dragon's ruined." I held up the Springfield. "Last stop. Let's go." I handed him the janitor keys and followed him to the door.

I scanned the stacks of secondhand goods. There was one older guy in a blue mechanic jumper examining a set of used metric tools. The husband and wife team were behind the counter. The woman looked in her sixties and wore a bright yellow tracksuit. The man was the same age and sitting at a desk sorting papers. He had a gray T-shirt that matched his shoulder-length hair.

"Everything, all right, Mr. Leo?" the man asked.

The woman stayed at the end of the counter, studying me. She eyed the bulky Kevlar vest under my shirt. She knew something was up.

"Everything's cool, Buddy," Leo said. "We're going in the office for a moment."

The man turned to me expecting an introduction. I smiled but didn't say anything. I watched his hands for any sign of nervousness. His wife occupied herself with something in the glass counter.

The mechanic decided he didn't want the tools and walked out the front door, triggering an electric bell. I pulled the Springfield and pointed it at Buddy. "Lock the front door."

Buddy's eyes shifted from me to Leo.

Leo nodded, and the man went to the door.

I walked behind the counter toward his wife. There was a small

TV monitor that showed four surveillance cameras. One pointed at the front door, one at the counter, one at the back door, and one at the back parking lot. They had watched us park and walk inside.

Buddy locked the front door and walked back to the counter. He stood beside his wife.

"Both of you go in the back room," I said.

Buddy and his wife looked at each other but didn't move.

"It's okay, Buddy. Do what he says," Leo said to them.

The husband and wife team reluctantly walked toward the back office. I motioned Leo to follow. We formed a single file. The woman went through the office door first, followed by Buddy. Leo went next. The door opened in.

Something moved in the shadows. I caught the outline of two men behind the door. I kicked the metal hard, then dropped to my knees.

Four quick shots exploded in the small space. Four holes appeared in the metal door at chest level. One of the men jumped from behind the door. I fired from my crouching position. The .45 slug caught him in the chest and blew him against the wall. The woman screamed. Three more shots rang out. The last one hit me in the chest. The Kevlar held, but the impact knocked me to the ground, sending shock waves of pain through my chest and down my arms.

The other man appeared out of the shadows. He wore sunglasses, a black T-shirt, and jeans. His hair was slicked back, and a skull tattoo covered the front of his neck.

"You fucked up, man," he said, aiming the pistol at my head. He dropped his guard, thinking I was hit or already dead.

I rolled quickly to my left and kicked him in the knee. He went down and dropped the pistol. I dove on his chest and grabbed him around the throat. He tried to counterpunch, but I pinned his arms with my knees. The woman was still screaming.

I was in the doorway on top of the thug. He kicked at my back.

The impacts jarred the wound in my chest. His core muscles contracted under my weight. I squeezed his neck, cutting off the blood flow to his brain. A minute ticked by, then another. His kicks got less frequent and weaker. Finally, he stopped moving.

I grabbed the door handle and pulled myself up. "Get the money."

The woman stopped screaming.

Leo opened the safe. He found a plastic trash bag and filled it with the money. I noticed a stack of computer disks on the top shelf.

"Take those too," I said to Leo.

He hesitated for moment. He was calculating his options. He looked from the contents to my .45, then to the unconscious man on the floor. He took the disks and dropped them into the bag.

"You stay inside," I said to Buddy and his wife. "Keep the front door locked until we're gone. Understand?"

They both nodded. I followed Leo to the Lexus, opened the door, and watched him toss the heavy bag in the back with the other two. I took the handful of computer disks to the front seat for closer inspection. Leo got in beside me.

"Where to?"

"Just drive."

CHAPTER FORTY-THREE

I DIRECTED LEO TOWARD LOOP 410, and we hit the on-ramp headed south. I wanted to put some distance between us and the pawnshop. Someone would have heard Buddy's wife screaming and the gun shots and called the police.

I needed to get out of the Kevlar. It was hard to breathe. When I moved to unroll the window, a stabbing pain shot through my chest. My bandage and the T-shirt underneath the vest were soaked with blood. I had to stay focused long enough to call Russell, then get rid of Leo.

"Get off here," I said, pointing to the South Presa Street exit.

He drove a few blocks north to the Mission San Juan Capistrano parking lot and stopped under a shade tree. I opened my door. A tour bus had just pulled up, and a couple dozen blue-haired ladies with their husbands in tow were slowly climbing down the steps and ambling toward the large wooden cross stuck in a patch of prickly pear cactus. Beyond that stood the eighteenth-century white limestone church surrounded by the remains of the eighteenth-century stone wall.

Leo sat behind the wheel, tapping his pinky ring on the center console.

"Ever take the tour?" I asked.

It took him a minute to focus on what I was saying. Finally, he said, "No. I went to the Alamo once."

"You should tour the missions. Bring your kids. Show them some Texas history."

"I'm from Greece. We invented history. The house I grew up in was older than this mission."

We watched the senior tour group gather around the cross.

"How much money do we have?"

Leo did a quick calculation in his head. "Two million three hundred and thirty thousand."

"You're pretty sure about that?"

"I'm always sure about money," he said.

"Call Russell. He'll take your call. You're the accountant."

Leo touched a button on the steering wheel. The dashboard lit up. The British female voice spoke: *Good afternoon, Leo. How may I help?*

"Call Russell Stevens," he ordered.

Calling Russell Stevens, the voice responded. After a series of electronic beeps, the phone rang.

The Dragon's raspy voice answered. "What is it?"

"I'm here with the accountant and a bag of your money, dickhead."

"Who is this?"

"Take a wild guess. The boys you sent were sloppy."

"Goddamn you, Nick Fischer."

"We can end this tonight." I pointed the Springfield at Leo. "Tell him how much we got."

"Two million three hundred and thirty thousand," Leo recited.

"You want it back, hand over Maya," I said.

"My people will kill you and your whole fucking family."

"Too late. I don't have a family. There's just me. So let's make a deal."

"I don't negotiate."

"That's too bad. I'll have to keep going."

"Fuck you! No matter what you do, you're dead."

"I'll sweeten the pot. You give me Maya, and I'll give you the money and throw in the stack of computer disks that you left in Leo's safe."

He didn't speak.

"Do we have a deal?"

"She made her choice."

"She doesn't know what she wants. She's eighteen. Let her go." I waited for Russell to respond. The silence stretched to thirty seconds.

"You're dead, asshole." He disconnected.

"Charming guy."

"No one has ever crossed the Dragon and lived. He is the devil. An evil spirit."

"Where is he?"

"I do not know."

I pressed the Springfield against his forehead. "Tell me, Leo. He's gonna kill you anyway."

He didn't move. "I-I would tell you if I knew. I don't owe the Dragon anything. He killed my wife. She talked about his money. She mentioned his name. She broke his code of silence, so he killed her. You asked why I didn't go to the police. I have two children. I do what he asks. My kids are all I have."

"What's on the computer disks?"

"Men with underage girls. Russell provides the girls and tapes what happens. Then he blackmails the men. There are dozens of men he's caught on tape. Police, judges, politicians. All perverts who like young girls."

"Get out," I said. "Out of the car."

His jaw clenched tight and his double chin shook. "You're gonna to kill me."

"No, Leo. Go home to your kids. Russell's going to come after you. Get the kids and take a little vacation." A wave of pain shot from my chest down both arms. I lost my grip on the pistol, and it dropped into my lap.

"God have mercy," he said and crossed himself. Blood had leaked from under the Kevlar vest and soaked the top of my jeans.

"Get out!" I yelled. I didn't want him there if I passed out.

Leo got out of the Lexus, and I climbed behind the wheel. He walked slowly toward the mission.

"Leo," I said.

He turned, expecting a bullet.

I tossed him his cell phone.

Leo caught the phone and let out a loud nervous sigh.

I drove north on Presa Street. I wanted to ditch the Lexus and get my old pickup. I'd left extra weapons and ammo in the back seat, and I would need them before this was over. The traffic was light. I passed the turn for Mission San José and Mission Concepción. Maybe Texas history didn't stretch as far back as the Greeks, but everyone should know something about the place where they lived.

I negotiated the traffic back to Leo's pawnshop on Culebra where I'd left my pickup, then stopped down the street and studied the front of the store. The open sign was on, but no one was going in or out. There were two police cars parked across the street. The officers were probably inside. I drove into the parking lot of the minimart next door and saw two more officers searching my pickup. The black duffle bag with my extra weapons and ammo was on the pavement. So much for my extra fire power.

I called Skeeter and told him what happened. I expected the police would send an officer to my house very soon. I told him to get the weapons and ammo out of the safe and take them to Rose's house. I wanted Sarge and Lucky to stay with Rose, so they weren't on the police radar.

"You don't sound good, man," Skeeter said.

"I'll be all right." I disconnected. It wouldn't be long before the cops or Russell's gang started looking for Leo's Lexus, so I got out, left the keys in the console, and began walking toward the corner convenience store. I needed water and something to eat. When I reached the parking lot, I hit the Uber app on my phone. With any luck, I could get a ride out of here in a few minutes. I took another step toward the store and blacked out.

CHAPTER FORTY-FOUR

THE EXPLOSION LIFTED THE HUMVEE into the air and turned the blue sky white. The windshield fractured into a thousand tiny pins that stabbed my face. The vehicle came to rest upside down. My legs wouldn't move, pinned to the seat by the crushed dashboard. To my left, Corporal Lorenzo bled through the mouth and ears. His arms hung down lifelessly toward the roof of the cab. Rifle bullets ripped into the metal frame. A dozen legs clad in desert boots appeared in the swirling dust and circled the vehicle.

"Get down!" I shouted. I pounded on the door and the dashboard. I was trapped.

The men stood their ground. Protecting me.

One of the men dropped to the ground, shot through the head. He was a giant of a man with a metal hook for a hand. Skeeter. He opened his mouth. Shouted:

"Mr. Fischer, wake up!"

I opened my eyes and saw Leo's jowly face staring down at me. The dream was back. For months after my last deployment, the nightmare of those final moments kept me up at night. The names and faces of my brothers were seared in my memory.

"You were screaming. You okay?" Leo asked.

I waited for my head to clear. There was pain in my chest, but it was manageable. I was lying on a bed with a clean sheet in a sparsely furnished room. I was naked down to my skivvies, and there was a fresh bandage over my wound. The Saint Jude medallion hung around my neck.

"What's this," I asked, holding up the necklace.

"Saint Jude. In my orthodox church he is Thaddaeus. The patron saint of lost causes. You will need his help fighting the devil."

"Where am I?" I asked.

"My house. I took a cab back to the pawnshop. When it dropped me off, I looked across the street and saw you lying face down beside my Lexus. A homeless guy was trying to use your phone to call 911."

"How long have I been here?"

He looked at his watch. "Four hours. You were out of it. Don't worry, no one knows you're here."

I found my phone and checked for messages. Two texts from Skeeter and a missed call from Detective Ochoa. I called Skeeter and let him know I was all right.

"Where are we?" I asked Leo.

"Ogden Lane in the Heights," he said.

The Alamo Heights was an upscale neighborhood north of downtown. There was old money there—businessmen who owned buildings and worked downtown. The perfect place for a mob accountant to hide in plain sight.

I passed along the address to Skeeter and told him to sit tight at my place and monitor the GPS signal from the manager's pickup.

There was a knock on the door. A young female voice said, "Papa?"

"My kids know you're here. I had to explain why we missed the soccer game. They helped me bring you inside. You're in my basement."

A teenage girl entered the room. She was seventeen or eighteen years old. Her hair was pulled into a ponytail. She wore soccer-style shorts and a team T-shirt with her number on the back and socks with athletic sandals.

"This is my daughter, Penelope."

"The wife of Odysseus. She looks brave enough," I said.

"I thought you only studied Texas history."

"It's not so different than yours." I sat up in bed and pulled the tangled sheet up around my waist.

"It's Penny," the girl said quickly. "Would you like something to eat?" She carried a bowl of stew and a glass of water to the bedside table.

"Thank you, Penny. I'm starving."

She put a hand on my forehead. "You have a fever. We should take you to the hospital."

"Penelope wants to be a doctor," Leo said proudly.

"I'll be all right after I eat some of that stew. Did you make it?"

"It's my father's recipe."

The bowl contained thick chunks of meat in tomato-based sauce mixed with carrots and potatoes and smelled like heaven.

"Would that be lamb?" I asked, holding up a piece of meat on the spoon.

She laughed a spontaneous, girlish laugh. She wasn't scared or intimidated in the least by a wounded man lying in the spare bedroom. "It's venison," she said.

"One of my clients has a deer lease. He lets me take the kids hunting," Leo explained.

I took a bite. It tasted as good as it smelled. It reminded me of my grandma's wild meat stew that always seemed to be cooking on the backburner of the stove during hunting season. Father and daughter watched me devour the stew and use the pita bread to clean the bowl.

When Penny took the empty bowl and left the room, I got out of bed.

"What're you doing?" Leo asked. "You need to rest."

"No time for that. You know how Russell operates. Maya's life is in danger. Now, you and your family are in danger."

Leo tried to come up with an excuse to keep me in bed, but there wasn't one that didn't involve putting him and his kids in more danger. He brought me my clean clothes. He'd had his daughter wash and dry everything. Most of the bloodstains were gone. I got dressed and slipped back on the Kevlar vest. It had already saved my life once. I was sure I would need it again before I found Maya and took her home.

He handed me back my Springfield .45 and my S&W .38. I strapped both in place. I would need more firepower, and I had no idea where I might get it.

"Thank you," I said. "For saving my life."

"Before you came, I was willing to follow orders to protect my children. The Dragon killed my wife. My kids are the only thing I have left. But you… You are willing to sacrifice your life to rescue the daughter of a family friend." He paused and looked at me. I was dressed, my Springfield strapped in a shoulder holster over the Kevlar vest, my ankle bulging with the .38. "I will fight."

"You sound more like Leonidas," I said.

He smiled at that. He understood the reference.

I was grateful for his help but wasn't really prepared to offer him absolution. I wasn't a priest. His hands were bloody. Maybe he still thought I would kill him. He would pay for his crimes one way or another. I had no doubt about that. You don't profit the way Leo did all these years and get off scot-free.

Leo showed me to a desk by the door where there was an open laptop. Beside it sat the stack of computer disks we'd taken from the pawnshop safe.

"This will help you bring the Dragon down." He loaded one of the disks.

We watched a video cue up on screen. The picture wasn't exactly a Hollywood production. The image was grainy, and the room was dark. The camera angle came from the ceiling above a bed in what looked like a cheap motel room. The two people in the frame were clearly visible. One was a naked young woman sprawled on the bed. She had dark hair and a forced smile on her face. The other was an older man with gray hair and a clean-shaven face. He had his shirt off, and his belly hung over the top of his black suit slacks. His face looked familiar, but I couldn't place it.

"That's Gordon Lozano," Leo said.

"The county commissioner?" I hit pause and studied his face. The bastard was enjoying himself. The girl was skinny. Her ribs were visible. She looked to be no more than sixteen, despite the heavy makeup. "How many of these are on here?"

"A dozen. Probably more."

I ejected the commissioner's disk. The date and city were written in black marker on the side. I shuffled through the rest of the disks. Each had a date and location. The last one was from this year. The city was Fredericksburg. I inserted the disk and booted up the video. There was a different girl in the same motel room. She was near the same age, naked and spread-eagle on the queen-sized bed. Thankfully, there was no sound. The girl's head was turned toward the bathroom.

After a moment, Mike Bauer walked into the frame, a towel wrapped around his round belly. He smiled like a kid at Christmas. I cut the video off. I didn't need to see any more. I knew why the Dragon was in Fredericksburg and why Mike Bauer had given him a job and an alibi for Lori's murder.

"I need a car," I said. "And I need to know where Russell's hiding." I took the disk out of the laptop.

"You can take my daughter's Camry."

"Where's the money?"

"Still in the Lexus. My best guess is that Russell went to his warehouse. South Highway 16, but I doubt he will be there long."

"Where's he going?"

"I don't know. I told you. I'm an accountant, nothing more. I hear rumors that he takes girls to Arizona and South Florida. Sometimes different cities in Texas."

"He's taking Maya?"

He shrugged. "That's what he does."

I gave him my phone, and Leo typed in the address of the warehouse. I followed him up the basement steps and into the kitchen. A boy was sitting at the bar doing homework. He looked like Penny's twin, only a couple of years younger with chubby cheeks.

"This is Leonidas Junior," Leo said.

The boy stood up from his textbook. He was built like his dad, already developing a gut. His hair was dark and cut short. He extended his hand and I shook it.

"Pleased to meet you, Mr. Fischer," he said politely. There were no secrets it seemed between father and children. They all knew who I was. I glanced at the textbook.

"Math?" I asked.

"Not my favorite subject," he said.

"Junior is my budding artist," Leo said. "My daughter's the scientist."

"The world needs artists, too," I said.

The kid smiled.

I followed Leo out the back door to the garage. After he'd given me the keys to his daughter's red Toyota Camry and helped me load the money bags and the disks into the trunk, he hit the garage door opener.

"You need to leave," I reminded him. "Take the kids. At least until I take Russell down."

"I have a gun here. I know how to take care of myself and my family. I won't run."

If he wanted to face the music here, there wasn't anything

I could do about it. I got in the Camry and started the engine. Penny's car smelled like perfume and Skittles. I unrolled all the windows and drove out of his winding driveway and into the quiet residential Alamo Heights neighborhood. The lots were big, and the houses set back off the street. Dense live oak trees gave the area an exclusive feel. It was easy to see why it was so hard for Leo to pack up and leave.

CHAPTER FORTY-FIVE

BY THE TIME I GOT to I-35 south, a cool city mixture of exhaust fumes and fall cedar pollen had replaced the sweet smell of Penny's hairspray and Gummi bears. I rolled up the windows and turned on the heat. The last thing I needed was an attack of cedar fever.

My phone rang. Skeeter. I hit accept.

"They're coming for you," he said.

"Coming where?"

"Alamo Heights. The GPS signal's headed east on Hildebrand. I don't think it's a social call."

"What's their ETA?"

"Fifteen minutes. There's no traffic. You want some help?" Skeeter asked.

"I left. I'm on the I-35 headed south."

"Sounds like Leo the Accountant is about to pay the piper."

"I need fire power," I told him. "SAPD impounded my pickup and took my bag."

"You can't come home. They got the street covered. Cruisers on both ends and an unmarked car out front. Rose has already been out to offer them coffee. You're hot right now."

"All right. Keep me posted." I disconnected.

Leo laundered money for the Dragon and whoever his bosses were. Money that came from drug deals and prostitution. He knew what he was getting into. Once you made a deal with the devil, you had to accept the consequences. The problem was, Leo had two kids that didn't deserve what was coming. Everybody has a choice. I knew what mine had to be.

I took the next exit ramp and made a U-turn under the interstate. I would never make it back in under fifteen minutes. Leo said he had a weapon. He was going to need it.

I cut through the Olmos Basin park, north of the zoo and the headwaters of the San Antonio River. The neighborhood was quiet. The park was a small piece of wilderness in the middle of the city.

I parked down the street from Leo's house and walked through the oak trees lining his property. The jacked-up Dodge Ram from the strip club was in the driveway.

The front door was kicked in, and fresh chunks of wood were scattered on the welcome mat. I pulled my Springfield and jogged to the back of the house. The kitchen light was on. I inched to the window and looked inside. Leo was sitting at the kitchen table. Arnold the Manager stood behind him.

"Where the fuck is he?" Arnold shouted.

"Gone. Stole my daughter's car," Leo said, not looking up.

"You brought him home last night."

"It wasn't my choice."

The bald-headed bouncer moved into view. He was wearing a Spurs basketball T-shirt and carrying a Glock 9mm. No sign of the other bouncer. I ducked away from the window and put my hand on the back door. Locked.

"You're lying to me, Leo." Arnold was angry and hyper-excited like he was tweaking on meth. The only advantage I had was he and his crew didn't know I was outside the back door.

There was banging on the interior walls.

"Let me go!" a voice screamed. It was Penny.

I slipped back to the kitchen window. The bouncer with the neck tattoo had Penny in one bear claw and Junior in the other. Junior seemed shell-shocked and ready to piss his pants. Penny was a fighter. She pounded Tattoo with her free hand.

"Take your hand off me!" she shouted.

"We can have some fun with this bitch," Tattoo sneered. He shoved Junior into a kitchen chair and pressed Penny against the counter. In one swift motion, he ripped Penny's T-shirt off, exposing her black sports bra.

"Stay away from her," Junior yelled, springing from the chair.

Tattoo backhanded him in the face. Junior dropped like a wet towel, blood spraying from his broken nose.

"Junior's got more fight than his old man." Tattoo laughed and turned his attention back to Penny.

"Leave them out of this." Leo started to stand, but the bald bouncer shoved his Glock into Leo's neck. Things were going downhill fast.

I used my folding knife to pry open the latch bolt. Leo hadn't locked the deadbolt. This time, it might have saved his life.

"Didn't you learn your lesson?" Arnold asked. He danced from foot to foot. Sweat rolled down his forehead despite the cool temperature. He wiped his runny nose with his fingers. "Did you tell the kids you watched while we took your wife down?"

"Leave them alone! I told you, I don't know where Nick Fischer is. He stole the car and took off. He took the money with him."

"I think you wanted to help him as payback for your wife," the manager said.

"That's crazy. How could I do anything? He had a gun."

"And now I have a gun," he said. "You can watch while we have a little fun."

Tattoo lifted Penny to the counter. She kicked and screamed

while he yanked her soccer shorts off and tossed them on the kitchen floor.

She screamed and clawed at his face. "Let me go!"

Tattoo hit her in the temple, and Penny slumped back against the countertop. The brute grabbed her black panties.

Boom!

I fired through the opening in the back door.

My .45 slug hit Tattoo in the back of the head. Blood sprayed Penny's half-naked body. She kicked the dead man to the floor.

I dropped to my knees outside the door and yelled into the room. "Put the guns down!"

They answered with gunfire that ripped through the door and the wall at chest level. I peeked through a bullet hole. The manager grabbed Penny from the counter. He held her from behind with his pistol jammed in her neck.

"Let her go!" I yelled.

"Who's out there?" he yelled. He was more nervous now than ever. He wouldn't hesitate to kill her or the whole family.

"Nick Fischer," I said.

"You motherfucker!"

"Let them go. I'll give the Dragon his money," I said.

"Where's it at?"

The bald bouncer and the manager pointed their pistols at the back door. Hearing I had the money got their attention, but they were waiting for confirmation before blasting me again.

"It's right here," I yelled and sprinted for the front of the house.

They opened fire, blasting toward my voice.

I ran through the front door and back to the kitchen. Arnold had his arm around Penny's neck with his back to me. Penny saw me coming and jerked her head sideways, giving me all the clearance I needed to hit Arnold in the head. He dropped his pistol and sank to the floor. Baldy spun toward me and pulled his trigger, but he was out of ammo. The slide on his Glock was locked back and empty. Maybe Saint Jude was on my side.

He went for the backup weapon in his jeans. I fired first, blasting him into the kitchen table.

Leo and his kids stared in stunned silence. Junior got to his feet, still holding his bleeding nose. I handed him a kitchen towel. Penny grabbed her shorts and slipped them on.

"Is there anyone else in here?" I asked.

"No," Leo said. "Just the three of them. Thank you."

"You need to leave. You know he'll be back."

CHAPTER FORTY-SIX

I NEEDED MORE THAN A COUPLE of pistols to break into a gangster's warehouse. The rifle, the shotgun, and the extra ammo I was counting on was locked up in the SAPD impound. I had extras at the house, but they might as well have been in Seattle. I called the only person I knew and trusted who had access to firearms. He might not help me, but it was worth a shot.

"You're fixin' to make the ten most wanted list, Junior," Sergeant Vera said when he came on the line. Calling me *Junior* was his way of saying he disapproved of my behavior. He'd used the same technique since I was in elementary school.

"I'll give you an autograph when I see you."

"What the Sam Hill's gotten into you?"

"I'm getting your deer blind ready. We should get together soon and catch up. Right now I need some firepower."

"If I saw you on the street, I'd have to arrest you."

"I promise to turn myself in when this is over," I said.

I explained my predicament with as few words as possible. When I was finished, there was silence on the line.

"You still there? I wouldn't ask unless I was desperate," I said.

"I don't like the sound of that, Junior," he said.

• • •

I got off the freeway and met Vera around the corner from the SAPD annex west of downtown. I parked Penny's red Camry on the street and got in the passenger seat of Vera's Chevy pickup.

"I'll do this on one condition," he said.

"I told you I'd take you deer hunting."

"That's a given. The condition is, you call Detective Ochoa and tell her where you're going."

I thought about that while he drove to the guard house at the back gate. He wasn't giving me a choice. "Maya might be at the warehouse. If she is, I want to get her out of there before the shootin' starts."

"All the more reason to have backup. It's your choice. Call her or go empty-handed."

"All right," I said. If it was anybody else but Detective Ochoa, I would have said no. I didn't want or need the interference. But I trusted her.

A plump female guard wearing cobalt-blue eyeliner stood under the streetlight by the gate.

Vera unrolled his window, gave her a flirty grin. "You're lookin' tight, girl. Did you cut your hair?"

"Don't try getting in my pants, *viejo*," she said and laughed.

"You can't blame me for tryin'," he said.

"That's sexual harassment."

"I can't help it. When I see a beautiful woman, I get weak in the knees."

"I could get you fired."

"I'm already retired. My wife wants me to chase younger women. She says she doesn't like sex anymore."

"That's not what she told me."

The two of them laughed like two bridesmaids at a nail salon. I drummed my fingers on the console of his pickup.

The guard shined her flashlight into my face.

"This is—" Vera started to say.

She cut him off. "Fischer. I know. Ochoa called me. Don't take too long." She opened the gate and went back inside the guard shack.

"You have a guardian angel," Vera said.

He drove to the back entrance and parked beside the loading dock. I followed him inside to a warehouse-sized room cordoned off by hurricane fencing. He walked to the nearest gate and produced a key for the lock.

"I talked to the officer who found your pickup. He's my cousin. Your bag of goodies is in here. He left it off the inventory."

"I owe you one."

"This one's for your father." He hesitated, deciding whether to go on. "I never told anyone this. I made a bad decision that should have got me killed. I was young and stupid, looking for a big payday. Luckily, your dad was the lawman who caught up with me. Anybody else, and I'd have been in prison or dead. Lee Fischer told me to put my gun away and go home. He didn't just mean sleep it off—he meant take a new path in life. I followed his advice and never looked back."

He went to the caged area that was stacked to the ceiling with weapons of every kind—pistols, shotguns, and dozens of AR-15s. Most people had no idea the kind of firepower the bad guys were packing on the streets of the Alamo City. My black duffle bag was on the floor near the front gate.

I sorted through my bag. Everything was still there. My AR-15 with the suppressor, the shotgun, the extra magazines, the ammo. It was like finding your lost pair of shoes on the lakeshore after a swim. The walk back to the car was going to be a lot easier.

Vera disappeared for a few minutes while I picked up my duffle bag and took it back out to his pickup. I stood under the blinking florescent lights of the building and glanced up at the clear sky and the few stars that penetrated the city lights. I tried to keep my mind clear and focused. Find Maya. Take out the Dragon.

Vera reappeared and closed and locked the annex door behind him. He was carrying a black duffle bag about the size of my own.

"I thought you could use a little extra help," he said and grinned. He handed me the bag.

Inside I found a tactical flashlight and a pair of night-vision goggles. Very useful.

"Came from a cartel bust last week. Those guys have military-grade weapons directly from the Mexican army. DEA was supposed to pick it up. There was a problem with the inventory sheet." He winked at me and started his pickup. "Ochoa called me yesterday. Asked me what I thought about you."

"That doesn't sound good."

"I told her everything I know. She still likes you." He chuckled.

"Diana Ochoa? Detective Diana Ochoa?" She and I had been at each other's throats since the first night I met her.

"Diana is a nice lady and a good cop. She knows her shit," he said. Coming from Vera, that was the highest compliment. "If it hadn't been for her, you would be in jail by now."

We drove back out the gate, and he parked behind Penny's Camry.

I unloaded the two duffle bags.

"I'm not gonna try to talk you out of this business because I knew your father and your granddad. Stubbornness is a Fischer family trait. I also think you're doing the right thing. It's what Lee Fischer would have done."

Vera held his hand out the pickup window, and I shook it.

"Opening weekend I expect you to have my feeder full of corn and my deer blind ready." It was his way of telling me to be careful. He wanted to see me at the ranch when deer season opened on the first of November.

"I'll find a nice big buck and tie him to a tree."

His pickup disappeared around the corner. I cranked the Camry, put it in gear, and focused on the mission.

CHAPTER FORTY-SEVEN

I FOLLOWED LEO'S GPS COORDINATES WEST on I-35, then south on Highway 16. The southern edge of the city consisted of industrial businesses, the occasional residence, and pastureland overrun with mesquite and huisache brush that stretched to Mexico, a hundred and fifty miles to the south.

The address was in an industrial park with an oilfield equipment company on one end and a Mexican food restaurant on the other advertised by a twelve-foot metal sculpture of a fat bullfrog wearing a sombrero and playing a guitar.

The Dragon's warehouse was in the middle, set back off the road about a hundred yards. Ten-foot hurricane fencing topped with razor wire surrounded the compound. The corners had surveillance cameras, and there were two guards inside a shack beside the locked gate.

I cruised by on the highway once to see if the guards paid any attention. They didn't seem to be watching the road. I made a U-Turn and parked behind the Mexican bullfrog.

I pulled my AR-15 from the duffle bag, screwed the Surefire suppressor in place, and loaded a thirty-round clip. I stuck two extra mags in my pockets and grabbed my binoculars. I had promised Vera I would call Detective Ochoa, and I would. But first I needed to find out if Russell was in the warehouse with Maya. Otherwise, the call would be a waste of time.

I skirted the light from the floodlamps and worked my way in the shadows to the back of the compound. The fence was neglected and covered with thick brush. I pushed my way through the prickly huisache limbs to the base of the wire.

The loading dock and back parking area were lit up like a football stadium. I wasn't going to get within fifty yards without being seen. There was a semi-tractor trailer backed into the landing, and two workers were busy offloading cargo with a forklift. A man with a dark jacket stood near the door holding an AR rifle.

I scanned the area with my binoculars. Whatever cargo was coming off the truck was in black plastic bags. They looked like the same size and shape as what I'd seen in the trailer in Gillespie County. The windows were blacked out, and the open warehouse door only gave a small glimpse of the interior. I searched the dozen cars in the parking lot. There was a black Jeep Grand Cherokee near the warehouse door.

Russell was there. I hoped Maya was with him.

I worked my way out of the brush and back to the Camry. I needed a way to cut power to the warehouse. I thought of shooting out the transformer. I'd used that ploy on my last case to gain access to the Allison ranch. It had worked then, but only because there was cover between the gate and the ranch house. This time, I'd be exposed in an open field for fifty yards. An easy target.

Then I heard the distinct downshift of a big diesel engine. I ducked as headlights flashed across the Camry. A semi-truck turned off the highway toward the warehouse gate. Opportunity knocked. I pulled the night vision goggles from the duffle bag and slipped them around my neck. I didn't have a clear plan, but being able to see in the dark would come in handy, thanks to Sergeant Vera.

I found Detective Ochoa's number and typed out a text message: *Possible location for Russell and Maya. Need confirmation. Will advise.*

As soon as I hit send, my phone vibrated. Ochoa was calling.

The two guards at the gate house approached the cab of the semi-truck. The driver set his air brakes. The phone vibration stopped. I ran to the edge of the Mexican restaurant, closing the distance to the gate and the truck.

My phone vibrated again. Ochoa wasn't giving up. I hit accept.

"I said it's not confirmed."

"Don't give me that. Where are you?" Ochoa said.

I told her the address of the warehouse and what I'd seen so far, while I watched the truck driver open his cab door and got out.

"Stay where you are," she said. "Do you hear me? Do not attempt to enter that warehouse until I get there."

The driver and one of the gate guards turned toward the back of the truck.

"I can't wait. Maya may be there," I said and disconnected.

I sprinted to the rear of the semi, keeping the trailer between me and the two men, then dove under the bumper and wedged myself against the trailer bed. If they did a search, I was toast. I only hoped they weren't that careful.

"It's locked, dude," a voice protested.

"Rules are rules," another voice insisted. "Open it up."

"You know what happens if I'm late?"

I heard the driver rattle the lock on the trailer door, his knees inches from my face. He had only to bend down to see me. I was clinging to the undercarriage with both hands. No chance to pull my pistol. The exertion caused pain to sweep from my chest to my shoulder and shoot down my arms.

The retractable trailer door rattled up.

"You see?" the first voice said. "Now can I get back to work?"

"All right, all right. What if you had something else in your trailer, huh? What would he do to me?"

They were worried about someone. I guessed that someone was the Dragon.

I heard the footsteps recede, a door slam, and the gate swing open. I kept my body tight against the bumper and the bottom of the trailer, hoping by butt wasn't visible. The truck slowed and made a U-turn. That was my signal to get off. He would be backing into the well-lit loading dock. When the driver hit the brakes, I let go and rolled to the pavement. The wheels immediately reversed. I dove clear and ducked under the nearest pickup.

The semi-truck backed to the loading dock, and I heard the door open and several men's voices. I worked my way toward the side door and slipped inside.

There was probably ten thousand square feet of space and three-quarters of it was filled with pallets stacked with black plastic bags. I didn't need to know what was in them.

All the activity was at the loading dock. There were shouts and some laughter as the men unloaded the truck and added to their bounty.

I worked my way along the wall to the base of the steps leading to the second-floor offices and found what I was looking for—the main electrical breaker for the warehouse. I'd seen three men, one armed with an AR. Judging from the voices, there were at least four others inside the warehouse. I was outnumbered and needed an advantage.

I opened the breaker box and pulled the main switch.

The warehouse went black.

I heard a crash that sounded like the forklift slamming into metal. Someone flipped on a flashlight. The light beam searched the warehouse. I pulled on the night vision goggles and walked up the stairs to the offices.

Crouching at the top of the steps, I scanned the warehouse

floor. There were five men on the inside. Three of them had rifles. Only one had a flashlight, and he was holding it so that two of the men could finished unloading the truck.

"Where's the fucking generator?" a raspy voice shouted from the office window less than ten feet away.

It was the Dragon.

"We're working on it," a voice responded from the first floor.

I pulled my Springfield and felt a warm dampness inside the Kevlar vest. No time to change the bandage. I opened the door at the top of the stairs. The first room was a breakroom area with a long table in the center and a refrigerator and sink in the corner. I checked my watch. It had been ten minutes since Ochoa called. I checked my phone. There was a text message from her.

Sit tight. On our way.

Too late. I stepped into the next room.

Russell Stevens stood behind a desk scanning the dark warehouse floor. I leveled my pistol at his chest.

The lights flicked on. Someone had found the breaker. I slipped the goggles off.

The Dragon didn't jump or flinch. He turned and smiled like he was expecting me.

"You're a real pain in the ass," he said.

"Where's Maya?"

"When you gonna get it through your head? Maya's not your concern."

"I'll make you a deal."

"You think you're gonna get out of here alive?"

Footsteps pounded on the metal stairs. At least two men were coming fast.

"In about nine minutes, San Antonio's finest will be here." I showed him my phone display with Detective Ochoa's message and caller ID. "Give me Maya and I'll tell you where the money is. You can get a head start."

Russell studied my face for signs that I was bluffing. I held his gaze.

"Maya!" he yelled.

Maya walked out of the back room. Four other girls about her age followed. They looked scared and hesitant. All were dressed like Boys Town hookers with their hair curled and layers of glitter makeup. Maya's dress was gold, shiny, and skintight.

Suddenly, I felt lightheaded. Warm moisture trickled down my skin under my Kevlar vest.

"Maya, your grandpa wants you back," I said. "He told me about the fight you had. He's willing to give you some space."

Maya chewed her bottom lip. She looked at Russell.

"It's okay, you can come with me." The room went blurry. I grabbed the back of a chair for support. The Springfield felt like a fifty-pound weight in my hand.

"You see? You wasted your time, Fischer. She don't wanna go with you. She likes it where she is."

The other girls looked at Maya then down at their feet.

"In a few hours, they'll all be in a new home," Russell said.

"You can't take them," I said, then lost my grip on the Springfield.

Russell saw the drops of blood on my boots.

"You ain't doing too good, partner."

The men behind me grabbed my arms.

Everything went black.

CHAPTER FORTY-EIGHT

I CAME TO UPSIDE DOWN. MY hands were zip-tied in front of me, and I was hanging from an A-frame engine hoist like a fresh-killed carcass ready for gutting and skinning. The bloody bandage on my chest was still in place, but they had stripped me of my Kevlar vest and shirt. A fresh puddle of blood pooled beneath me on the concrete floor.

"Where's the money?" the Dragon yelled.

He stood five feet away, wearing a self-satisfied smile, like he'd just drawn an inside straight. I must have been out for only a few moments, long enough for his men to bind my feet and hoist me in the air.

"What're you after, man?" he asked. "You come here to steal my money?"

"I came here to get Maya."

He laughed. "She's just a cunt."

"Not to me."

Maya and the other girls stood near the exit, listening.

"Tell him, Mr. Fischer," Maya shouted. "He's going to kill you."

"She's a smart one."

I struggled to focus with the blood rushing to my head. "This time it's over. I found your CD collection in Leo's safe," I yelled. "I already turned it over to Detective Ochoa. Your enterprise is about to crash and burn."

"You're lying. You wouldn't call the police. They're after you. Cops hate a vigilante."

"Give me Maya, and we'll cut a deal."

Distant sirens cut through the silent warehouse. For once I was glad the cavalry was on its way.

"Let me go and cooperate. Maybe you can cut a deal," I said.

Russell's jaw tightened. He didn't panic, but he was weighing his options. Still cool and in control. "Kill him. Blow the place." He strode to the exit, his square boot heels clicking on the concrete floor, and disappeared with Maya and the other girls.

One of the thugs stepped toward me, smiling. He pointed his pistol at my head.

The sirens got louder.

"The money's all yours if you let me go," I said.

The thug lowered his pistol and stepped forward. "Where, asshole?"

"It's in..." I whispered.

He was curious and greedy. He stepped closer.

I swung my head with everything I had and connected with the bridge of his nose. Blood instantly covered his face and sprayed down his shirt.

He fired his pistol.

The bullet careened off the warehouse floor and hit the metal wall.

An explosion ripped through the building. Part of Russell's escape plan. The Dragon was destroying the evidence. The room went white, then burst into flame. Pieces of metal roof crashed down around me.

The thug with the broken nose sprinted for the exit.

I swung my torso forward and lifted my bound hands to the

edge of the A-frame. The plastic tie caught on a metal spur. I jerked my arms down and freed my hands. I grabbed the top bar and pulled my body up to ease the strain on my legs, then pulled my feet loose and dropped to the floor. Pain shot through my chest and down both arms.

The building erupted in flames. I ran into the parking lot. The Dragon's Jeep Cherokee was gone.

Emergency lights approached on the horizon along with the surging sirens.

The two gate guards jogged toward me out of breath.

"What happened?" one of them shouted.

I didn't respond. I stood still watching them approach, holding my hands at my sides. The heat felt good on my naked back. The outside temperature had dropped another five degrees.

The two guards came closer, eyeing me suspiciously. My torso was naked and covered in blood, and my feet were bare. The one on the left raised his pistol.

I grabbed his wrist and hit him in the ear. He went down. I grabbed the weapon and pointed it at his partner.

"Put it down," I ordered.

He dropped his pistol.

I picked it up and shoved it in my waistband. "Let's go," I said, waving the pistol toward the gate.

I followed him inside and made him take off his boots. They were a little too small, but they would work until I found something bigger. I took a black leather jacket from the peg on the wall and put it on over my bloody bandage.

"Where's your boss?" I asked the guard.

"I don't know," he said.

I hit him on the side of the head with the pistol.

"Where's the Dragon?"

"He'll kill me if I tell you." He put his hand to his bloody face.

"What do you think I'm gonna do if you don't?"

I hit him again. He went to his knees, clutching his bleeding ear.

I shoved the pistol into his forehead. "Talk."

The sirens were coming fast. I needed to move. I didn't want to get arrested or have to explain myself to Ochoa until I caught up with Russell and Maya again.

I pressed the barrel harder against the guard's skin. "Tell me where he went."

"There's an airstrip, man, on 1604."

"Off Weller Road?" I asked. I knew about the private airport.

He nodded, still holding his ear. I jogged out to the Camry. The sirens were less than a mile away, and the emergency lights on the horizon lit up the sky like a weekend carnival.

I jumped into the Camry and fired the engine. The flames from the warehouse leaped fifty feet into the air. I drove past the Mexican bullfrog. Another explosion ripped through the night. I cleared the front of the building and accelerated toward the highway.

Before I reached the road, a dark blue Crown Vic cut me off.

CHAPTER FORTY-NINE

Detective Diana Ochoa calmly got out of her car and walked to my driver's side window. She wore jeans and tactical boots with a dark blue jacket. Her hair was in a ponytail under an SAPD cap.

"Your twenty-four hours are up, hotshot," she said. "I hope Russell Stevens is in that warehouse and you're going to pick up Maya Chavez."

"He was in that building, now he's gone. But I know where he went."

"You're done, Fischer. You better have some good evidence or I'm placing you under arrest."

"I've got everything you need in this car, but right now Russell is getting away with Maya."

"How do you know that?"

"One of the guards said he was going to a private airport. He won't be there long. He blew up his own warehouse. I didn't have anything to do with it. He heard you coming."

She eyed me suspiciously.

It was hard to look convincing wearing a borrowed leather jacket soaked in blood. "I have to go, now."

"No, Fischer. I'm not letting you out of my sight. What evidence have you got?" She wasn't going to back off or let me leave.

"Two million dollars and a stack of computer disks that show the Dragon's blackmail victims."

"And none of that's admissible because you burned down half the city to get it." She was pissed. I understood. I hadn't used the most legal tactics, but Maya's life was at stake.

"I've got an eyewitness. Russell's accountant, Leonidas."

"An eyewitness to what?"

"Murder. The Dragon killed his wife ten years ago."

"That's a long time to keep quiet."

"He was scared to talk."

"You changed his mind?"

"He grew a backbone."

She studied my face. "You better be on the level."

"You have to trust me. We need to go now."

"Take my car. I've got a shotgun and an AR in the trunk." She opened the Camry door. In the dome light she saw the bloody bandage on my chest. "Jesus, Fischer. You're bleeding." She helped me out of the car.

"It's been a long night."

She opened her trunk and got out a first aid kit. I was still pumped full of adrenaline and wasn't feeling any pain. I reached for the AR.

"He's got a ten-minute head start."

"We do this my way, or I put you in handcuffs," she said. She stood her ground. I put down the AR and unzipped the jacket.

She peeled off the old bloody bandage. "How are you still up running around?" she asked, wiping my chest with a paper towel. "You should be in the hospital."

I grabbed her hands. I needed her undivided attention. I knew what was at stake, and I needed her to believe me. "After I find Maya."

She held my gaze, studying my face. "You never give up, do you?"

I let go of her hands, but she didn't move away.

"Take off the coat," she insisted.

She helped me take off the coat, then quickly finished wiping away the blood.

"I didn't know you had a tattoo," she said, noticing the small Chinese character inked into my right deltoid.

"A small act of rebellion when I turned eighteen," I said.

"Why am I not surprised?" She finished taping a large gauze patch over my wound. "What does it stand for?"

"Family."

She smiled, appreciating the irony. "You're a piece of work."

CHAPTER FIFTY

THE CROWN VIC WASN'T JUST a big comfortable car, it could get up and move when you hit the accelerator, and Ochoa had her foot on the floor. I checked the AR and loaded a full thirty-round magazine. I also checked her police issue 870 shotgun. Both were ready to go.

"Where's Kelly?" she asked.

"She went back to Lubbock."

I felt her staring at my profile. "I thought she was a part of this."

"She changed her mind."

Ochoa didn't comment.

Ten minutes later the lights from the private airport hangar popped up on the horizon. The terrain was flat, and most of the brush had been recently bulldozed. The runway lights were visible from the road and were surrounded by a ten-foot hurricane fence. Ochoa cut the headlights and stopped by the locked access gate five hundred yards from the hangar. She pulled a pair of binoculars from under the seat. There was a plane parked near the fuel pump.

Ochoa studied the aircraft. "It looks like a Beechcraft King Air. Nice."

"You know planes?"

"I learned to fly in high school. My dad was a pilot. I always thought I would follow in his footsteps."

"What happened?"

"I found something I liked better."

"My grandpa liked to fly. I still have his plane. A Cessna 172."

"I love those. It's a workhorse." She was looking through the binoculars. "There's Russell."

"Is Maya with him?"

"I can't see her, but there are three or four females inside the hangar. I count six men besides that. All armed. You were right, Fischer."

"Did you ever doubt me?"

She rolled her eyes.

"How many passengers will that plane hold?" I asked.

"It's a beast. It can hold ten people and take off with a full tank of gas and gear. A smuggler's dream. If he gets off the ground, he's gone."

"That's not gonna happen."

Ochoa reached for her cell phone. "I'm calling for backup."

She made the call. San Antonio's finest were on their way. Ochoa drove with her lights off and parked behind the hangar.

We both got out and walked to the edge of the building on the outside of the fence. The front gate was open, and one thug with an AR-15 stood guard. He was nervously puffing on a cigarette and blowing smoke into the cold night air.

I motioned for Ochoa to follow me, and we jogged to the far end of the building. The Beechcraft engines fired up. Time was running out. It was now or never.

"Over the fence," I whispered.

"No, wait for backup."

"You can wait." I grabbed the fence and hoisted myself up. A sharp pain shot through my arm. Ochoa saw me flinch and the grimace on my face.

"Do you ever follow orders? I thought you were in the military," she said and grabbed the fence wire below me.

"I was, and no I don't. That's why I got out." I cleared the top strand of barbwire and dropped down on the inside.

Ochoa was hard on my heels. She was quick and agile and moved like a gymnast.

"You've done this before," I said.

"We do go after bad guys occasionally."

We jogged to the open back door of the hangar. A half dozen small four-seater planes filled the space with room for maybe a dozen more. The Dragon stood in a small waiting area on the opposite end surrounded by four men. Two had AR-15s. The females were seated. I spotted Maya's gold dress.

I motioned for Ochoa to follow me, ducked back out the door, and jogged in the shadow along the outside of the building. At the front corner, I stopped and crouched down. Ochoa did the same. She had the shotgun ready, and her face was all business. The revving Beechcraft engines told me SAPD wouldn't get here in time.

I lay on my belly and inched to the edge of the building. The hangar opening was around the corner. The Beechcraft stood thirty yards away with the stairs extended to the tarmac. Fueling was over. They were ready to fly. A man stood on the tarmac shouting to someone inside the plane.

I was close enough to see the faces of the people in the waiting area. Russell wore a bomber jacket, his hair in a ponytail and a smug expression on his face. The other four men were on high alert. The two with rifles watched the airplane, the other two watched the females.

Maya sat with her legs crossed, chewing on her index finger, the gold dress sparkling in the light. Whatever circumstances led to this point didn't really matter. If I failed, she'd be wearing that gold dress for a long time. I hoped she trusted me. I hoped when the moment came, she'd make the right choice.

"Now would be a good time for your backup to arrive," I whispered to Ochoa.

She shrugged and inched closer to the edge so she could see the plane and the hangar opening. "What's your plan?"

"We need to separate the girls from the boys."

She studied the waiting area and the plane. "I've got an idea. Wait here." She took off running for the back door.

I aimed the AR toward the man near the plane.

Suddenly, the lights in the hangar went out. Ochoa had found the light switch or the electrical line. Dragon pulled a pistol from his bomber jacket. A loud boom echoed through the metal building. Ochoa had fired her shotgun. Lights from the runway cast deep shadows inside the hangar.

The two men with rifles ran through the shadows toward the back door. I hoped Ochoa was ready for them. It was my turn. I put the AR's open sights on the thug by the Beechcraft and pulled the trigger. He slumped to the tarmac.

Another shotgun blast ripped through the hangar.

The Dragon shouted something into the dark. He motioned in my direction. One of his men took off running. I stood and pressed my back against the building, listening to his footsteps come closer.

When he cleared the edge of the building, I jammed my fist in his throat. The man went down, clutching his windpipe.

The odds were better now. The two men, who disappeared after Ochoa, hadn't returned. Now it was Russell and one man left.

Suddenly, Maya screamed.

I looked around the corner into the shadows. Russell had her by the neck.

"Is that you, Fischer!" he yelled. He pressed his pistol into Maya's ear.

There was nothing else to do now but confront him. I leaned the AR against the side of the building, pulled my Springfield, and stepped into the open.

"Let her go, Russell," I shouted over the engine noise.

He turned toward me, forcing Maya in front of him. The other thug had his pistol out and took several steps to Russell's right.

I quickly closed the distance between us, stopping ten feet from Maya. "I told you it was over. The police are on their way. Drop the weapon and let her go."

"Fuck you, Fischer. I've got Maya. My plane is fueled and ready. You can't stop me." He took a step toward the Beechcraft, keeping Maya between us.

"I brought the money," I yelled over the engine noise.

He jammed his pistol harder into the side of her head. A trickle of blood ran down Maya's cheek. "Liar," he shouted.

I took a step closer and lowered my pistol. Maya was shaking like a leaf. Her tight gold dress glittered in the runway lights.

"Two million is a lot of money," I said. The Beechcraft engine roared. "I told you I'd trade it for the girl."

He was thinking about it. He couldn't pretend two million dollars didn't matter. I caught and held Maya's eyes with my own. We stared at each other. *If I could get her to move…*

She mouthed, *Help me.*

It was all I needed from her. I nodded once and mouthed, *Drop.*

She buckled her knees and dropped like a rock.

My .45 slug caught Russell in the right eye and took the top of his head off.

A shotgun exploded off to my right.

The girls screamed as the other thug's blood rained down on them.

Ochoa pumped another round in her 870 shotgun, waiting for any more of Russell's crew, but that was the last of them. Sirens approached from every direction. The cavalry had arrived. Better late than never. Red and blue emergency lights lit up the dark hangar. Tires squealed, voices shouted, and running feet crossed the tarmac.

I laid my pistol on the hangar floor so SAPD wouldn't shoot me and knelt beside Maya.

"You okay?"

She grabbed my hand as if I were going to run away. The smell of blood from Russell's head was overwhelming. She gagged and threw up at my feet.

SAPD officers swarmed the hangar.

Detective Ochoa wrapped her SAPD jacket around Maya's shoulders. "Are you hurt?" she asked.

Maya shook her head and wiped her mouth with the back of her hand.

"You are one lucky girl," she said.

"I do wanna go back," Maya finally said. "I was scared to say anything. I'm sorry. He—he threatened…" She couldn't finish.

"It's okay. Don't worry. I'm gonna take you home."

CHAPTER FIFTY-ONE

DETECTIVE OCHOA DROVE ME BACK to Fredericksburg the next day in her Crown Vic. Maya was spending a few days in the hospital. After her two-month ordeal with the Dragon, she wasn't in any shape to be traveling. The doctors said they wouldn't know if there was any long-term physical damage until she was completely detoxed and rested. I wanted to complete this business before I took any time off, so they gave me a few pints of blood, and by morning I was ready to go. The nurse wrapped my left arm in a sling to keep me from opening the wound in my chest again.

Leo didn't take my advice. Instead of packing up the kids and getting out of town, he had contacted someone at SAPD who put him in touch with Detective Ochoa. Ochoa and her staff wasted no time combing through the computer disks and getting warrants issued for the men on camera, who included an assortment of local politicians, policemen, and one former state congressman from El Paso. There were raids taking place all over the city based on the videos. The FBI was in the process of tracking down the rest of the girls who were scattered across Texas, Louisiana, New Mexico, and Arizona. Many of the girls came from Mexico, but there were others like Maya. The Dragon didn't discriminate. It was the biggest sex trafficking bust in years. The agent in charge said I'd done them a favor. I told her I didn't do it for them.

Outside, the sky was gray and overcast and the temperature hovered near fifty. Not cold, but a pleasant reminder of the season. I had Ochoa drive the back roads through Boerne and Sisterdale. A few oak and maple trees along the highway added orange and yellow hues to the fall scene, but the mesquite trees still clung to their yellow-green foliage. They were always the last to lose their leaves. If all went well, I'd be in a deer blind for opening day and enjoying Sergeant Vera's company.

Ochoa had changed and showered since the shootout in the hangar. Her hair smelled of lavender soap with a hint of perfume. Her shoulder-length hair was curled, and she wore faded Wrangler jeans with cowboy boots. Her badge and pistol hung from a turquoise belt that matched her short leather jacket.

"Are you studying me?" she asked.

"I was wondering why you didn't let the Fredericksburg police take care of Mike Bauer," I said.

"Why let them have all the fun?"

"So, you like taking down the bad guys?"

"Especially perverts like Bauer," she said.

"What about the arrests in San Antonio? Aren't you missing out on them?"

"I know my team will take care of business in SA. I was a little worried about Officer Zeller. When I talked to him on the phone, he sounded hesitant."

"He didn't believe the evidence?"

"Let's just say he was less than enthusiastic."

"You could've called the sheriff."

"I did. And the DPS. I'm having Mr. Bauer transported back to San Antonio. That's where the crime took place. That's where he'll stand trial."

"What about his son?"

"That's up to the judge. We didn't find any drugs on him, and he's still seventeen."

"I have a recommendation."

"Join the Marines?" she asked.

"Why not? His football career is over. Everybody needs a second chance."

"He'll end up like you."

"Is that such a bad thing?"

She laughed and gazed out her driver's side window.

The farm fields were plowed under and ready for winter. Stacks of hay stood under bright blue tarps. I unrolled my window a few inches to get a breath of air mixed with fresh hay and cedar trees.

"You love this country, don't you?" she said.

"It's in my blood."

She slowed down for a closer look at a ten-point whitetail deer standing just inside the barbwire fence.

"You won't see him in a couple of weeks."

"Why's that?" she asked.

"Hunting season is coming."

"You would shoot that beautiful animal?" she asked.

"Honoring my pioneer ancestors."

She laughed while she passed a rancher on a John Deere tractor pulling a flatbed trailer stacked with hay. It was a pleasant, spontaneous laugh that was genuine and down to earth.

"Why else did you come out here with me?" I asked. "The sheriff and the DPS would have done their job, even if Zeller was reluctant to make an arrest."

She studied my face. "Don't get any ideas about us."

I raised my one good hand. "I don't get ideas. I'm a country boy, remember?"

Her face turned serious. "Don't start something you can't finish, Fischer."

We pulled into town, and I directed her toward Mike Bauer's

winery. There were three state trooper SUVs in the parking lot along with the sheriff's pickup and two local police cruisers. Officer Zeller stood by one of the cruisers. He had a kolache in one hand and a cup of coffee in the other.

"Hey, Les," I said when I got out of the Crown Vic.

"Hey, yourself," he said, licking the powdered sugar from his fingers. "What're you doing here?"

"I was gonna ask you the same thing."

"My town. My jurisdiction. What's with the sling?"

"I got a little banged up," I said.

"Not surprised."

Ochoa stepped between us. "I'm Detective Ochoa," she said. "We spoke on the phone."

Zeller held out his sticky hand.

Ochoa didn't take it.

"The sheriff's inside with Mike," he said and pointed toward the front entrance.

I turned to follow Ochoa inside.

"Not you," Zeller said. "Just the detective."

Ochoa hustled inside and left me with Les.

"No hard feelings," I said.

"You don't know, do you?"

"What?" I said.

"Your mom's in there with Mike."

I shook my head. I didn't know. I had hoped she'd gone back to Colorado. "Why should that bother me?"

"Just thought you'd wanna know."

Zeller pinched the pastry bag from the front seat of his cruiser. He held it out to me. I wasn't really hungry but took one anyway. I recognized the white bag as coming from the German Bakery. They had the best kolaches in town. He offered it like a peace pipe at an Indian treaty meeting. The Comanche had tobacco. The Fredericksburg police department had kolaches.

"We're not real close," I said.

We stood chewing in silence. I wondered if Helen understood that Mike was finished in Fredericksburg. It wasn't her style to give support when the ones around her needed it. She had left my dad when he was elected sheriff—said she couldn't stand the long nights at home waiting for a phone call telling her he had been killed. It sounded like a good excuse, but it didn't explain why she left her son.

"You gonna keep doin' the private eye thing in San Antonio?" Zeller asked.

"Gotta make a livin' somehow," I said. "I like workin' for myself."

"What ya gonna do with your grandpa's place?"

"I'll keep it as long as I can pay the taxes."

"That's good," he said. "It wouldn't be the same without a Fischer in town." He was trying to bury the hatchet. He would never admit that he was wrong, but at least he wasn't going to arrest me.

"You got a place to go huntin' this year?" I asked.

Les grinned.

Before he could respond, the posse burst through the winery door. At the same time, a San Antonio news station van pulled into the parking lot. A cameraman jumped out with his camera rolling, followed by a reporter in a long red coat and carefully coiffed TV hair.

Les sprang into action. He had been assigned to crowd control. He held up his hands and instructed them to stay behind the barrier set up thirty feet from the police vehicles.

Mike Bauer lead the posse, his hands cuffed behind his back. A burley state trooper followed. Mike looked as white as the limestone bricks supporting the winery porch. He saw the camera rolling and tried to duck his head. Too late. It was the second time he'd been caught on camera.

Ochoa and two other state troopers followed, along with the

county sheriff and one of his deputies. She stood out among the well-fed law enforcement good ol' boys like a female reporter in an NFL locker room but wasn't intimidated in the least.

Helen appeared at the entrance beside Brenda, the teen server who'd tried to push the Bauer wine. Helen put a hand on her shoulder and gave Brenda a little shove just as the news camera swept across the building. She wasn't protecting her; Helen wanted a solo pose for the camera. She put her hand to her mouth in fake concern. Tears would be next. She was too easy to read.

"Hey, Mike," I yelled over the commotion.

Mike looked up and saw me. His eyes had lost the bravado of our last visit.

"I'm gonna hang on to the ranch. Thanks for the offer."

"Fuck you, Fischer! You did this to me," Mike yelled.

The burly trooper held Mike's head and guided him into the back seat of the SUV. Zeller answered questions on camera for the news station reporter, putting on a serious expression and clearly enjoying the attention.

Ochoa joined me in the parking lot. "Bastard denied everything. Said you set him up."

"Does he know about the video?"

"He will soon enough."

"Nicky," Helen called from the porch.

"*Nicky?* You know her?" Ochoa asked.

"No," I said.

"Nicky, I need to talk to you." Helen walked off the porch and started across the parking lot toward us.

I opened the driver's side door of the Crown Vic for Ochoa to get in.

"You just gonna ignore her?" she asked.

"Yes," I said.

Ochoa got in the car, and I closed her door. Helen caught me before I could get to the passenger side. She studied my sling.

"Did you hurt yourself again?" she asked as if I'd fallen off the swing set.

"I'll be fine."

"Did you have anything to do with what happened to Mike?" Helen asked. She was blocking my path to the passenger door in full view of Ochoa.

"Not in the way you think. Mike's guilty. He's goin' to prison."

Her face fell like a kid who'd lost her ice cream cone in a mud puddle.

"You'll need to find another sugar daddy," I said.

"Don't be cruel. I'm still your mother." She glanced through the front windshield at Ochoa. "Who's this?"

"An SAPD detective. She handled the case."

"Nicky, I need to talk to you. Is there somewhere we can go?"

"No, Helen. There's nowhere we can go," I said and stepped around her to the door.

"Please," she said. "Don't make me beg."

I'd heard that line before. It hadn't worked then, and it wouldn't work now. I opened the door and got in.

"She's your mother?" Ochoa asked and started the engine.

Helen stood outside my door holding her hands palms up. Tears streaked her makeup.

I felt Ochoa's stare on the back of my neck along with my own guilt. I knew I was opening a can of worms when I unrolled the window. "Come by the ranch next week. We'll talk."

Helen reached for the window. "Thank you, Nicky. I wanted to—"

I rolled the window up and turned to Ochoa. "You goin' back to San Antonio now?"

"Yeah, but I'll drop you off if you want."

"Why don't you come out to the ranch? I can show you Grandpa's Cessna 172."

Her face turned serious. "I told you not to start something you can't finish. I have a little boy who is the love of my life."

"Does he like to ride horses?"

She studied me for a full minute before she smiled. "All right, Fischer. Show me the plane."

CHAPTER FIFTY-TWO

I STOPPED IN HELMUT'S DRIVEWAY. MAYA got out to open the gate. She walked past the iron cowboy kneeling in front of the large cross. He seemed to be saying a prayer for her as she unhooked the latch. She paused for a long moment to study her grandfather's barren hay pasture and the hills beyond covered with dark green live oak trees. Woodsmoke rose from the single-story ranch house. Another norther had swept down from Canada while she was in the hospital in San Antonio and dropped the temperature into the thirties. Good news for the deer hunters whose season started in a few days.

The cold air put color in Maya's brown cheeks. Luckily, the drugs she'd been given hadn't done lasting physical damage. It would take her some time to get over the mental aspects of the ordeal. The fact that she wanted to go back to her grandpa's ranch in rural Gillespie County said a lot about her. She wanted to start over. It wasn't going to be easy. No one understood that more than Maya. Ochoa had suggested a rehab facility. She knew of one in Bastrop County, east of Austin. They took girls under nineteen who had been rescued from thugs like Russell Stevens. They had a charter school and provided counseling to help the girls recover. Maya wanted to give her grandfather's ranch a try first.

I drove through the open gate and waited for Maya to hop back in the cab.

"You have my number," I said. "Diana left you hers too."

She was silent on the drive to the house. Helmut had wanted to visit her in the hospital, but I told him to wait and give Maya time to recover. I wanted her to be sure of her decision before Helmut saw her again. I wasn't going to force her to live with her grandfather. I parked facing the front porch and reached over to open the door. Maya touched my arm.

"Wait." She studied the worn porch that had held up generations of the Geisler family. I thought she was having second thoughts.

Helmut held the front curtain back and peeked out. I'd known him all my life and had never seen him get particularly sentimental, but I thought I saw a tear in his eye as he gazed at his granddaughter. Maya had changed him.

"Do you want to leave?" I asked her. Helmut Geisler's ranch was about as far from urban San Antonio or Southern California as she could get.

Helmut stepped out the door with his silver Stetson cowboy hat pulled low over his eyes and his felt-lined brush jacket buttoned to his chin. He was the nineteenth century, and she was the twenty-first.

Maya squeezed my arm. "No. I want to stay. Thank you for not giving up on me." She leaned over the console and kissed me on the cheek. "I won't forget what you did." For the first time, her face was full of hope and determination.

"Come in out of the cold," Helmut called from the porch.

Maya smiled. She jumped out of the pickup, ran up the steps, and into her grandpa's arms.

THE END

If you enjoyed this Nick Fischer adventure, please stop by Amazon and Goodreads and write a quick review. Your support will be much appreciated.

To receive your FREE e-copy of "Alligator Gar" and other short stories from Nick Fischer Country, sign up for the mailing list at GeorgeLeeMiller.com. Along with the free material you will receive additional book deals and insights from Nick Fischer Country.

Visit George Online:
GeorgeLeeMiller.com
Facebook.com/George.Lee.Miller
Twitter.com/GeorgeLeeMiller

COMING SOON...

Last Rodeo (Fall 2020)

A rodeo cowboy turns up dead at the San Antonio rodeo clutching an empty snuff can inscribed with Nick Fischer's name and a pocket full of painkillers. Was it a cry for help—the young cowboy was a veteran—or was it an accusation? Nick finds himself on the wrong side of the law, again, as he struggles to find the answers that will clear his name and catch a killer before it's too late.

ACKNOWLEDGMENTS

I would like to thank my daughter Ruby and sister MaryAlice, who continue to chide and encourage me through the writing process, and Gus, my friend and guide to the Alamo City. Also, I would like to thank my editor, Lisa Gilliam, for her continued patience and guidance. Prost!

The historical events mentioned in this book are derived from three main sources of historical research: A Fate Worse Than Death: Indian Captivities in the West, 1830-1885, by Gregory Michno and Susan Michno; Myth, Memory, and Massacre: The Pease River Capture of Cynthia Ann Parker; and Empire of the Summer Moon by S.C. Gwynne.

I would also like to acknowledge Pastor Joseph A. Travers and his organization, Saved In America, for being true heroes in the battle to rescue trafficked and exploited children. If you know someone in need of their services or would like to donate to the organization, contact SavedInAmerica.org.

ABOUT THE AUTHOR

George Lee Miller is a former cowboy, Navy corpsman, and theater director who splits his time between teaching at a local college and writing the next Nick Fischer adventure. He currently lives with his Labrador retriever in Central Texas.

www.ingramcontent.com/pod-product-compliance
Lightning Source LLC
Chambersburg PA
CBHW020612310726
48979CB00008B/1452/J